The Wisteria Tree Cottage

HOLLY MARTIN

CHAPTER ONE

Meadow walked out of her treehouse and stood on the decking looking out over the sea, enjoying the rare quiet of the morning as she nursed her cup of coffee. It was another gloriously hot day and the sea was a gorgeous teal, sparkling in the early morning sunlight.

She glanced at the tattered old purple notebook on the table, her diary from when she was seventeen, the year her life had changed. She'd found it a few days before stuffed in a box and had spent some time since then reading it. She smiled. Young Meadow had had hopes and dreams, she was going to be a fashion designer of the world's most glamorous dresses, she was going to have a shop of her clothes in every major city across the globe and every famous woman would want to wear her beautiful outfits.

Meadow smiled as she glanced around the wood which was her home. Life had turned out completely differently but she knew she wouldn't change it for the world. She lived and worked at Wishing Wood, a luxury treehouse resort on the south coast of Wales filled with magical fairy-style treehouses that guests could come and stay in. The guests were always so enchanted with the place when they came here for the first time. Every treehouse had so much character: wonky turrets, round windows, spiral staircases and an abundance of fairy lights everywhere. Meadow lived in a treehouse herself built around a beautiful old wisteria tree, which bloomed with incredible purple flowers every year. Across the little rope bridge from her treehouse was another treehouse where her ex-husband, Heath lived. Their daughter Star would happily spend some nights with him and some nights with her, just wherever took her fancy. Meadow adored Heath, he was her best friend. In fact she had been best friends with all three of the Brookfield brothers for as far back as she could remember.

Despite the fact that her life was nowhere near what she had dreamt when she was younger, it was pretty much perfect. She loved her job as manager of the Wishing Wood treehouse resort, she enjoyed helping the guests to have the most magical holiday possible. She loved living here in the woods with Heath's brothers, Bear and River, along with River's daughter Tierra and fiancée Indigo. They were a team, a family, and she wouldn't want to be without any one of them. But more than anything in the world she loved being a mum to her brilliant, clever daughter Star.

It was funny, seventeen-year-old Meadow had never thought about children other than someday, far off in the future she thought maybe she would have some, but when she had found out she was pregnant shortly after her seventeenth birthday there was no question in her mind that she wasn't going to keep the baby. Star had changed her life completely but there hadn't been a single day in the last seven and a half years that she had ever regretted that decision. And there was not a better place in the world to raise her daughter, living here in the middle of all this nature, playing on the beach with her every day, Star's wonderful uncles and cousin to love and support her.

Up until a few months before, life had just ticked along, they were happy. The brothers would go out on dates now and again, although she never did, but none of them had ever found someone they wanted forever with.

Until Indigo Bloom crashed into their lives with her purple hair and the small matter of carrying River's child from a one-night stand. After a bit of a bumpy start to their reunion, it was clear for anyone to see that River and Indigo were now completely head over heels in love with each other. What they had was that forever kind of love and it had made Meadow start to look at her own life and how it had always been completely lacking in that department.

Heath was a wonderful father to Star but getting married purely because she was pregnant had been a stupid decision. They had never had a romantic relationship, they had simply been two best friends who had raised Star together. A few years after Star was born, they had separated, at Meadow's insistence, so that Heath could live like any other man in his early twenties, date other women, lead the life he should have had if they hadn't married. He and River had built the treehouse next door and he'd moved in so he could always be close to his daughter. He had dated and that was totally fine but she had never wanted to.

A movement caught her eye and she looked over to the top of the steps that led up from Pear Tree Beach. There was a topless man walking through the trees, evidently wet from having a swim, and although she couldn't see the man's face as it was hidden under the leaves of a tree, she knew who it was, her heart and body responding to him before her brain could even identify him. Bear Brookfield, Heath's youngest brother and the man she'd been in love with for probably most of her life. Young Meadow had just two dreams, according to the diary she'd found: become a fashion designer and marry Bear Brookfield. He came into view and he immediately looked up, maybe instinctively knowing she was there too. He flashed her a big smile and a wave and she waved back. She couldn't take her eyes off him as he walked back to his own home, his broad shoulders, his strong, muscular arms, his tanned skin wet from the sea. He was beautiful, there was no denying it, but her love for him went way deeper than that.

There were a few reasons why she hadn't wanted to date before now, but Bear was one of those reasons, or rather several of them. He had broken her heart when she was seventeen, when he'd slept with Milly Atherton, the girl who'd made her life a living hell at school, and she'd never wanted to put her heart out there again for fear of getting hurt. But despite that, she had never ever stopped loving him. He had been her first kiss what felt like a lifetime ago but she was a hundred percent sure he had never thought of that kiss again like she had, especially after what had happened with Milly Atherton, and he just saw her as his friend, nothing more.

But maybe it was time to move on. Having seen how

happy River and Indigo were together, she'd decided it was time to find her own happiness. Her divorce to Heath had finally come through a few weeks before and now felt as good a moment as any to let go of the heartache of the past and move on once and for all. She finished her coffee and went back inside to finish getting ready for the day.

CHAPTER TWO

'Smoking or non-smoking?' Heath asked as he tapped away at Bear's computer.

'It sounds like I'm looking for a hotel room rather than someone I'm hoping to spend the rest of my life with. I just want someone lovely, is there not a box for that?' Meadow said, finishing the details of a booking on her own computer.

'You'd think there would be, but sadly you have to answer a million stupid questions and then Connected Hearts will supposedly find your dream match. Do you care if they smoke or not?' Heath said.

Meadow sighed. 'I suppose I'd prefer it if they didn't.'

'This is the point of all this. If you're looking for someone to have a bit of fun with, then none of this stuff matters, but if you're looking for someone to be your soul mate, your husband, your life partner, then why not be picky? You don't want to settle, you want the perfect man. And I'm not saying they have to be exactly six foot three, weigh exactly fifteen stone of pure muscle, have blue eyes, be a heart surgeon and speak five languages kind of perfect, but if something like them smoking turns you off, then you should absolutely put that on your dating profile.'

'OK,' Meadow said, doubtfully.

This all seemed so convoluted. Surely people didn't really meet their soul mates through online dating. What was wrong with walking into a pub and your eyes meeting with a handsome stranger's across the room? Although she hadn't actually been in a pub without Heath or Star for a long time. Or ever met anyone in that way.

'As your ex-husband I have no right to tell you who to date – I want someone who is kind and respectful to you and Star, but other than that I have no stipulations – but I have to say, I would prefer whoever you end up with didn't smoke around our daughter. We manage her asthma really well right now with her inhalers and she's never had an attack. But I wouldn't want it to be aggravated by someone who smokes.'

'No, I agree with that,' Meadow said. 'It's just that some of these questions seem so petty. Like that one on ethnicity. Do people really choose a life partner depending on the colour of their skin? That's horrible.'

'Thankfully most people don't care what colour skin the people they date have, or what country they come from, or their faith, but for some that would be a deal-breaker. Anyway it's good that you're open to meeting a range of men and you don't have too many rules or requirements for your perfect match. It will make the search easier. Besides, you've done all the hard stuff with your introduction note, that was warm, funny and chatty. Most people will read that rather than bother looking at these tiny questions. I do think it's a bit weird though that this dating site doesn't allow photos.'

'Connected Hearts is about finding that real deep connection with someone, not choosing a partner based on their appearance. I quite like that. There's this new dating event happening around here and one of the dates is dating in the dark. You have a meal in this completely dark room and you chat to your date but you have no idea what they look like until after.'

'It certainly brings a new meaning to the term, blind date,' Heath said. 'Anyway, I have to go to work. We're making great progress with the wedding chapel treehouse, but I know River would like it finished by the end of the summer.'

'We've had some enquiries already since we put a few teasers out as Facebook ads. Bear ran some "Coming soon" promos with some confetti and some wedding ribbons and flowers but nothing more than that, but we must have had ten or fifteen phone calls about it already. I've told them what we intend to offer, a beautiful place to get married, but I've said right now it's a bit up in the air as to when it will be finished and I will get in touch with them as soon as I know. We also need to get it registered as an official wedding venue too, which is quite hard to do when it's just a few pieces of wood.'

'Hey, it's a bit more than that,' Heath said, clearly affronted. 'The basic shell is there, although the roof isn't finished. I also think that River would like to marry Indigo there. He said the other day how he couldn't think of a better place to tie the knot and with Indigo nearly six months pregnant, I think River would like to do it before the baby comes.'

'I guess that makes sense. How wonderful though that they might be our first wedding. I'm so excited about holding weddings here. There is something so beautiful about getting married in the middle of the trees, surrounded by nature. I remember when I was a child I went to my mum's cousin's wedding. It was a Wiccan ceremony held in the woods. There were candles and flowers and they did the traditional handfasting. My parents thought it was ridiculous, but I remember thinking it was the most beautiful thing I'd ever seen. Ever since then I've always wanted to get married outside in the woods too. It was a childhood dream and not something I ever grew out of. Building that little wedding chapel treehouse here in the woods is a great way to offer that kind of ceremony to people who want something more natural and simple.'

'Maybe if this online dating malarkey works out, you can get married here too.'

'That may be a little while off since I haven't even been on one date yet, but maybe one day I will.'

She imagined herself in a simple dress, a flower crown on her head, walking through the trees to where Bear was waiting for her.

She shook her head with a smile, she'd played that ridiculous fantasy in her head far too many times.

'Right, I better go,' Heath said. 'I'll see you later for dinner. If you need any further help with your dating profile, I'm sure Bear would give you a hand.'

Meadow waved him off and then sat back in her chair. The reception area of Wishing Wood was a bit quiet today.

They had enjoyed the success of the opening ceremony of twenty new luxury treehouses a few weeks before and with the twelve older ones they were pretty much fully booked for the rest of the year. But being in the middle of a glorious heatwave, and located right on the coast, all the guests were out enjoying days at the beach or sunny walks through the nearby countryside rather than hanging around here in the woods so she was set for another quiet day.

Tomorrow would be another story. The tents, yurts, gazebos and food stalls were arriving for their annual Dwelling festival which would kick off the day after. Dwelling had started off as a very small thing several years before, with just a few large tents where people could come for the day to learn back-to-nature skills, like making flower crowns or garlands, wood whittling, willow weaving, clay pots and den building, but it had grown every year to include more activities. Small bands would play music and it had now become a three-day festival. People would come from all over the world to learn new skills or just hang out with strangers who quickly became fast friends. It was a chilled-out, peaceful vibe. People would listen to music and there was lots of painting, printing and crafts for the children to do too, not to mention the excellent food that was always available. Many of the guests and workshop leaders had booked to stay in the treehouses but some guests would just camp in their own tents or sleep in the yurts. As tomorrow would be really busy, Meadow was making the most of the quiet spell today.

She wouldn't even have Indigo, the receptionist and events manager, to talk to for the first few hours as she and

River were going for their second baby scan. Poor Indigo was already huge and she still had over three months to go. But then with the sheer size of the Brookfield men, there was never going to be any doubt that Indigo's baby would be big too. River, Heath and Bear were all around six foot seven, broad, muscular, with dark curly hair, but while they all looked similar, there was only one brother Meadow was attracted to.

Just then Greta, one of their ground and maintenance crew, walked in carrying a large vase of flowers. Greta had spent a long time planting a multitude of different flowers throughout the woods and fields, ensuring there was a kaleidoscope of colour almost all year round.

'Morning Greta,' Meadow said, as she walked in to put the vase behind Meadow and the desk.

'Good morning, it's another beautiful day,' Greta said.

Meadow smiled, Greta had a fabulous Dutch accent and she always sounded so happy.

Greta turned round after positioning the vase of flowers in the perfect spot to catch the sun through the skylight and must have spotted what was on Meadow's computer.

'Oooh, you're signing up to Connected Hearts. My little sister is on there. She hasn't found her prince yet but she has had a lot of fun kissing all the frogs, if you know what I mean.'

Meadow smiled. She had wondered if online dating was all about sex rather than deep relationships, but that's why she had chosen Connected Hearts which seemed to be more of an advocate of finding that real connection rather than just casual sex. Not that there was anything wrong with that, it just wasn't for her.

'I'm kind of looking for something more than… kissing frogs,' Meadow said, tactfully.

'Ah, you want the fairytale. I'm not sure it exists.'

'Greta, you've been happily married for years. Surely you've found your fairytale.'

'I hated my husband when I first met him. He didn't sweep me off my feet, he knocked me off my feet, with his stupid great big dog. Then he was rude to me and I was very rude back to him and that started a love/hate relationship for the next three years. He was my neighbour and I enjoyed insulting him and being antagonistic, winding him up every time I saw him, and he gave as good as he got. Then one day, after another ridiculous argument, we ended up having hate sex and it was wonderful. We kind of never looked back. We still wind each other up, but I do love him. It definitely wasn't the fairytale.'

Meadow sighed. Was it too optimistic to think she might find someone she could fall head over heels in love with? Or did that kind of thing only happen in the romance novels she loved so much?

'Bear is on Connected Hearts too,' Greta said, gesturing to his empty chair.

'Yes, I think he is, though he hasn't dated for a while.'

Greta nodded. 'My sister was matched with him. But when she messaged him he told her he was coming off online dating for a while, said he wanted to take a break. Maybe he might go back on there now you're on there.'

'I'm not sure if that will be any incentive.'

'But if he does and you two get matched, would you go out with him?'

'I, erm… hadn't really thought about it,' Meadow lied.

'Well, if it's the fairytale you want, then you probably should think about it.' Greta gave her a wave as she walked out the office.

Meadow bit her lip as she watched her go. She wondered how many people knew about her inappropriate feelings for her best friend. She thought she'd been discreet but clearly Greta had seen something.

Right on cue, Bear walked into the office. He had the loveliest smile and gentle eyes and despite seeing him every day it didn't stop that little flutter in her heart when he was around her. What had started as a silly crush on a boy in her teens had developed into something much more powerful over the years and the boy was now very much a man.

'Morning,' Bear said as he sat next to her at his computer.

'Hey, how was the swim?'

'Wonderful, you should come and join me one day, it's my favourite way to start the day.'

Her mind suddenly conjured up a much more romantic scenario than he was probably suggesting, the two of them together, not wearing much or anything at all as they swam together, kissing with salty lips, under a sunrise-coloured sky.

'Bring Star too, she would love it,' Bear said, popping her little fantasy bubble.

'She would.'

'Where is she today?'

'She went with River, Indigo and Tierra to see their baby on the scan. She was so interested in it, I asked if she could come too. River and Indigo were happy to oblige.'

'I bet she'll have a ton of questions when she gets back.'

He turned to the computer and he started singing to himself, slightly out of tune which made her smile. God she loved this man.

She watched him fondly as his fingers flew across the keys as he logged in to the website and did his daily check to make sure everything was running smoothly. It almost always was. He had designed and built their website and booking system by himself. He was also responsible for all their social media and marketing and had helped with all the electricity and lighting around the resort, too. As a kid he'd always been taking apart computers and fixing them or building new computers from the old parts of others. He was super smart and an expert in all things techy and electrical.

Meadow often wondered what would have happened between them if she had accepted his offer of a date shortly after that first incredible kiss. They had both been so young, she'd just turned seventeen, he was sixteen. Would they have stood the test of time or would they have fizzled out after a few weeks? Would these feelings for her best friend have faded away too if they'd gone out with each other because she'd been there and done that rather than all these years of wondering?

She thought back to their one and only kiss. She had read that little chapter in her diary just that morning. Despite being her first kiss it had been wonderful. He had been away on four weeks' work experience in London and when he'd come back she had practically thrown herself into his arms because she had missed him so much. The hug had turned to a kiss, one that had made her feel like she was floating on air.

She'd gone home that night practically bouncing with excitement. Her parents, well her dad mainly, had always been so strict about her staying out and dating boys, which was why her first kiss had happened so much later than all her other friends'. When she told her mum about kissing Bear, her mum had laughed and said it was foolish to fall in love with a boy like Bear because he would leave her and break her heart. And Meadow had known she was right. Not because Bear was a womaniser or one of those love-them-and-leave-them types, it was because he was always destined for bigger and better things than a sleepy village in Wales. Everyone knew that. He was so smart that Meadow had known that one day the move to London or New York or some other big city somewhere in the world would be permanent. He would follow his dreams to work in designing computer programs. And she wanted that for him. She wanted him to grab every opportunity that came his way, for him to see the world and be successful.

The next day she'd bumped into Heath who excitedly told her about Bear being offered a three-year apprenticeship with Strawberry, one of the biggest computer software companies in the world. Someone from his work experience in London had been impressed by him and had used their contacts at Strawberry to get Bear an apprenticeship. It was two years in London and one in California. It was an amazing opportunity for him.

So when she'd seen Bear later that day and he'd asked her out she had said no. She didn't want him giving up his life for her. She hadn't wanted him to miss out on an incredible experience. And selfishly, she hadn't wanted to get involved with him, fall even more in love with him, only to watch him leave in a few weeks' time. So she'd laughed off the kiss, told Bear that it didn't mean anything and to prove it she'd started dating other boys. But Bear had never left. He turned down the apprenticeship and she'd never known why. And almost as if he was trying to prove he wasn't bothered about the kiss either, he started dating other women, rubbing salt into the wound when he'd slept with Milly Atherton. But then she'd discovered she was pregnant with Star and the diary she'd found had pages of regret and messy complicated feelings after that.

She knew she had hurt Bear when she fell pregnant and got married to Heath, especially after they'd shared such an incredible kiss, but what was worse was that she could never tell him why. Only she and Heath knew the truth and she was determined it had to stay that way.

Bear turned to face her, flashing her a smile that warmed her heart.

'I just saw Heath, he said you needed a hand with something.'

'Oh, I'm just trying to set up my dating profile on Connected Hearts, but I think I'm done now. I just have to hit submit and I will be on the market as if I'm selling my house. They want to know my entire life history. It seems so complicated. I just don't believe that two people can share a real connection from ticking boxes on a website.'

'You see, that's where me and you differ. These dating websites are built on algorithms, finding a match is about a computer program finding matching patterns in a sea of different patterns. It stands to reason that if your pattern matches someone else's – if you like and dislike the same things, you have the same attitudes and beliefs, not necessarily religiously, but the same moral compass – then you at least have a common ground to start from. Human beings are like very sophisticated computers and if you can find one with compatible software then you can connect very easily.'

'But what about that old adage, opposites attract? Your algorithms and software don't consider that random chance meeting, that connection that comes from nowhere. That kind of thing can only be found by meeting someone in real life.'

'Yes, but how often does that happen?'

'It happened for River and Indigo. That love at first sight kind of thing.'

'I think what they have is very rare,' Bear said. 'I think you have a better chance of having a computer find you a match than try to bump into your soul mate in a pub or on the street.'

'He could walk in here any second, looking for love.'

Bear looked towards the door and she did too but there was not a soul to be seen.

'Well, that doesn't prove anything,' Meadow said. 'I'm not sure why you're so supportive of online dating. You've tried it and I don't see you happily married to your soul mate. In fact, you gave up looking.'

'Soul mates are tricky to find. If you believe those romance books you love so much, we only ever get one. Some people never find theirs. A lot of the women I was getting matched with were looking for sex. I'm looking for forever. And I haven't given up, I just had a run of bad dates and now I'm taking a break for a while.'

'See, that's not a good advert for online dating, is it?'

'But at least I had things in common with these women. You walk into a pub and see a man with a nice smile, you might not have anything in common with him. He might enjoy fox hunting or eating sprouts. Or in all seriousness, he might not want to get involved with someone who has a child and, honestly, someone who doesn't want to get to know Star isn't worth you wasting your breath on because she is an amazing little girl. These are things you can find out before you even get as far as meeting them. I understand your reluctance. Online dating is weird and there are many men online I wouldn't want you to meet. But I do think that a dating site that uses a program to match you with someone similar to you is a really good place to start.'

'I get that and I guess online dating has its merits but there is so much more that happens when you meet someone new face to face; eye contact, body language, a comment that warms your heart, a smile that makes your heart flutter. Look, I saw this the other day,' she dug out the leaflet she'd seen in a café. 'There's this new dating company in the area and they have different ways to find your perfect match. They ask you to go to five events and at each event they match you in a different way. They measure your heart rate, they have a body language expert, they even have a pheromone night where you can find your match by scent. By the end of the five events you should have found your perfect match.'

Bear arched an eyebrow, 'You're going to walk around smelling everyone?'

'I'm not quite sure how it works. But this is a more realistic way of finding your soul mate. This is based on science.'

'You're talking about sniffing people's armpits to see if you find them attractive,' he said.

'No, of course not,' Meadow laughed. God, she hoped it wasn't that.

'OK. How about a bet?' Bear said. 'You try both ways. Online dating and sniffing armpits to see what works out the best for you. Let's see which one leads to a meaningful relationship. If online dating wins you give me twenty pounds and if sniffing armpits wins—'

'Not just sniffing armpits, the face to face stuff, body language, smiles, that kind of thing.'

'OK, if that wins I pay you twenty pounds.'

'How do we know who has won? What counts as a meaningful deep relationship?'

Bear clearly thought about this for a moment. 'Three months. You date someone for three months, then that's a sign it's going somewhere beyond the initial getting to know each other. Three months means you want something more than that, it means that you could have something special.'

She couldn't imagine what it would be like to actually meet someone and go out with them for that length of time. But then she had never really dated anyone, apart from a few silly, nothing dates with a few teenage boys.

She sighed, feeling like she was being coerced into doing something she didn't want to do.

'If it makes you feel any better, I could resurrect my

dating profile and then we can go on dates together,' Bear said.

Her heart missed a beat. Had Greta been right? 'Together?'

'Yeah, I could arrange to meet my dates at the same place you're meeting yours and then if any weirdos or axe murderers turn up I can see them off, or at least take video evidence for comedy value.'

Meadow laughed. 'There is no way I want you there to watch me make a fool of myself. I haven't been on a date for… well, forever. I have no idea what I'm supposed to do.'

'Any man would be lucky to go on a date with you. Just be yourself and I'm sure they will fall in love with you.'

She smiled. Bear was so lovely. He was always saying stuff like that to her.

'OK, if you do it with me, including all the armpit sniffing, then you have yourself a deal,' Meadow said.

Bear pulled a face and then offered out a hand. 'I must really love you if I'm agreeing to sniff armpits for you.'

She shook his hand to seal the deal, sighing to herself because, if he really did love her, then all this dating malarkey was completely pointless.

CHAPTER THREE

Bear put the phone down after disappointing someone who wanted to know if they had any vacancies August bank holiday weekend and glanced over at some guests who were checking in. Meadow was explaining where everything was and how to get to the beaches in her usual efficient manner.

He noticed the woman was heavily pregnant, dressed in dungarees. It reminded him of Meadow when she was pregnant with Star, she'd practically lived in her dungarees once she started showing and she looked so damn cute in them.

'So you're staying in Honeysuckle Cottage,' Meadow said, handing over the key. 'Do you have a lot of bags?'

'Quite a lot, yes,' the woman giggled, looking at her husband who rolled his eyes good-naturedly.

'I'll take you down in the buggy,' Bear said.

He got up and walked round the desk.

'We hope you'll enjoy your stay, Mr and Mrs Lovegrove, and if you need anything at all, please do come and see us.'

'Emma and Jason,' the man said. 'Mr and Mrs Lovegrove are my parents, I always feel so old when people call us that.'

'Then we'll call you Emma and Jason from now on,' Meadow said.

The couple followed Bear outside to their car and Bear jumped on the buggy and pulled it up next to their boot. He grabbed the bags and loaded them onto the back and then helped Emma to get in. Jason climbed in the other side and Bear drove off, a lot slower than he normally would considering the precious cargo he was carrying.

'Oh my god, will you look at those treehouses,' Emma said.

'I feel like we're in Disneyland,' Jason said. 'It's so wonderful.'

Bear couldn't help feeling proud as he looked at it through the guests' eyes. The treehouses were so unique and quirky and he loved seeing the customers' excitement when they arrived.

'That one has a helter-skelter slide, does ours have a slide?'

'I think it does,' Bear said. 'Although perhaps given your condition, you might want to give that one a miss.'

'Spoilsport. You non-pregnant folk get to have all the fun,' Emma said.

'When are you due?' Bear said, taking the slightly longer coastal path over the cliff tops so it would be less bumpy for them and so they could enjoy the spectacular view of the sea that stretched out for miles before disappearing into a pink hazy horizon.

'Not for another five weeks yet, we thought we'd get

away for a few days, make the most of the quiet nights before our lives change forever,' Emma said, fondly stroking her belly.

'Well, you've come to the right place for a bit of rest and relaxation. There is a festival happening here for the next few days but your treehouse is very far away from it so you won't hear any noise and it's not a festival in the Glastonbury sense, it's more of a back-to-nature, wood-whittling, harp-playing, flower-garlands kind of thing. Feel free to come and have a look or just chill out in your treehouse.'

'Thank you, we'll probably be going out for a few little walks and to see the sights, but nothing too strenuous,' Jason said.

Bear pulled up outside Honeysuckle Cottage just as Felix, one of their grounds crew, was pulling out a weed at the bottom of their steps.

'This is Felix, your own personal gardener,' Bear teased.

Felix laughed and started helping Bear take the bags off the back of the buggy. Jason went ahead to open the door and Bear headed up the stairs with Felix and placed the bags inside the treehouse.

Emma came up last and stepped inside, her eyes lighting up in wonder. 'This is magical, thank you.'

She hurried off to explore, squealing as she no doubt saw the skylight above the bed.

'Thank you,' Jason said, offering out a tip.

Bear shook his head. 'Oh no, thank you, but it's not that sort of place where you give tips. It's all part of the service. Enjoy your stay.'

'We will, thank you.'

Bear and Felix went back downstairs.

'Thanks mate,' Bear said, getting back into the buggy. 'Can I offer you a ride anywhere?'

'No, I'm good.' Felix rested his arm on top of the buggy and leaned in as if he was about to discuss something private or salacious. 'Greta said that Meadow has signed up for online dating with Connected Hearts.'

Bear smiled. He loved working here but the staff thrived on gossip.

'Yes, that's correct.'

'And you, are you going to do it too?'

Bear cocked his head wondering where Felix was going with this. 'Yes, I said I'd do it with her.'

Felix nodded. 'Interesting.'

And with that, he walked away smiling as if he'd found the Holy Grail.

Bear drove back through the woods, smiling at two children who were chasing each other with water pistols, and pulled up outside reception again.

He walked back in to see Meadow scowling at her computer.

'Problem?'

'I've got fifty-eight matches already,' Meadow said.

Bear looked at her staring at the screen in disbelief. Why did he get the feeling that encouraging her to do online dating was a terrible idea? Fifty-eight men who could potentially be the man she would marry and it was only half past ten in the morning. How many more men would she be matched with before the end of the day?

And why had he agreed to go on dates with her? Talk about being a glutton for punishment. The very last thing he wanted was to sit there and watch her fall in love with someone else.

'How can there be fifty-eight?' Meadow said, scornfully. 'As you said earlier, we only get one soul mate but according to Connected Hearts I have fifty-eight of them, oh wait, fifty-nine now. This is ridiculous.'

'You don't have to meet them all,' Bear said and then regretted it because although it would kill him to watch her find her happy ever after with someone who wasn't him, he wanted her to be happy more than anything else and he didn't want to put her off finding that.

'Isn't that the whole point? If the computer algorithms have matched me with all these people, don't I need to meet them all to see if we are destined to be together forever?' Meadow said.

'Honestly, no. That's not really how online dating works. What is the percentage of these matches?'

She glanced at the screen again. 'Some of them are around fifty or sixty percent match, some of them are in the seventies, one or two are in the eighties.'

'If you match with someone at sixty percent that means there is forty percent of things you didn't match with. That's quite a large chunk that is not compatible with you. When I did online dating I would only really look at someone who was a seventy percent match or over to reduce the chance of meeting someone I'm not compatible with. So focus on the bigger percentages to start with. Then I'd read through all their profiles, their introduction, the answers to their questions, especially the longer answers, to get a sense of who they really are, and that will help you whittle it down even more. After that you might have five or ten people you would actually consider dating. You can start messaging them, chat to them online, and that will give you a really clear picture of whether you'd like to meet.'

'OK, that makes sense.' She started scanning through the profiles. 'I haven't got any matches in the nineties.'

'I doubt you will. The highest I ever got was an eighty-seven percent match. I was really excited. But she didn't want any children so I didn't even bother contacting her.'

'Yeah, that's quite a big thing to disagree on,' Meadow said. 'You would make a wonderful dad. Would you be happy to date someone who already had children?'

'Yes I would. But I'd want my own too. I'd love a big family and I'd be more than happy if stepchildren were a part of that as well.'

'I wonder if me having Star will put some men off.'

'I think some men won't want to date someone with a child, but some of them will embrace it. Some men might even have children of their own. This is why you chat to the men you match with online before you meet them so you can find out if they tick the important boxes for you. Otherwise it's a wasted date.'

'How long do you chat to someone for before you meet them?'

'There's no rules. Just whatever you feel comfortable with. I always think it's harder for women because for you it's not just about meeting someone you like, you also have to feel safe. Always meet in a public place, don't go anywhere alone with them.'

Meadow smiled and rolled her eyes at his overprotectiveness but he'd wrap her in cotton wool if he could.

'Connected Hearts is actually really hot on safety,' Bear said. 'They don't encourage you to give out your real name unless you are meeting them, same goes for any personal details like a phone number or your email address, all the messaging is done through the website. And if you are talking about your friends or family, they encourage you to give fake names so any scammers or weird stalkers can't find you in real life. Did you give yourself a cool codename?'

'Yes.'

'What did you go for?'

'I'm not telling you that, you'll laugh.'

'Why will I laugh?'

'Because you will.'

'Try me.'

She hesitated. 'Iris Starfish.'

He smiled. 'That's... different. Why did you go for that?'

'Irises are my favourite flower and Starfish because Star loves them. Heath said it sounds like a porn star name.'

He screwed up his face. 'I'm not sure it does. But anyway, it's better to be safe in these matters.'

'You know, with all your doom-mongering, you're not exactly selling this online dating malarkey to me.'

'I'm sure you will be fine, but a little bit of caution won't do any harm.'

She rolled her eyes and turned her attention back to the screen and after a few moments let out a heavy sigh.

'Why are you sighing? Fifty-nine matches is a great start. The last thing you want is to have one match at thirty-seven percent and find out that he kicks puppies for fun. At least this way you have choices,' Bear said.

'I just don't know where to start. I feel like I'm buying a car and I'm comparing one with electric windows versus another with a built-in sat-nav and I'm not interested in either of those things. This man enjoys cricket and says he has a good sense of humour. What does that even mean?'

'Probably that he laughs at his own jokes.'

'This one built his own model railway in his loft. That doesn't exactly get me excited.'

'Star would love it,' Bear said.

Meadow smiled. 'She really would.'

'And it shows that he's creative, has attention to detail and has hobbies. Everyone needs some kind of hobby, otherwise you're just sat in front of the TV every night watching crap.'

'So you think I should meet him?'

'What percentage match is he?'

Meadow studied the screen. 'Seventy-two percent.'

'He might be worth having a chat with, if nothing else. You might find he's lovely even if he is a nerd.'

'I don't mind nerds. I have a bit of a soft spot for them actually.'

'Is that so?'

'I love the smart techy types.'

Not for the first time, Bear wondered why they'd never got together. They clicked in a way he'd never had with anyone. His grandmother, Amelia, would tease him whenever they were alone that his relationships never lasted because none of them were Meadow. And there was some truth to that. What he had with Meadow was something special, something deep and powerful, and while it wasn't fair to compare that with what he'd had with women he'd dated, he couldn't help doing just that. Of course, his connection with Meadow was built on years of friendship and you couldn't have that bond with someone you'd just met, yet every woman he dated, he always found himself looking for that special something he had with his best friend and was always disappointed not to find it. He knew he'd set himself an impossible goal, no one was going to match up to her.

They'd shared a kiss together, back when they were still kids, and, despite only being sixteen, he'd known then she was the woman he was going to marry. But she'd practically run away the next day when he'd asked her out. She tried so hard to prove she wasn't interested in him, she'd dated a few other boys, but it almost seemed as if she was only doing it to push him away. Being the petty sixteen year old he was, he dated a few girls to prove he wasn't interested in her either, which he knew had upset her. But before he could get to the bottom of it, she was suddenly pregnant with Heath's baby and they were getting married. He'd hated her a little bit because of that. Sleeping with his brother had taken the point-scoring to a whole new level.

But then Meadow had gone into premature labour at thirty weeks while Heath had been away. Bear had rushed Meadow to hospital and held her hand while she had given birth to a tiny little girl barely bigger than his hand. For the briefest moment that Meadow was allowed to hold her before they whisked Star away to intensive care, she had looked at her daughter with such love and adoration and any hatred and pettiness had gone straight out the window. He'd immediately fallen in love with his tiny niece too and the hows and whys of who said and did what had no longer mattered. Heath had arrived later that night and the next four weeks had been a constant vigil at the hospital for all of them as they sat next to the incubator. Meadow had told the hospital staff that while Heath was the father, Bear was the stepfather so he was allowed to stay, although he wouldn't have left unless he'd been forced to. Star had rallied very quickly and they were all allowed to hold her for short periods, being careful of the cables and monitors she was hooked up to. They'd all had to grow up and be responsible adults once there'd been a child to look after. Meadow and Heath were amazing parents and Bear had tried to share the load as much as he could. But those feelings he'd had for Meadow as a kid had never gone away and here they were nearly eight years later, Meadow freshly divorced and he'd kind of hoped that she'd leave one brother and fall straight into the arms of another, so her decision to do online dating was a bit of a galling one.

'I'm sure we can find you a load of nerds to date,' Bear said. 'Us nerds are normally single. Most of them are rich too so they can take care of you.'

'You're single by choice. I'm sure once you reopen your dating profile, you'll have hundreds of women messaging you. You're the perfect man.'

'Oh well, if you think that then maybe me and you should date. I'm definitely a nerd, love kids and puppies, I'm tidy, have all my own teeth.'

Meadow laughed. 'If only life was that simple. Two best friends fall head over heels in love with each other. Maybe in a Hallmark movie that kind of thing happens. I don't think real life is that straightforward.'

He swallowed. 'It doesn't need to be complicated.'

'Love and dating *are* complicated. These are murky waters to navigate. And I don't need to marry another man who wants to take care of me. I want to get married to a man who loves me so much he can hardly think straight. I want to be a man's everything, his every breath, his every waking thought. I want a love that's exciting. I know it sounds ridiculous and I've probably been reading way too many romance stories, but I want that big soul mate kind of love. I want to love someone so completely and utterly and have that love returned. I've never had that. I have no idea what that feels like.'

'You've never been in love?'

'Oh I have, it never worked out. I've never had someone love me.'

He stopped himself from telling her that he had always loved her. 'I'm sorry my brother never gave you that.'

She waved it away. 'Me and Heath have always been best friends, it's never been more than that between us. I never loved him either, not in that way. I know you feel he let me down by divorcing me but I don't feel like that at all. We should never have got married in the first place. And he will always be a big part of my life and Star's so I'm never going to be lonely in that sense. But in here,' she pointed to her heart. 'That has ached to be filled for a long time.'

He stared at her. 'Then we need to find you someone amazing.'

CHAPTER FOUR

Meadow smiled as the entourage of River, his fiancée Indigo and his daughter Tierra arrived late morning with Meadow's daughter Star and the Brookfield brothers' grandmother, Amelia. It had been a big family trip out to go for the baby scan. Tierra had been desperate to see her future sibling on the scan and River and Indigo had decided to let her come so they could all find out the sex together. Star had also been really keen to see her new cousin too but Meadow knew that was more from a scientific inquisitive perspective than anything else. Amelia had been tasked with looking after the two girls in the waiting room while the sonographer checked everything was OK and then they were going to bring the girls in to have a look.

'I'm going to have a brother,' announced Tierra loudly as soon as she burst into the reception area.

Meadow adored Tierra, she was a five-year-old whirlwind of excited energy who gave her opinions freely.

'We could see his willy,' Star giggled.

'Finally a boy,' Bear teased.

'Hey!' Star said, feigning indignation. 'Girls are best.'

Bear scooped her up to sit on his lap and kissed her head. 'Yeah they are.'

Meadow couldn't help smiling at them; it was clear they adored each other.

Indigo and River walked in with Amelia.

'How was it?' Meadow asked. 'Was everything OK?'

'All fine, a big strong boy,' Indigo said, stroking her belly fondly.

'He is big,' River said, his voice holding a note of concern. 'They said we might have to discuss a caesarean or an early induction but they won't make any decisions on that until nearer the time.'

'I'm sure they will do what's best for Indigo and the baby,' Bear said.

Indigo stroked River's arm. 'It will be OK, I promise.'

'His heart was beating really fast,' Star said.

'And he waved at me,' Tierra said.

'I thought the sonographer was quite a hottie,' Amelia said, fanning herself. 'A right silver fox.'

River stared at her incredulously. 'The first time you get to see your great-grandson, and that's what you were looking at?'

'What? A lady like me has to take the opportunity when it arises. What do you want me to say, that the baby was cute?'

'Well that would be a start?' River said.

'I thought he was cute,' Tierra said, protectively.

'We couldn't really see his face though,' Indigo said, 'just an outline on the screen.'

'I'm sure he will be cute,' Amelia said. 'He has the Brookfield genes.'

'I thought it was really interesting,' Star said.

'She asked a ton of questions,' Indigo said. 'The sonographer was wonderful, he explained everything to her.'

'Did you get any photos?' Bear asked.

'The printer was broken but they are going to email over a load of pictures so we can print them off ourselves,' River said.

'I said we should name him Olaf,' Tierra said.

'We're going to discuss lots of different options for names,' Indigo said, diplomatically.

'Olaf is a good name,' Bear said and Star giggled.

'Right, come on then you,' River said to Tierra. 'Let's get you back to craft club.'

'Yay!' Tierra said, excitedly. 'We're making a puppet this afternoon, the ones that hang from the ceiling and you pull the string and they move. I said I wanted to make a pterodactyl.'

Meadow smiled. Tierra loved anything to do with dinosaurs. As it was the summer holidays there was no school for the girls. Tierra had begged to go to a daily craft club where she spent the days up to her eyeballs in glitter and came home with an armful of things she had made. Meadow had asked Star if she wanted to go, but she was such an outdoorsy girl, she was happiest spending her days in the woods or on the beach.

River gave Indigo a kiss on the cheek and she took her normal place behind the reception desk as they walked out the door, with Tierra chattering excitedly about the pterodactyl she was going to make.

'And you missy, do you want to take me down to the beach to show me the starfish you found yesterday?' Amelia said to Star.

Star quickly scrabbled off Bear's lap. 'They're not really fish, you know. They are echinoderms. And marine biologists are trying to change their name to sea stars.' She took Amelia's hand and walked off. 'Did you know if they lose an arm they can regrow it?'

Meadow smiled as she watched her go then she turned back to Indigo. 'Thank you for taking her, she's been so excited to go and see the baby.'

'It was my pleasure. She's such a smart girl, she had such fascinating questions. I'm sure she'll have many more for you tonight so be prepared for the birds and the bees talk.'

Meadow smirked. 'I'll look forward to that.'

CHAPTER FIVE

Meadow watched Bear chase Star across the sand as she walked across Pear Tree Beach with Heath. He was so good for her and Meadow counted her blessings every day that Star had three such wonderful men in her life.

Meadow's dad had wanted nothing to do with his granddaughter. He'd kicked Meadow out as soon as he found out she was pregnant and they'd never spoken since. And while Meadow was hurt by his attitude, she could only really find relief that such a vile man was not a part of Star's life. He'd made her and her mum's life a living hell with his huge drinking problem and his terrible temper. He'd never hit either of them but he was permanently angry, belittling and nasty. He had been part of the reason why Meadow had never felt inclined to date or have a relationship with anyone. The last thing she wanted was to follow in her mum's footsteps and end up with a man like her dad.

Their relationship was such a bad example of what married life was like, it had done nothing to make her want that. They had possibly been in love at one point for them to have got married in the first place – she'd seen the wedding photos and they looked happy. But growing up, Meadow had never witnessed that and, while she could accept that you could fall out of love with someone, the way her father had treated her mum with so much contempt had made her wonder if he'd ever loved her at all.

Her mum had stayed with him, even after all these years. She had never stood up for herself, never defended Meadow when his temper turned on her, which it frequently did. Her mum had stood by and done nothing when her dad had kicked her out at seventeen for being pregnant and she too had made no attempt to see Meadow or Star in the nearly eight years since Star had been born. Meadow had gone round there once after Star had been born on a day she knew her dad would be at his bowls club. She hoped to introduce her mum to Star. Her mum had flat refused to answer the door. She felt let down by that too. If the two people who were supposed to love you more than anything or anybody in the world didn't then it didn't exactly give her a lot of faith that any man would love and respect her either.

'What are you thinking about?' Heath said.

'My parents' relationship and how I don't really have any good role models for a proper loving relationship.'

'I wouldn't let their relationship put you off finding love for yourself. There are far more decent men out there than horrible ones.'

'I'm going to give it a try. I have a date tomorrow night, a man called Josh. I'm cautiously optimistic. Mainly because he hasn't sent me a dick pic yet. I've had five of those so far.'

'Oh god, I take it all back, men are the worst,' Heath said.

Meadow grinned. 'Some of you are OK. So I've made a bet with Bear over which will be the most successful dating path. He thinks online dating is the way forward because the computer has matched our algorithms. I don't think that is the way to meet my soul mate. I think I'll have more luck at these dating events I've signed up for with Mix n Match where I get to meet people face to face.'

'You meet people face to face with online dating too, eventually you'll meet these people in person.'

'I know, even if chatting online is far easier. I just meant with online dating we're matched with silly questions like dog or cat, beach or city holidays. We're meeting face to face because we know we've already been matched by some computer, only to find we may have a ton in common but we don't have that spark. If I meet someone by chance where we're both attracted to each other, the connection is there through a smile or eye contact or a touch, I think that connection is far more real and long-lasting than if we'd been connected because we both like cheese.'

'Fair point.'

'I'm quite excited about some of these dating events. There's speed dating and dating in the dark and even a kissing event which sounds a bit gross as I have to kiss thirty men in one night but I guess it could be fun. I'm nervous, I've never really dated before and I'm not sure what to expect, but I hope at the end of it all I find someone to love, who loves me.'

'I hope for that for you too. You've spent far too long hiding yourself away.'

'I'm not sure if I've been hiding,' Meadow said, awkwardly, knowing that she probably had been. 'Star has just been my priority.'

'And she is a brilliant, clever, happy little girl because of it. It's time to make you a priority for a change.'

'She will always be at the forefront of my mind when I date these men, will she like them, will they like her.' Meadow watched Bear throw Star over his shoulder and Star squeal with delight, her laughter loud and infectious. 'I want someone for her like Bear.'

'And while I would love for someone like him to end up being Star's stepdad, you have to look at the kind of man *you* want, too, not just go shopping for Star. Star has a wonderful fun uncle in Bear, you don't need to provide that for her. You need someone who ticks your boxes.'

Meadow didn't mention that Bear ticked every one of her boxes too and not just because he was so good with Star.

'I'm just saying that as long as the man you end up with is kind to Star, that's all you can really hope for. It could take many years for Star and your new boyfriend or husband to develop the kind of bond she has with Bear, so I wouldn't necessarily look for that.'

Meadow knew he was probably right but she decided to change the subject. 'I'm going to be out a lot over the next few nights and I know she'll be totally happy with you, she's with you three or four nights a week anyway, but what should I tell her about where I'm going and what I'm doing?'

Heath clearly thought about it. 'I don't want to lie to her but equally I don't think she needs to know that you'll be going out with a different man every night, she might find that a bit unsettling. I think we tell her that you're going out to meet some new friends, which is the truth. If it gets serious with any of them, then we can tell her you're dating or in a relationship and we can arrange for the two of them to meet.'

'I like the sound of that. I'm sure she would have a ton of questions if she knew and my answers may not always be appropriate.'

'It gives you a bit of breathing space to have some fun without having to think about them meeting Star just yet, get to know them properly before we involve her.'

Meadow nodded.

'And keep an open mind, especially when you're dating men you've met online. You never know when and where the right man may come along.'

'I will. And what about you? Are you not going to date again now you're officially divorced?'

There had been quite a few women for Heath over the years. Meadow had been insistent about him going out and having some fun because theirs was never a real marriage anyway, but he had only ever had casual flings. She wasn't sure if that was because that was what he was looking for or whether he didn't want anything serious because of Star and being technically married. At the beginning of the year, he'd spent an incredible weekend with Scarlet, some woman he'd met and fallen instantly in love with, or rather instantly into bed with. But when he'd told Scarlet he was married she hadn't wanted anything to do with him, which Meadow thought was a little unfair, Scarlet hadn't even hung around to hear his side of the story. Although she knew what she shared with Heath was definitely not the most conventional of relationships and if Heath had said, 'My wife is totally fine with me sleeping with other women,' how many women would actually believe it, despite it being the truth?

'I look at River and what he has with Indigo and I want that,' Heath said. 'But I can wait. I was with quite a few women while we were married and you had no one. I'd like you to find someone first.'

'We don't have to take it in turns,' Meadow said.

'I just don't really like the idea of you bringing home a new man to meet Star at the same time I bring home a new woman. I feel that could be quite unsettling for her. Let her get used to the idea of you having a boyfriend and that it's a good thing before I introduce her to my new girlfriend. That's not to say that if I go out with my friends to the pub, meet a woman, I'm going to turn down a night of sex if it's offered to me, but in terms of actually dating, pursuing something serious, I think I'll put that on the back-burner for now.'

'But one of these women you have casual sex with could turn into something serious if you let it. You shouldn't push it away, we can figure it out. Star is a bright girl and she knows she is so loved, I think she will be totally OK with us dating, because let's face it we're never going to bring home someone who is a dick.'

'If it happens, it happens. But it's going to take someone

really special to fit into my life. I don't want to change the fact that I live next door to my ex-wife, that I have breakfast and dinner with you and Star almost every day, but not every woman I meet is going to be OK with that.'

Meadow thought about that for a moment. Had she ruined his life? That's what her dad had said when she told him she was pregnant; she remembered how, in amongst the diatribe, he'd said that if she went ahead and had the baby she would ruin her life and that of the baby's father too. Although she had never thought that was true. But even though she and Heath were divorced now, she'd never realised how their co-parenting arrangement would add a complication to Heath's relationships that didn't really need to be there.

'Do you ever regret... what we did?'

Heath stopped dead and turned to face her. 'Oh my god, no. Not for one second. Don't ever think that. You gave me a daughter and she is the most incredible thing that ever happened to me. You gave me a reason to get out of bed in the morning, you gave me something to fight for, and I will always be grateful for that. She is the single most important thing in my life and I could never ever regret that. She is the best thing that happened to my brothers too. We were all drifting through life with no purpose, no hope. River had this big plan to build the treehouse resort but we'd never got off our arses to do anything about it. Back then, I couldn't ever see a way out of our hole, the resort was a pipe dream, I didn't think it would ever happen.'

He smiled as he thought. 'Bear was building a website for it even though we hadn't got a single treehouse built, he was always the optimistic one of us. He did research about how much to charge and what kind of facilities other places had. He was really excited, while River and I would go down the pub to discuss plans and then just get stupidly drunk. We were pathetic and hopeless and Star being on the way was the incentive we all needed to make it happen. She changed our lives for the better, all of us. And if we'd… told the truth I don't think any of that would have happened. And I'm glad we got married. I know we never loved each other, not in that way, but if we hadn't got married, if we'd lived separately and I just popped in to help now and again, it wouldn't have been the same. We handled the sleepless nights, the feeds, the dirty nappies and the uncertainties and worry together. We raised her as a family. We were a team, we still are, and Star knows that even though we are divorced. I wouldn't change any of that for the world. And so what if I have to aim high to find someone who will fit into my life rather than just settling for an easy life? It's OK to have high standards.'

Meadow smiled at that, but then frowned.

'But what about what happened with Scarlet? If you weren't married to me that could have turned into something.'

Heath shrugged. 'I met her the other day actually.'

'You did?'

'She seemed delighted that I was divorced, she said she'd call me. So far I've heard nothing. I will always wonder if she was the one that got away, I felt we had this incredible connection but maybe what we really had was great sex. And who knows how that relationship would really pan out. Maybe she didn't run because I was married but because I had a daughter, in which case that relationship would have been very short-lived and she clearly wasn't the one at all. I have no doubt that my perfect match is out there and maybe it's Scarlet and maybe it isn't but when the time is right I'm sure we will meet.'

Meadow smiled at that utter confidence of finding that perfect person. She wished she shared that attitude.

CHAPTER SIX

Meadow poked her head around Star's bedroom door to see she was fast asleep, sprawled across the bed like the starfish she adored so much. She loved spending her days playing in the woods or on the beach but she always went out like a light when it was bedtime, exhausted from the day's exertions. Meadow softly closed the door and went into the spare room. Standing in the middle was a mannequin wearing a wedding dress and she couldn't be prouder about how it was turning out.

She'd started sewing when Star was little, partly because she wasn't happy with the choice of clothes available for little girls, which were mostly pink and delicate – not great for a little tomboy who had a love of climbing trees – and partly because she wanted some time just for her. As much as she loved being a mum, it was a completely all-consuming part of her life. Sewing gave her a hobby that was just for her. What started as making clothes for Star and Tierra had progressed to making dresses for herself and then making dresses for other people too and she absolutely loved it.

This was her first wedding dress. She was making it for a local woman who was having a very low budget wedding and who had seen Meadow's dresses online and asked her if she would be willing to make her wedding dress, which felt like a big responsibility. But it made her smile so damn much every time she was working on it. She carefully removed the dress and sat down in her chair, selecting a beautiful turquoise embroidery silk so she could start embroidering some flowers on it.

This made her happy, she could spend hours doing this. Going out and meeting new people was so far away from what she really wanted to do.

She had always struggled with making friends. Growing up, her parents had never let her play with anyone after school or go over to anyone's house because her dad had said he'd then be expected to have those children round to his house too and he didn't want children in the house, something Meadow often thought included her.

But Bear, Heath and River had, at least in their early years, lived right next door so she would often climb over the fence to play with them. Their parents and later their various guardians hadn't minded her presence and the boys had no desire to come and play in her house with the grumpy man so everyone was happy.

But at school the girls would often mock her for her closeness to the Brookfield brothers so she hadn't made any real deep female friends there. There had been a few girls later on that she'd thought she could count on, Sally and Fliss, but no sooner had Meadow announced her pregnancy, she hadn't seen them for dust. They had all gone off to university the following year and she had been forgotten. And while she had attended some mother and baby groups, the other mums were quite a lot older than she was, with most of them being mid to late twenties in comparison to Meadow's seventeen, and quite a lot more judgemental than she'd been expecting, too. So apart from a weekly yoga class where she had a nodding acquaintance with the other participants, she had largely stayed at home, as Heath said, and hidden herself away. It was easier than putting herself out there to be rejected, and not just in her relationships with men but also in her friendships with women.

But this, sewing, following a pattern, embroidering, creating a dress from scratch, this she found peaceful. She smiled wryly because a love of sewing didn't exactly make her a great catch for the men she was going to date. She was sure men wanted women who surfed or danced or went backpacking around the world. Unless she went out with the guy with the train set in his loft. He could have his boring hobby and she could have hers.

She sighed because that didn't exactly fill her with joy either.

CHAPTER SEVEN

Bear lay in bed that night and idly logged in to his online dating account. He'd reopened it earlier that day but he hadn't yet looked at any of his matches. His heart really wasn't in it, but he had promised Meadow that he would do all this dating stuff with her so he supposed he'd better chat to a few women online so he could get a few simple dates out of it.

He went to his matches and saw that he had forty-nine. And one of them had already messaged him earlier that afternoon. Twilight Rose. He rolled his eyes. He wondered if the woman was a *Twilight* fan. Meadow had made him watch all the movies with her and he'd hated them. The acting was terrible, the plot was wispy thin. She did say she loved the books better than the films but the films had certainly never made him want to pick up the books. It was one of the things they agreed to disagree on and one of the things he teased her about. He had made her watch *Star Wars* with him and she'd hated that too, so he supposed they were even.

He clicked into Twilight's profile and then sat up straight. Ninety-six percent match. He'd never matched with anyone with such a high percentage before. He read through her information and her introduction to herself and it made him smile.

He clicked into her message.

Hello, I read your profile and you seem really lovely. Please don't spoil it by replying to this message with a dick pic, I've had three of those already and I'm not sure I can cope with any more.

He groaned. Some men were twats. No woman deserved to be sent that kind of message. He hoped Meadow had been spared that but he sincerely doubted it. He carried on reading.

So I have a question for you. If you put a coat on a snowman will it melt?

He laughed. What a brilliant starter question. She'd skipped straight past the typical favourite holiday destination question and what's your favourite movie and gone for something fun. And this kind of question was right up his street.

He opened up a reply box.

Hello Twilight, lovely to hear from you. Your profile made me smile. Can I take this opportunity now to apologise for my gender about the dick pics. I'm not sure why some men do that and if it has ever worked for them. It's not something I've ever done or feel inclined to do, so I promise you're safe there. As for your question, the jacket would actually protect the snowman or snowwoman from warmer air getting to it and keep the cold air trapped inside the jacket. So I have one for you.

Until I am measured I am not known, but how you miss me when I have flown. What am I?

He pressed send. She would get an email notification to say she had a message and if she was free she might come online to reply, although it was quite late now.

He waited a few moments and he couldn't help but smile when he saw her little green online light come on. She must have read his message because the little three dots appeared to show she was writing a reply.

I'm lying in bed, half asleep, and I can still tell you the answer to your riddle is time. You've picked the wrong girl to challenge with a riddle, I am the riddling queen, and you're right about the snowman, but of course you knew that.

He liked that she was into riddles. Meadow loved a good riddle but he knew this wasn't her as she was the rather randomly named Iris Starfish. Twilight was still writing more so he waited for her next message to pop through.

And thanks for no dick pics, it is an extraordinary thing why men would do that. I'm new to online dating, well dating at all, so that was an unpleasant surprise. I'm still not really sure I want to enter the dating world, I've been happily single for a very long time. Well, maybe not totally happily but I've done OK. Letting someone else into your life feels like a big step. Have you done much online dating before?

Bear liked her honesty. He wrote his reply.

I've done it before, came off it for a while, came back on again, I'm fortunate enough never to have been sent any dick pics though.

He smiled when she immediately sent back a crying laughing emoticon.

I should hope not.

He quickly wrote his reply. **I can understand your caution about dating and there's absolutely nothing wrong with being single, I think a lot more people nowadays are finding being alone the better option. But there's a big difference between doing OK and being happy. My brother has recently got together with someone who makes him blissfully happy and I look at them together and I want what he has, that forever kind of love. Sorry, I'm sure that sounds very soppy.**

Her reply was almost instant. **Not soppy at all. And you've given me hope that some men on here are looking for the same thing I am. From some of the messages I've had so far it's clear a lot of men are on here just looking for sex.**

Bear replied. **Yeah, a lot of women are on here just looking for the same.**

She sent her reply. **Thank you for being so lovely. I'm going to go to sleep now, my daughter gets me up early most days and as it's the school summer holidays she wants to go out and enjoy the outside as early as she can. I will message you tomorrow with another riddle. Be prepared. Night x**

He smiled. **Goodnight Twilight x**

He watched her little green online light go out. Now for once that felt like a positive exchange.

CHAPTER EIGHT

When Meadow and Star walked into the restaurant the next morning, only Bear was sitting there by himself eating his breakfast as he typed away on his mini laptop. Their breakfasts were normally early, the guests would all trickle through much later.

Meadow and Star went up to the counter to get their food, chatting briefly with Alex, their chef, and then went to join Bear at the table.

'Bear, I've been thinking,' Star said, plonking herself down next to Bear as Meadow went and sat opposite them. She watched as Bear turned to face Star, giving her full and immediate attention.

'What you been thinking about?' Bear said.

'I was watching *Hedgerows* last night and—'

Bear let out a little gasp. 'You watched it without me?'

Star grinned. 'It was last week's episode, the one we've already watched together. I wanted to watch it again because I love the badgers. I think we should set up some webcams in the wood so we can capture the different animals that live in the forest, especially at night. Just like they do in *Hedgerows*.'

Meadow smiled. That TV programme, *Hedgerows and Woodlands*, had been wonderful for Star. She had always been interested in the animals that lived in the wood but the show had developed in her this huge passion and excitement for them. There were animals featured on that programme that Star nor Meadow had never seen before. The best thing was that Bear watched it with them and it was a joy to see Bear and Star talk about it with so much enthusiasm.

'We can totally do that,' Bear said. 'It might be a good thing to feature on our website too so people feel like Wishing Wood will allow them to get back to nature. But we need to figure out where the best place to set up the webcams would be first. How should we do that?'

Meadow smiled. He would make such a good dad one day. He would totally know how to find the best place to put the webcams, but he wanted Star to come up with the ideas to push her and challenge her.

Star thought about it for a moment. 'We can put food out in different places in the wood and see where the most food gets eaten.'

Bear grinned. 'Great idea. What kind of food should we put out?'

'Fruits and vegetables for the herbivores like the rabbits, squirrels and voles. Cat or dog food for foxes, badgers and hedgehogs, though they will probably eat the fruit too,' Star said, knowledgeably.

'OK, great, we can set up a few feeding stations with different food around the wood,' Bear said.

'And fresh water too,' Star said.

'Good idea.'

'And we need to put some fruit and vegetables away from the meat too, so that the voles are not eating next to where the foxes are eating, otherwise the voles might become fox dinner too,' Star said.

'That's true,' Bear said, solemnly. 'I'll order some webcams.'

'Can we have webcams in the trees too so we can catch birds like owls and woodpeckers?'

'That's a bit more tricky, birds don't tend to sleep in the same place every night and they don't use a nest either, apart from when there are chicks. And we won't see any chicks at this time of year, except maybe with some pigeons,' Bear said. 'We can put some nestboxes up and put webcams inside but I don't think we'll see much action there at this time of year. I can certainly put a few webcams up some trees to see what we capture. We might get lucky.'

'Can I just remind you that any webcams that get put up can't be recording or pointing towards any treehouses,' Meadow said, with her manager hat on.

Bear grinned. 'Definitely not.'

'Why not?' Star asked. 'There are animals living in those trees too.'

'Because we might see naked people,' Bear said, honestly, and Meadow laughed when Star pulled a face.

'Ewww.'

'Exactly,' Bear said,

'And because our guests have a right to privacy,' Meadow said.

'OK, I'll get some food today,' Bear said. 'And tonight

before bedtime, me and you can go out into the woods and lay it out for any animals. And then tomorrow after breakfast we can go and see where the most food was eaten.'

'Yes, that will be awesome,' Star said, excitedly.

Meadow smiled at Bear with complete love as he chatted happily with her daughter.

She spotted Greta and Felix, their grounds crew, walking in together to grab breakfast and Meadow waved at them. Greta gave her an exaggerated thumbs up in return, gestured to her and Bear and gave her another thumbs up. She must have said something to Felix because he also gave her two thumbs up. Meadow watched them go to the counter in confusion. She always had breakfast with Bear, Heath, River and Indigo so that felt like a weird reaction to seeing the two of them together.

'And you never know, we might see the Wishing Wood wolf,' Bear said, mysteriously.

Meadow rolled her eyes. It was Heath who had started this silly rumour the week before. He'd been on his way back from the pub after a pool competition and he said he saw a wolf running through the trees. He said he'd only had one pint and was adamant about what he saw but obviously no one believed him. But then at least two different guests had mentioned about seeing a wolf in the trees too over the last few days. One had even captured a very grainy, shaky video of something grey, white and furry, but it was too far away to really see what it was.

'I really don't think we need to worry about wolves here,' Meadow said.

'I'm not worried,' Star said, excitedly. 'I've never seen a wolf before, I'd love to see one.'

Meadow smiled at her brave, brilliant, clever girl. She loved her so much. When she'd talked with Bear about her dating and the potential match being OK with her having a child, she knew now how important that was. But despite what she'd talked about with Heath last night on their walk, she knew she needed much more than that, she needed someone who would love and adore Star as much as Bear, Heath and River did and that was a tall order. For now, she would enjoy meeting different men and going out on dates but it would always be at the back of her mind if any of the relationships started turning serious.

'That would be cool to see a wolf,' Bear said. 'But we don't have any wild wolves in this country. I'm not sure what people are seeing but it's not a wolf. It could be a white deer, we've seen that a few times in the area. I can't think what else it could be.'

'A yeti,' Star giggled.

'Now that could be a possibility. But if Bigfoot is out there, we'll catch him on the webcams.'

Star clapped her hands together excitedly.

'What's going on?' Heath said.

He bent to give Meadow a kiss on the cheek and then moved to sit on the other side of Star, giving her a huge hug and a kiss. Star moved to sit on Heath's lap so she could hug him properly. Heath kissed the top of her head, holding her tight. Star used to be a real daddy's girl when she was small, always going to him for cuddles. It had never failed to make Meadow smile so much to see them together. As she'd got older, Star seemed to need less cuddles but, sometimes, she would still sit on their laps like she used to.

'We're going to trap Bigfoot,' Star giggled.

Heath nodded seriously. 'That sounds like fun. Although I kind of feel sorry for poor Bigfoot.'

'We'll let him go if we catch him, we just want to get a selfie with him,' Star said.

Meadow loved her overactive imagination.

'We're setting webcams up in the woods so if your wolf is out there, we'll see him,' Bear said, clearly mocking his brother.

'Oh, you tease me now,' Heath said, obviously not taking any offence. 'But when you see him, you'll be laughing on the other side of your face.'

'Bear thinks you saw a white deer not a wolf,' Star said, practically, climbing down from his lap to resume her breakfast.

'I'm pretty sure I could tell the difference between a deer and a wolf,' Heath said. Bear made drinking motions over the top of Star's head and Heath grinned. 'Even then.'

'We're actually setting up webcams to try to capture foxes, badgers, stoats and voles,' Star said.

'Now that sounds like a much more sensible idea,' Heath said. 'I've seen a few foxes in my time here, plenty of rabbits and squirrels, but I've never seen a stoat or a vole and I've only seen a badger once or twice.'

'And a wolf,' Star said.

'Yes, let's not forget that,' Heath said. 'It'd be good to see them on the webcams. And you've definitely chosen the right person to set it all up for you. I'm sure there isn't a single thing about webcams, night-vision and motion sensors that Bear doesn't know about.'

Bear looked momentarily stunned at the compliment from his brother.

Just then River, Indigo and Tierra arrived. They went to get their breakfast first and then came and joined them. Tierra was clutching something in her tiny hand.

'This is my brother,' Tierra said excitedly, thrusting the picture of their unborn baby under Meadow's nose.

Meadow slid an arm around Tierra to look at the photo. 'Wow, look at him, he is going to be huge.'

She glanced at Indigo who smiled weakly.

'I mean…' Meadow trailed off. There was no rescuing that comment.

'It's OK,' Indigo said, as she tucked into her waffles. 'There was no way this baby wasn't going to be big. Look at the size of the Brookfield men. Tierra was nine and half pounds when she arrived. I bet Star was big too when she was born.'

Meadow's heart leapt and she glanced over to Heath.

'Star was premature so she weighed four pounds nine ounces when she was born. I don't think she had time to put on that Brookfield weight,' Heath said, calmly.

'Oh my god, I didn't know, why didn't you tell me?' Indigo said to River.

'I didn't want to worry you,' River said. 'There are lots of reasons a baby is born prematurely, I doubt it's hereditary. Tierra was born with no issues at all, in fact she was two weeks late, so there's no reason to worry that our baby will be born earlier than planned.'

Meadow cringed. There were times when she wished she had been truthful about Star from the beginning and this was one of them, she didn't want Indigo to worry unnecessarily.

'Was she OK?' Indigo asked Meadow, despite the fact that Star was sitting there quite clearly full of life. But Meadow knew Indigo was now worried about her own baby.

'She was in an incubator for four weeks but not all the time, we were able to hold her and feed her for a few hours a day. She was strong, a fighter.' Meadow decided to change the subject slightly so as to not have to focus on the stress of the first few weeks after Star's birth. 'She loved being held by Heath and Bear. She would always open her eyes and look at them when they were holding her as if she knew she was completely safe in their arms.'

'Bear, you were allowed at the neonatal unit too?' Indigo said.

'He was there when I gave birth,' Meadow said. 'Heath had gone to London for the day with some friends. There had been no indication at all from the scans or health checks that I would go into labour ten weeks early, so I'd waved him off safe in the knowledge that everything was fine and then two hours later my waters broke. Bear was incredible, so calm and reassuring. He drove me to hospital and held my hand while I gave birth. Any other seventeen-year-old boy would have run a mile but he was there, by my side throughout the whole ordeal. And then when Heath arrived and they realised he was the father not Bear, they wanted to kick Bear out so I told them he was the stepfather, so all three of us were allowed to stay.'

'There was no way I was going to leave,' Bear said.

Meadow smiled at him gratefully. He had been her rock and she'd never forget that.

'I was so glad he was there too,' Heath said. 'When I arrived to find my daughter in an incubator hooked up to tubes and cables, I was a complete mess. Bear was… incredible, I'm not ashamed to admit I cried on his shoulder. He was solid, constant. I'm not sure how we would have got through those weeks without him.'

Bear looked awkward for a moment, focussing on his coffee mug.

'You pretended to be my stepfather?' Star said.

Bear nodded.

'That's funny.'

Bear leaned over the table to look at the photo and Meadow passed it over. Tierra immediately ran round to Bear and he pulled her onto his lap.

'I can't believe we're going to have another baby around the place, it's very exciting,' Bear said.

'Do you want children, Bear?' Star asked. 'River and Indigo will have two and Mummy and Daddy have me. You could have one too.'

'Oh, I'd love to have children, the more the merrier,' Bear said.

'Why don't you have one then?' Star asked simply.

'Oh, only women can have babies,' Bear said.

'I know that,' Star said, rolling her eyes. 'The daddy puts the baby in the mummy's tummy and the mummy grows it until it's big and then lays it like a giant egg.'

Bear choked on his coffee. Indigo turned a snort of laughter into a cough.

'But you need to find a woman who can give you a baby,' Star said, practically.

'I probably need to marry a nice woman first,' Bear said. 'Before we start thinking about having children.'

'River and Indigo aren't married and they are having a baby together,' Star pointed out.

'But we are engaged,' River said, quickly. 'We will be married soon.'

'But you gave Indigo the baby before you got engaged and before she came here to work. How did you give her the baby when she wasn't here?' Star asked.

'We met before she came here,' River said, honestly, but clearly downplaying the one-night stand that had brought Indigo here, which was a good thing as it turned out, they were clearly head over heels in love with each other.

'So Bear could give a baby to someone without marrying them?' Star said.

'I could,' Bear said, slowly. 'But normally, when you're giving babies away you do that with someone you love.'

Star clearly thought about this and then turned her attention to Meadow. 'Mummy, you could have Bear's baby now you are divorced from Daddy. Winnie from school, her mum and dad got divorced and Winnie's mummy had a baby with her neighbour a few weeks later. Bear could give you his baby to grow in your tummy and, once you laid it, Bear would have a baby too and he wouldn't be lonely any more.'

The strawberry Meadow had been eating lodged in her throat and she quickly took a big mouthful of tea to wash it down. Good lord. She hadn't been expecting that kind of conversation this morning. She thought she could hear a pin drop as everyone waited with bated breath to see how she would deal with that question. The thought of being married to Bear and having his babies made her go all gooey inside. But Bear didn't think of her that way.

'I don't think he is lonely, he has us and you and Tierra and lots of friends,' Meadow tried.

'But he wants children, he just said,' Star said. 'And you two love each other so it's perfect.'

Meadow glanced at Bear who was watching her, probably waiting for her to explain how they didn't love each other in that way, but she couldn't do it, because she did love him like that.

'You do love Bear, don't you Mummy?' Star said.

'I do,' Meadow said, buttering her toast, focussing on getting the butter into every corner. 'Very much.'

'And do you love Mummy, Bear?'

Bear cleared his throat. 'Yes I do.'

Meadow looked up at him and he was staring at her. If only she could read what was going through his mind because his face was showing a mixture of emotions.

'We all love each other,' Heath tried to explain. 'In the same way that you and Tierra love each other and Indigo and Meadow love each other because we're all family. But River and Indigo love each other in a different way to the way Bear and your mummy love each other and that's the kind of love you need to have a baby.'

'How is it different?' Star said.

'There are lots of different kinds of love,' Meadow said. 'You love pizza but you're not going to marry it. You love living here in Wishing Wood, but you're not going to marry the wood.'

Star giggled.

'And you love me and your daddy, but you're not going to marry us either. When you're in love with someone you choose to spend all your time with that person. They are your favourite person in the world and so that's why you choose to marry them.'

'But I choose to spend all my time with all of you, you are my favourite people,' Star said.

'Mine too,' Tierra said, then waved the photo she was holding in the air. 'And Olaf.'

Bear leaned forward. 'When you go to the fair or a theme park, you always like to go on the carousel, that's your favourite ride, right? It goes round and round and doesn't really do much more than that, but it's still your favourite because you love the painted horses. That's kind of what family love is, it's constant, always there, unwavering, it never changes. The horses are solid, dependable, just like the way your mummy and daddy love you. But you also love the big rollercoasters, they're exhilarating, exciting and make you squeal with delight as you go up and down and do the loops. Your stomach does these funny leaps. You feel this wonderful, delicious feeling of anticipation as you go up to the top and then you go over the edge and plummet to the bottom and it almost feels like you're flying, nothing beats that incredible feeling. And that's what the love River and Indigo have for each other feels like.'

Meadow's heart filled with love for him. He had described it perfectly.

Star stared at him with wide eyes. 'That kind of love

does sound wonderful. So you and Mummy don't feel like that for each other, the rollercoaster love?'

Bear looked at Meadow and she was surprised when he didn't immediately say no. He was clearly waiting for her to answer and she didn't know what to make of that. Meadow chose her words carefully.

'The thing about love, is that it changes. One day chocolate ice cream is your favourite but then you try strawberry somewhere new and then suddenly you love it and it becomes your favourite ever flavour. You can't go back then. You thought chocolate was your favourite but when you tasted that strawberry you know it will always be your favourite from then on. Maybe one day the love that Bear and I feel for each other might change too.'

Meadow saw River and Indigo exchange glances. Heath was looking confused and Bear didn't seem able to take his eyes off her.

Star nodded. 'I never used to like olives but now I do, Daddy said our tastes change as we get older. So when you two are older, you might like the taste of each other more.'

She giggled at her own analogy but then carried on eating her breakfast as if the conversation had come to an end.

'My favourite ice cream is honeycomb,' Tierra said. 'Especially the one with crunchy bits in it. What's your favourite, Bear?'

Bear's eyes were locked on Meadow's when he answered. 'Strawberry, always has been, always will be.'

Meadow's heart was suddenly beating so hard in her chest she felt sure everyone at the table would hear it.

CHAPTER NINE

The first yurts and tents started arriving for Dwelling not long after Meadow and Indigo arrived at reception. Meadow decided she'd be better placed outside in an attempt to direct proceedings, which was not easy when the organisers and workshop leaders were so laid-back they were horizontal. The field where the festival was taking place was right behind the reception area and was normally used for camping. There were a number of people milling around saying hello to each other as cars and vans drove around aimlessly looking for the best plot, despite there being an actual plan telling them where they were all supposed to set up.

It was like this every year: the organisers would have a strict plan of locations for the workshops, tents and food stalls and a tight schedule for when the workshops and bands would be on and every year people just suited themselves with where they would go, what time they would run their workshop or play their songs. Yet somehow this laid-back attitude not only worked but was completely contagious. Guests who had never been before would invariably get a bit annoyed that the wood-whittling workshop was an hour later than advertised or perhaps on a different day entirely, but after hanging around with the organisers and regular guests for an hour or two they all mellowed out and just accepted that the workshops would happen at some point. There was no rush, no panic, it was what it was and it would never change.

Meadow spotted Greta talking to one of the stall holders who was selling candles, while Lucien, one of their housekeeping crew staff, was admiring the wooden ornaments on another stall and Sharon Ecclestone, one of their regular guests at Wishing Wood, was chatting to a lady with a gigantic harp.

Meadow looked around and saw Amelia flirting with an older gentleman dressed in a splendid purple cloak with a silvery beard curled into a point. Amelia seemed to be going all out lately to find herself a man. Meadow had to admire her confidence with men. Amelia was in her eighties and was fabulously glamorous but Amelia knew that. Maybe Meadow should ask her for some tips.

Meadow glanced around for Star and spotted her sitting on a chair having her hair braided with pretty ribbons and beads by one of the regulars, Leah, who was wearing a long flowing beaded dress of every colour in the rainbow.

Meadow gave up directing cars and vans to where they should be going as no one was paying her any attention anyway and wandered over to talk to them.

'Star, you look beautiful, Leah is doing a wonderful job,'

Meadow said, giving Leah a big hug. It was then that she noticed the large baby bump. 'Oh congratulations.'

'Thank you,' Leah said, a huge smile across her face. She gestured to a young man in a red velvet waistcoat with curly hair tied back in a short ponytail, currently entertaining the smaller children with his fire breathing. 'It's Charlie's in case you were wondering. We finally decided to stop messing around with the best friend thing and become a couple, as we should have been all along. One night we were sitting out, watching the stars, putting the world to rights as we always do, and he suddenly stopped and said he loved me. I told him I loved him too and there was no going back after that.'

Meadow smiled, she knew Leah and Charlie had been friends as far back as Dwelling had been running and even longer than that. Meadow had originally thought they were a couple as they were so close. It was funny to think that what they were looking for was right under their noses the whole time.

'The carousel kind of love or rollercoaster love?' Star said, as she admired her braids in the little hand mirror.

Leah frowned slightly in confusion and then her face cleared as if she understood. She had a knack of seeing things that others didn't. 'Rollercoaster love presumably being the exhilarating ups and downs, the delicious stomach-churning loops and the screams and shouts of pure and utter joy? And I guess carousel love is slow, steady, constant, the kind of love you have for your best friend? I can tell you that with Charlie it's definitely a bit of both.'

Meadow smirked and shook her head. They had clearly defined the difference between family love and romantic love over breakfast and now Leah was blurring the lines all over again.

'Charlie is my best friend and he always will be and I love him as a friend – that constant companion, that loyal, unwavering kind of love – but when I kiss him, when I… cuddle him in bed, when I look at him sometimes and realise he is my forever, it's pure, wonderfully delicious rollercoaster love. And I wouldn't have it any other way,' Leah said.

Meadow knew exactly what she meant.

'Mummy and Bear have carousel love and River and Indigo have rollercoaster love,' Star said, passing Leah a purple ribbon to use in her hair.

'Did River get himself a girlfriend?' Leah said, incredulously, weaving the ribbon into Star's hair.

'A fiancée actually. She's five months pregnant too. They are completely head over heels in love with each other, I'm really happy for them,' Meadow said.

'That's wonderful news. Oh, I'm so pleased for him. I never thought he would ever settle down. He always seemed so distant and lonely. I'm glad he found someone to love him for who he is.'

'Indigo is lovely, you'll really like her.'

Leah smiled and then frowned again. 'And what's this about you and Bear having carousel love?'

Meadow forced a smile on her face. Leah had been telling Meadow that she was destined to be with Bear for years. 'We're friends.'

'Uh-huh,' Leah said, not sounding like she believed Meadow for one second.

'But one day their love might change just like yours and Charlie's love changed,' Star said, knowledgeably.

'It might change, yes,' Leah stared at Meadow with wide comical eyes, as if that was the most obvious thing in the world.

'And then Bear can put a baby in Mummy's tummy for her to grow and they can get married and he can live in our treehouse with us.'

'It's funny you should say that, Star, because knowing I was going to be seeing your mummy today, I did her cards for her last night,' Leah said, talking of the tarot cards she always carried around with her as if they could predict the future or answer an important question.

Meadow smiled. 'I'm not sure I want to know.'

Leah finished Star's hair. 'Right, you're all done, why don't you go and watch Charlie perform his tricks.'

Star hopped down from the stool and ran over to join the other children who were all watching Charlie with awe.

Leah was studying Meadow patiently.

Meadow sighed. 'Oh go on then, tell me, what did you see in my cards?'

'A wedding and a baby.'

'Well that will be River's obviously. I just told you that.'

'I did your cards, not River's.'

'But surely, if I'm going to their wedding and I'll be here when their baby is born, if the cards are able to pick up my future that's what they've seen.'

'That's not how the cards work. The baby is yours.'

Meadow swallowed a lump in her throat at that thought and then pushed it away. 'I suppose it's possible. I've decided to try dating after all these years of living a spinster life. I've signed up to online dating and I'm also doing these dating events like speed dating where I'll be meeting people face to face. I suppose I might get lucky and find someone I want to marry one day and I guess one day there might be more children.'

'The wedding will be this year, the baby shortly after.'

'Wow, that's fast work, even for me,' Meadow said, not believing in any of this despite wanting to.

'Me and Charlie married four weeks after we'd said we love each other for the first time. It would have been sooner, but the registry office won't let you do that. There was no point hanging around for us, we both knew we wanted forever with each other, so why wait?'

'That's lovely that you two have found each other after so long,' Meadow said, trying to distract her.

'The cards say you marry a dear friend too.'

'Oh come on, you've been trying to get me together with Bear for years,' Meadow laughed.

'Because I can see what you two absolutely refuse to see. You love each other, and that is as clear as day and now the cards have backed it up.'

'Well, I promise to invite you to the wedding if we do get married.'

'The cards predicted that too. Apparently I wear a big hat.'

CHAPTER TEN

Bear stepped inside the wedding chapel treehouse and looked around. River and Heath were busy in one corner, hammering and drilling away, and hadn't noticed his arrival yet. It was the first time he'd been inside since they'd started building it a few weeks before. He had to give it to his brothers, once they put their minds to building something, it often came together very quickly. River just had an eye for these things whereby he could see the bigger picture and Heath was quick and efficient with the way he worked. This place had been Meadow and Indigo's idea; he'd looked at the plans and the drawings and he could see his brothers had captured what Meadow and Indigo wanted perfectly.

It was going to hold thirty guests so future weddings would be small affairs, but the rustic walls, and the candles and the fairy lights they were going to have, were the perfect backdrop. It didn't need to be anything extravagant. He could imagine how some simple flowers around the room would be the only other decoration they'd need to have. The roof was partly finished but the part that wasn't was up the far end near where the couple would stand while getting married, and actually the lack of roof enhanced the beauty of the place, letting nature inside. There was a large open arch-shaped hole at the end, too, where the plan was to have some kind of modern stained-glass window. At the moment there was no glass in it, but with the stunning view of the sea and the woods just outside, maybe they didn't need a stained-glass window after all.

He watched his brothers working seamlessly together, passing each other tools or parts mostly without any kind of instruction or request. They had always been more practical than academic but what they had achieved here at Wishing Wood was nothing short of spectacular. With thirty-two incredible treehouses, each one charming, unique, luxurious and strong enough to withstand the fiercest storms, he couldn't have been prouder to be a part of this place, even if his contribution wasn't as hands-on as his brothers.

He smirked and shook his head as Heath danced and sang along to the radio. While his carpentry and architectural skills were second to none, his singing and dancing left a lot to be desired. Heath didn't seem to care though. He was always upbeat and happy about everything.

The three of them had always been so close growing up, despite Heath being three years older than Bear and River two years older than Heath. They had to be close because in reality they only had each other. Both of their parents had walked out on them when they were little and they'd been raised unofficially by a host of different friends and relatives who would come and stay for a few weeks before passing the baton to the next person who wanted a few weeks' holiday by the beach.

Their uncle Michael, who had owned this place, had been there for them more than any other relative so it made sense that they came to live with him when their parents died in a car accident. The powers that be needed something more official in place for their upbringing than the casual arrangement that had been in place for the many years before then. Michael fed them, looked after them, went to all the school events. On the surface he did everything a parent would, but he'd never been able to give the brothers the complete and unconditional love they'd needed. He was definitely lacking in any kind of visible affection, which just made the bond between the three brothers even stronger. So it had been a hard pill to swallow when Heath had got Meadow pregnant and then married her. Although Heath had had no idea about Bear's feelings for her so he couldn't really be angry at his brother. And when Star had been born premature and Heath was a complete mess, Bear had known he had to be there for him just like Heath had been there for him so many times before. And although there were times when Bear had thought Heath was wrong for sleeping with other women while he'd been married to Meadow, the three of them had still remained close over the years. And that was one of the things he loved about working here: he was part of the team and he liked that the team now included children and other halves too.

'This place looks great,' Bear said. 'You two have done a fantastic job.'

River turned to look at him, a big grin on his face. 'It's looking good, isn't it?'

'It really is. I actually like that there's no roof up that end. I know it isn't practical if it rains but we could put a glass roof up instead. The light is wonderful and you can see the tops of the trees and the sky, it feels more natural.'

'I was thinking that too,' River said, standing up and looking over at the missing part of the roof. 'Maybe get some white blinds for those days when it's really sunny.'

Heath stood up as well, stretching his back. 'It's a good idea but you'll have to clear it with the one in charge.'

'Who's in charge?' Bear said. Meadow was the manager of Wishing Wood but Indigo was now events manager so maybe it was her baby.

'Well it's definitely not me, I don't think I've been in charge of anything since Indigo arrived,' River said.

'You were never in charge.' Heath laughed.

'I'll suggest it to Indigo,' Bear said.

'You should probably talk to Meadow too. The wedding chapel was Indigo's idea but this design mainly came from Meadow,' Heath said. 'She told me that when she was little she wanted to get married in this wood. I think she's been dreaming about something like this ever since then.'

Bear suddenly had a vivid flashback to when he and Meadow were around Star's age and the smile stretched across his face. 'She did get married here. When we were about seven or eight, we were playing up here in the woods and she made me act out a whole wedding ceremony. I was the groom, she was the bride *and* the registrar so I don't think it really counts.'

River grinned. 'Probably not.'

'That's hilarious. You two were always so inseparable growing up,' Heath said. 'I need to get some more wood. I'll be back in a minute.'

Heath clapped Bear on the back and walked out.

'Well, your little wedding ceremony obviously struck a chord with her,' River said. 'She was really enthusiastic about designing this place and creating the perfect wedding venue. Although maybe it was the man she was marrying rather than the wedding that struck the chord.'

Bear ignored the comment. He was fairly sure, like their grandmother, Amelia, that River had guessed about Bear's feelings towards Meadow, but Bear wasn't going to take the bait.

'Maybe I'll leave it then if this place is so important to Meadow,' Bear said. 'I was going to suggest scrapping the stained-glass window too as that view out there is far more impressive than anything a stained-glass window could recreate.'

River went to the window. 'Yeah, that's one of the best views in the resort.'

Bear moved to stand next to him. He could see several treehouses peeping through their trees with their turrets and wonky chimneys. The peacock-blue sea twinkling under a cloudless sky followed the butter-yellow sand of Pear Tree Beach. It was stunning.

'That's actually one of the selling points for using this chapel to get married. We can sell that view in the adverts.'

'Good point. Talk to Meadow about it. She listens to you.'

Bear frowned. 'She listens to you too.'

'But with you it's different, you know that.'

Bear looked at River. 'What do you mean?'

River grinned. 'You two just get each other more than anyone I know.'

'We're friends. Just like you and Meadow are friends.'

'I adore Meadow, but what you share with her is very different to what I share with her.'

'Well, we're the same age, we were in the same class at school, we're bound to be closer.'

'And Heath and Meadow were married for nearly eight years and raised a child together, they're close, but still nothing compared to what you two share.'

Bear swallowed, focussing on the view, the way the golden light of the sun danced on the turquoise waves.

'How do you feel about her going on a date tonight?' River asked.

Bear didn't look at him. 'I want her to be happy.'

'And that tells me everything I need to know. Why don't *you* just ask her out?'

Bear sighed. 'She wants the big love story.'

'And why do you doubt you can give her that?'

'She wants excitement and passion. We've known each other forever, I'm like putting on a favourite old sweater. I'm the carousel, slow and steady, she's looking for the rollercoaster.'

'Why can't you be both? I can't think of anything more exciting than two people who have loved each other their whole life finally getting together. I think your love story could be amazing if you're brave enough to go after it.'

Just then Heath walked back in, carrying a huge plank of wood over his shoulder. He looked at them both standing by the window. 'We having some kind of tea party here? If River is going to marry Indigo here before the baby is born, we need to pull our fingers out.'

Bear nodded and moved over to the opposite wall to put up some lights that looked like brass lanterns. He glanced around. Meadow was making her dreams come true with this place and with being brave enough to go out and look for love. Maybe it was time he made his own dreams come true too.

CHAPTER ELEVEN

Meadow caught up with Amelia as they wandered round the different stalls that were being set up, although they wouldn't open officially until the next day. Star was a little way ahead, fascinated by someone whittling wooden animals.

'I saw you chatting to that dashing gentleman earlier, so are you looking for love too?' Meadow said.

It felt good to turn the tables on her for once, Amelia was always interfering in her grandsons' lives.

'I'm... seeing what's available,' Amelia said, as if perusing a menu in a restaurant.

'And was he?'

'Oh very much so, but I'm not sure if he is to my taste.'

'Too chewy?' Meadow teased.

'Too... eccentric.'

'Says the woman who walks around here in gold hot pants and sparkly red wellies.'

'That's simply fashion, my dear. I'm not sure a cloak is the in thing, unless you're at a fancy dress party.'

'So what are you looking for?' Meadow asked.

'I'm not sure I am. But I've been on my own for far too long, I feel like it's time to get back in the saddle again. Just like you, it seems.'

Meadow smiled at how quickly Amelia had turned the tables back on her. 'I'm not sure I'm ready either but I do have a date tonight.'

'With Bear?' Amelia said.

'No. He will be there but on his own date with someone else.'

'Why would you bother with someone else? You two are crazy in love with each other.'

'I don't think it's as simple as that.'

'Love is simple, there's nothing more simple in the world than two people being in love with each other.'

'And terrifying and heartbreaking and—'

'Wonderful and exhilarating,' Amelia said.

'When it goes right.'

'I have never been so certain about anything as I am about you and Bear. You were made for each other, any fool can see that.'

'So I shouldn't bother dating anyone else, I should just divorce one brother and marry another?'

'Sounds pretty simple to me,' Amelia said. 'But in all honesty, I think you should date other people because then you will see that no one will ever compare to what you have with Bear. I'll give it a week before you realise the perfect man has been right here under your nose the whole time.'

Meadow knew she didn't need a week to realise that, actually, she had been in love with Bear her entire life.

CHAPTER TWELVE

Bear had just got back from helping Star place food around the wood ready for their webcams experiment. He just hoped that the food would be eaten by something, otherwise Star would be bitterly disappointed.

He logged on to his online dating profile. He needed to find a date for tonight so he could support Meadow on her first ever proper date. He couldn't help thinking her first ever proper date should be with him but clearly she didn't agree. He'd read Josh's profile, the man she was meeting tonight, and he seemed nice, well… normal enough. And while if Meadow was going to fall in love with someone who wasn't him, he'd prefer someone amazing for her, he knew this night was a box-ticking exercise for her. They'd chatted earlier and she'd said she was nervous about her first date and really wanted it to go well, not because she had any illusions of finding *the one* on her first ever date but just so she could pat herself on the back and consider it done. The first one was always going to be the worst, the others would come easier. While he couldn't sit with her and hold her hand, as much as he'd have liked to, he could be there for moral support and to help her if the bloke turned out to be a weirdo.

There was a group chat forum on Connected Hearts where people would sometimes go rather than talking to people individually and privately. Sometimes people would be looking for a date just to accompany them on a works do or some other event where they felt they needed a plus one, and sometimes people were in a certain area and just wanted a date for that night. Those people were generally just looking for sex, which Bear had no problem with – he'd had many a casual arrangement with various women – but it wasn't what he was looking for any more.

He clicked into the forum and scanned through some of the comments and posts. His eyes widened in surprise. There was a woman called Claudia who wanted a date tonight, specifically at the exact same restaurant that Meadow was meeting Josh but half hour before. That felt like a bit of a convenient coincidence to him but he wasn't going to look a gift horse in the mouth. He'd dated a few food critics over the years, those sent to do anonymous reviews of restaurants and who needed a date just so they didn't look suspicious sitting in the restaurant alone. This could be one of those things.

He quickly replied. **I can meet you at that time in Joseph's.**

Her reply came instantly. **Good, wear something smart.**

His eyebrows shot up at the blunt request but he'd play along. He wasn't in this to find everlasting love and it didn't seem Claudia was, either.

He agreed to her terms and then logged out of the forum.

He spotted that he had another message from Twilight Rose and that made him smile. He clicked into it to see what she said.

Hello, I promised you a good one so here it is. I have cities but no houses, mountains but no trees, water but no fish, what am I?

He smiled because he actually knew the answer to that one. He quickly wrote his reply.

I was thinking about you today and I admit to going online to find some really hard riddles to stump the self-proclaimed riddling queen. And while this one is good and clever, I did see it on a website so I'm afraid I already know the answer. It is a map. But I do have one for you. A bucket of water weighed 22lbs, someone put something in the bucket and it now weighs 10lbs, what did they put in it?

He waited a few moments to see if she replied and then he saw the three little dots to show she was typing.

Damn it, I thought the map one would stump you for sure. I don't know whether to be flattered that you were thinking of me enough to spend time looking up riddles or annoyed that you have all the answers. I can however answer yours. When I was at Brownies I had to sing a song dressed as a farmer as part of some kind of talent show. If we ever date and get married, I may even show you the video evidence of this. The answer is, there's a hole in my bucket, dear Liza, dear Liza, there's a hole in my bucket, dear Liza, a hole.

He laughed, loudly, and then wrote his reply, adding some crying laughing emojis.

I'm going to need to see that video.

She replied. **Not a chance. I can't sing.**

Still need to see it.

And see you running for the hills? I'm quite enjoying our little chats, I don't want to scare you off.

OK, promise me you'll show me if we get married.

Maybe on our tenth anniversary, then you're kind of committed and unlikely to run away.

Bear smiled. **I promise never to judge you on the things you've done in the past.**

There was no reply for a moment and then Twilight started typing. **I've done some stupid things in my past that I look back on and cringe. Good to know you won't judge me on it.**

He bit his lip as he thought. That sounded like something that was a lot more serious than singing a song dressed as a farmer. He thought for a moment before he sent a reply.

We've all done things we regret or in some cases we regret not doing them. But I think we grow because of our actions and decisions, hopefully become better people. I'm more interested in the person you are now than who you were or what you did in the past.

That's lovely. I like that attitude. I haven't received too many messages on here so far and certainly nothing as lovely as that. I think I might have put off a few men with my snowman question.

He smiled. **Then they are fools.**

He could see she was typing again. He liked chatting to

her, it was nice and easy, comfortable. Her reply came through.

I have a date tonight actually. I haven't been brave enough to ask anyone myself but he asked me so I figured it was probably a good time to dip my toe into face to face meetings.

He tried to think of some good advice to give her. There was a fragile quality to Twilight and it reminded him of Meadow and her decision to date even when she wasn't really sure she wanted to. But before he got a chance to impart some pearls of wisdom another message popped through.

Sorry, is that weird telling a man I potentially might date in the future that I'm dating someone else?

He quickly replied. **Not weird at all. We're on an online dating site, of course we are going to be chatting with and dating multiple people. I have one tonight too. If we get to the stage where we're dating seriously, then I would expect a monogamous relationship, but until then we can chat about this kind of thing. I think the important part of any relationship is honesty. I also think a great start to a relationship is a good friendship. If we were friends in real life, we'd tell each other about our dates so feel free to talk to me about this stuff.**

Thank you. I am a bit nervous, it's been a long time since I've done any kind of dating. I'm not sure what to expect.

Bear rubbed his hand across his chin and then sent back a reply. **Just be yourself, relax and try to have some fun. Tonight is just about finding out whether you want a second date, whether there's something about this man** that makes you want to find out more. So if you get stuck for something to talk about beyond the weather, which is a must on all first dates, ask him questions about himself. Men love nothing more than talking about themselves.

Thanks for the tip. And if I get really stuck I can ask him my snowman question.

He grinned. Why the hell not? The fact that your first message to me had that question was something unique and different and I really liked that. If he doesn't get your sense of humour then he's probably not the man for you.

Thank you. I better go and get ready. Hope you have a fabulous night too. I'll message you tomorrow and we can compare notes.

Look forward to it. Good luck Twilight.

And you xx

He watched her little online light go out and sat back. He really liked Twilight. He hadn't wanted to date for a while now but for the first time in a long time he'd found someone he wanted to get to know better.

CHAPTER THIRTEEN

Meadow was running around her treehouse trying to get ready for her first date. She was wearing a pretty blue satin dress that had sequins and embroidery around the bust and she just hoped it wasn't too over the top. It was the first time she'd worn it after spending weeks measuring, sewing and embellishing it. She was really proud of it. She had been going to wear the silvery sandals with it but she could only find one, so she'd resorted to putting on a pair of black sandals instead. She had her favourite earrings in though, little diamante octopuses that crawled around the ear. She had seen them in a jewellery shop in the local town when she had been with Bear and fallen in love with them. The next day Bear had given them to her. He was so thoughtful like that.

She looked at her watch, she still had plenty of time, she didn't know why she was in such a flap. She just needed to do something with her hair and she was ready to go.

'Mummy, you look really pretty,' Star said, from her

position on the sofa, cuddled into Heath's side as they read a book together.

'She's right, you do,' Heath said.

'Thank you. Do you think it's too much?'

Just then there was a knock on the door and Bear stepped inside.

He stopped when he saw her and just stared.

'Hey, you all right?' Meadow asked.

'Meadow… you look… sensational,' Bear said, softly.

The way he was staring at her made her feel warm inside. Not just warm, hot. He looked like he wanted to pin her to the nearest hard surface and make love to her. She mentally shook her head. She was seeing what she wanted to see. He was probably just admiring the dress.

'Bear, you're looking at her like a groom would look at his bride walking down the aisle,' Heath said, interrupting their little reverie.

Christ, Heath had seen it too.

Bear looked away, brushing his hand through his hair in embarrassment.

'Bear, why don't you come into the kitchen for a second,' Meadow said, keen to get him away from the teasing of his brother. The kitchen was tucked up round the corner away from the view of the lounge. Bear followed her inside.

'I won't keep you, I'm leaving to meet my date now,' Bear said. 'But I'll see you there. I just wanted to wish you good luck. But I can see that you are absolutely going to knock him dead. You look magnificent.'

She looked down at the dress, feeling a huge element of pride in his words. 'Do you think it's over the top?'

'No and any man who thinks so is an absolute idiot. I love your hair when it's loose, it suits you.'

'Oh, I was going to put it up.'

'Whatever makes you happy.' He stepped closer and gently moved her hair away from her ears, causing goosebumps to erupt all over her body. He smiled when he saw her earrings. 'I love those on you too.'

'They're my favourites, probably because you bought them for me.'

He stepped back slightly to look at her and she immediately regretted saying that, it was too much. But then he had just told her she looked sensational and magnificent, so maybe not.

'You're looking especially handsome this evening,' Meadow said, admiring his suit, experiencing a sudden sharp kick of jealousy. 'Your date is a very very lucky woman.'

He shook his head. 'This isn't a date. I'm just going so I can be there for you. And it's definitely not a date for her, she just wanted someone to accompany her to the restaurant tonight, not sure why.'

'Oh.' She thought about what he'd said for a moment. 'Are you going on these dates to find someone or just so you can be there for me?'

He paused.

'Bear, I don't need you to babysit me, I'm quite capable of going on dates on my own. I thought we were doing this properly. You need to be open to finding someone otherwise there's no point in doing it. I don't want you to just go through the motions for me.'

'I am open to finding someone. If I'm honest I sort of

gave up looking a while back because I can never find what I'm looking for. I suppose, like you, I find it all a bit daunting. You go on dates and you never know what you're going to find until you get there. A lot of the time you don't click with someone within the first few minutes, yet you have to endure a whole evening with them to be polite. And it just made me feel a bit jaded about it all. But maybe it's time to try again. I've actually been chatting to a lovely woman online. She makes me smile. A lot. I would definitely be open to seeing how things progressed with her. But yes, I do want to be there for you too. I know you're nervous and by being there tonight I can metaphorically hold your hand.'

She stared at him. 'You are the loveliest man I've ever met. I want you to find someone wonderful who will appreciate how absolutely amazing you are. If this woman you've been chatting to online makes you smile then you definitely need to meet up with her.'

'I will. And for the record, I think you're pretty spectacular too. I hope this Josh appreciates that.' He looked at his watch. 'Look, I better go. Good luck.'

He bent his head and kissed her on the cheek, which almost made her go weak at the knees from his gentle touch. And then he was walking away leaving her wishing more than anything that she was going on this first date with him.

CHAPTER FOURTEEN

Claudia had told Bear what she was wearing so he could recognise her, a navy-blue trouser suit. It sounded a bit formal, but maybe it was a works thing.

He had been waiting at the bar for twenty minutes and she hadn't come yet. He was on the verge of giving up but he'd promised Meadow he would be here.

And then he saw her. A woman walked in dressed in a very smart suit like she was going to a job interview or even a funeral.

He waved and she looked at him disapprovingly, clearly hoping he wouldn't be her date for the evening. She was about to be sorely disappointed.

'Claudia?'

She sighed and held out a hand for him to shake. 'Yes. Shall we grab that table.' She moved over to the table, not checking to see if Bear was following. No apology for being late either. It was going to be a long night.

She sat down and he sat opposite her. 'Let me explain the rules,' Claudia said. 'I have no interest in dating you or getting to know you better. You will not be getting laid tonight. Do not touch me or attempt to kiss me. Do not play footsy with me under the table, I can't stand feet. I am only here tonight because my brother is on a date and I need to see if she's good enough for him.'

Bear nodded. 'At least we're clear on the expectations. Is your brother Josh by any chance?'

Her head shot up to look at him. 'How did you know?'

'Because my friend is his date. I'm here to make sure your brother isn't a weirdo.'

'My brother isn't a weirdo,' she snapped.

'Well I wouldn't know that, would I? But this...' he gestured to their little situation, '...doesn't bode well.'

Her eyes widened. 'Are you saying I'm weird?'

'You come across as a little intense.'

'How is what I'm doing any different to why you're here? I want what's best for my brother, you want what's best for your friend.'

He nodded to concede this. It wasn't that she was coming across as intense because she had come to keep an eye on her brother, it was because of the insane list of demands she had given him at the start of their date.

A waitress appeared at their table. 'Can I get you two a drink?'

'Yes, a beer please,' Bear said.

'I can't stand men who drink,' Claudia said.

'Then it's a good job this isn't a real date,' Bear said.

'Water for me please,' Claudia sniffed.

'Would you like to see the menus?' the waitress said.

'No, we won't be eating,' Claudia said.

Bear sighed. He was starving. He was tempted to order

some food anyway but, if Josh was anything like his sister, the date would be over very quickly.

Just then the door was pushed open and Meadow walked in. God, she was magnificent. She glanced around and caught his eye but she was obviously trying to be discreet for the sake of his date as she didn't wave. Little did she know.

'Is that her?' Claudia said, her voice dripping with disdain.

'That's Meadow, yes.'

'What the hell is she wearing?'

'We can't all look as fabulous as you do in that suit, Claudia,' Bear said, without missing a beat.

She seemed strangely pleased by that even though he hadn't meant it. She seemed to appraise him for the first time. 'I suppose we could have sex later, if you're interested.'

Bear felt his eyebrows shoot up into his hair. 'Thank you, that's a very kind offer, but I'm not sure I could cope with all the rules.'

CHAPTER FIFTEEN

Meadow took a sip of her wine while she waited, nervously tapping her fingers on the bar. What would he be like? Would he be attractive? Would he be kind? Would he make her laugh? Would he like her?

She glanced up as the restaurant door opened and saw a young man wearing a white shirt with a red hanky sticking out of his pocket, just as Josh had said he would. But she was thrown by the fact that the man was escorting a much older lady into the restaurant with him.

Josh looked around the bar and he waved when he saw her, obviously recognising her from what she'd told him she would be wearing.

He pointed her out to the older lady and they both came over.

'Meadow?' Josh said.

'Yes, hi. Josh, I presume?'

He nodded. 'This is Barbara, my mum.'

Barbara held out a hand as she gave Meadow the once-over. 'Hmm, you're not what I expected.'

Meadow forced a smile. 'Sorry about that.'

What was going on here? Surely he hadn't brought his mum on the date with him. Maybe Barbara was meeting someone else here and he was just giving her a lift.

'Shall we sit down?' Josh said.

'OK,' Meadow said, uncertainly.

Josh caught the eye of a waitress. 'Table for Mr Blake.'

The waitress consulted her book. 'Yes, right this way.'

She escorted them over to a table laid for three people near the front window and Meadow's heart sank. The waitress placed three menus on the table and left them alone. Meadow watched as Josh pulled out a chair for his mum and then sat down himself. She glanced across at Bear who was watching her with undisguised shock and amusement. Surprisingly, his date was watching them avidly too.

Meadow sat down. 'So this is nice, the three of us together.'

'I always go on Joshua's dates,' Barbara said, sniffily. 'I don't want my boy going out with any old tramp.'

'Mother, I'm sure Meadow isn't a tramp.'

'You have terrible taste in women. I haven't forgotten the last one you brought home who turned out to be a prostitute,' Barbara snapped.

'I didn't know that.' Josh squirmed uncomfortably in a way that suggested that he absolutely did know. 'And I thought you'd be in bed.'

'She stole my best tea cosy too, I dread to think what she did with it,' Barbara shuddered.

'Well, I can understand that you want the best for your

son,' Meadow said, glancing at her watch to try to gauge how quickly she could get out of there without being rude.

'So you're divorced?' Barbara said, getting a notepad and pen from her handbag.

'Yes, but it was all very amicable. We're still good friends.'

Barbara couldn't look any more disapproving if she tried. 'In my day, you made a marriage work, you didn't give up on it at the first hurdle.'

'It wasn't really like that with me and Heath. We got married because I was pregnant but we didn't really love each other. We were friends but it seemed silly to stay together just for the sake of our daughter. Heath is still a huge part of mine and my daughter's life but now we are free to find someone we love.'

Barbara's eyes bulged. 'You have a child, I didn't know that.' She glared at Josh. 'I wouldn't have let you come if I knew she had a child.'

'I... I didn't know,' Josh said.

'Umm. You absolutely did know,' Meadow said as Josh made frantic gestures with his hand to get her to stop talking. 'It was one of the first things I told you and you said that you loved children and you couldn't wait to meet her.'

'How old is the child?' Barbara said.

'Seven, nearly eight.'

Her eyes widened to comic proportions. 'You must have been a child yourself when you got yourself pregnant.'

'Seventeen.'

'Slut!' Barbara muttered underneath her breath.

Christ, this night couldn't get any worse. Should she get

up and walk out now? She couldn't endure another hour or two of this.

'Let's have a look at the menu, shall we?' Josh said.

Barbara leaned forward. 'Just so you know, my son will not be paying for your meal, so don't go choosing something expensive expecting him to foot the bill because it isn't going to happen.'

'That's fine,' Meadow said.

'And we are both vegetarians, we don't want any disgusting meat at our table.'

'Right,' Meadow said with disappointment. She'd just spotted the spit-roast half chicken which she'd quite fancied. 'Is fish OK?'

'Nope. No food with a face.'

'Potato smileys have a face, am I allowed them?' Meadow said, obtrusively.

'Don't be so stupid,' Barbara snapped.

Meadow sat back in her chair and surveyed the situation for a moment. There was absolutely nothing that could salvage this date right now. She had no desire to go out with Josh ever again, let alone get to know him any further. So what was she doing here?

'Excuse me for a moment,' Meadow said, picking up her bag and walking into the ladies. As soon as she was in there she looked around for a way to escape. There was a small open window over the sinks. It didn't look like it would be big enough to be able to accommodate her but the only other option was to go back into the restaurant and tell Josh and Barbara that the date was over and she really didn't want to do that.

She hoisted herself up onto the shelf surrounding the

sink and then started pulling herself through the window. It was a tight squeeze but with a bit of wiggling around she thought she could get out.

Just as her arms and shoulders were hanging outside and her bum and legs were still dangling inside, the bathroom door opened. Judging by the shadow, it was a man coming in. Oh god, to have Josh find her like this was mortifying.

'What are you doing?'

She sighed with relief to hear Bear's voice behind her. This was still embarrassing but not quite as bad as if Josh had found her.

'What does it look like I'm doing? I'm running away.'

'You could just walk out the front door,' Bear said, coming up behind her.

'And face the wrath of Barbara? I don't think so. Look, just give me a shove and get back to your date. No reason why both our evenings should be ruined.'

'My *date* is Josh's sister who also wanted to come along and make sure you were suitable for her big brother. She lives at home with her mum too and has a pet tarantula. I'm really not in any rush to get back there. Here, let me help.'

He climbed up onto the sink unit and then took her feet and slowly started feeding her through the window until she was dangling upside down, the dress she was wearing hanging over her head as she blindly groped around for the ground. She prayed that Bear wasn't looking out the window as he'd get an eyeful of her bum and knickers.

With his hands round her ankles, she finally found the ground. 'OK, I'm down,' Meadow said and he released her.

She fell in a heap on the floor, among the rubbish and squalor of a darkened alley. The night couldn't get any worse.

She picked herself up and dusted herself off.

'Bear, I'll see you back at home,' she called through the window but there was no reply.

'Or we could go and get something to eat,' Bear said, from behind her.

She turned round. 'Where did you come from?'

'I came through the fire exit,' he gestured to a door that was a few metres from where they stood.

'You could have told me there was a fire exit.'

Bear grinned, picking a dried-up bit of noodle gently from her hair, making her heart race in her chest. 'But where's the fun in that?'

She rolled her eyes.

He offered out his arm. 'Fancy a McDonald's?'

She grinned. 'Yes I do.'

She slipped her hand into the crook of his arm and he escorted her down the alley and out onto the street.

'What a disaster. I'm not sure what was worse, that he brought his mum, that she was disapproving of me being a divorced mum, or that Josh clearly uses prostitutes. Oh, that and I was banned from ordering any meat.'

'Claudia said the same thing when I told her I was hungry. I was just about to order a big steak when I saw you making a run for the toilets.'

'As that was my first date in… well, forever, we can put that down as a spectacular disaster. Tell me it gets better than this?'

'Oh, we can't have your first ever date ending badly.

Why don't I take you on a date tonight, show you what it should be like?'

Her heart thundered against her chest and she tried to calm it down because this wasn't real. 'To McDonald's?'

'I think I can do better than that,' Bear gestured to a little Spanish restaurant that was perched on the harbour wall, overlooking the sea. 'Give me two minutes and then come on in.'

Before she could stop him, he'd left her side and run across the road, letting himself into the restaurant. She watched through the window as he spoke to the waitress and she nodded and gestured to a table that was facing the sea. Bear nodded and sat down, pointing to the middle of the table. The waitress nodded and hurried off. A few seconds later she returned with a small candle.

Meadow smiled, her heart melting at the effort he was going to.

She walked across the road and pushed open the door. As soon as Bear saw her he stood up, waiting for her.

She moved across the restaurant and, as she reached him, he bent down and placed a kiss on her cheek, making her heart gallop so loudly she felt sure he'd hear it.

'Hi, I'm Bear,' Bear said.

Meadow grinned. 'Meadow.'

Bear moved behind her and held out her chair for her and she couldn't help smiling as she took a seat.

He sat down opposite her.

'Very smooth,' she said.

'Oh, I'm going to pull out all the stops for you.' He cleared his throat. 'So Meadow, shall we order some food to share and then you can tell me all about yourself?'

Her mouth twitched with a smirk. 'OK.'

She looked at the menu. There were lots of little bite-size dishes here, it was the perfect place to come to share food.

'These tapas dishes are going to be really small so we should probably get five or six to share. What do you fancy?' Bear said.

She looked across the table, her eyes locking with his, and she had to stop herself from saying that she fancied him.

She refocussed on the menu. 'The tiger prawns look good and the marinated chicken wings.'

'Excellent choices. How about the meatballs and the sautéed mushrooms?'

'Yes, they sound delicious. Shall we also get a sharing board – it has ham, olives, nuts, roasted tomatoes and cheeses?'

'OK, looks like we have a plan.' Bear studied the menu a bit more. 'How do you feel about calamari?'

'Never had it, but willing to give it a go.'

'Brilliant.'

They called over the waitress and gave their order. Meadow realised the girl was Frankie, Greta's teenage daughter. She had only met her a few times but Meadow wondered if Frankie would recognise her and whether their little impromptu date would find its way back to Greta. The staff at Wishing Wood loved a bit of gossip and word travelled very quickly but, as Frankie left to take care of their order and Bear reached across the table and took her hand, she suddenly didn't care who knew about this.

He gently stroked his thumb across her palm, sending tingles of desire through her body.

'So Meadow, I feel like I already know you so well... through your dating profile obviously.'

'Yes, of course, my dating profile, not from twenty-odd years of friendship.'

'So tell me something I don't know, something that no one knows.'

Her mind went instantly to the dress that was hanging in the spare room. 'When I was little my dream was to be a—'

'Fashion designer,' Bear interrupted.

She let out a little gasp. She hadn't spoken about that for years. That dream had faded away. 'How do you know that?'

'I remember. You were always sketching out designs for different dresses when we were younger. I was always impressed with them. What happened to that dream?'

She smiled. 'I love my daughter completely and utterly but when she was born my only priority was her, providing for her, looking after her, making sure she was happy. Everything else went out the window. But a few years ago, once Heath had moved out into the treehouse next door, I decided to use the spare room for something just for me. I bought myself a sewing machine and I set about making some clothes for Star, dungarees mostly and I still make those, they're fun and easy to make. Leah has said she will sell some of them at Dwelling for me at her clothes stall. But after I had mastered that I tried to make my own dress. It was a lot of trial and error and a lot of research and watching YouTube videos as I'd had no training or experience, but eventually I made my own dress. The bright pink one you admired so much when I first wore it.'

'I remember that dress vividly. It had silver ribbons from the shoulder to your hip. You looked so beautiful wearing it.'

She stared at him, swallowing a lump of emotion in her throat at his choice of words. Not that the dress looked beautiful but that she looked so beautiful wearing it.

'But I didn't know you'd made it,' Bear said.

'Well, since then I've made a few more. This is one of them.'

'That dress is... magnificent. You should be very proud of that.'

She smiled. 'I made a few for Star and Tierra too. And then last year I opened up my own Etsy shop. I still make and sell children's clothes, but I also sell women's dresses. I had a few staple designs and people were able to choose their own fabrics. I didn't think I'd get any orders at all but I've made twenty-three dresses so far for different customers. I have expanded my choice of designs and I even worked with one customer to make a design just for her, from her specifications. A few weeks ago, I got my first wedding dress commission and I can't tell you how excited I am to be making someone's wedding dress. I'm no Christian Siriano and I'm a million miles away from my guru Jenny Packham but it feels so good to be designing and making beautiful dresses. It's not about making money, it's just about the pure joy I get from designing and making a dress from scratch, the sewing, the embellishments, it's something I love.'

Bear's face lit up into a huge smile. 'I love this. I had no idea you were doing that. Why didn't you tell me?'

She shrugged. 'I don't know really. It wasn't really a secret but I liked having this... other life outside of Star and the treehouses.'

'Do you have photos?'

'Yes but I don't want to bore you with them.'

'Please do, I'd love to see them.'

Meadow dug out her phone and scrolled through her gallery to find the right folder. She clicked into it and passed it over the table to Bear.

Bear started flicking through. 'These are incredible. And the embroidery on some of them is perfect.'

'Oh, I enjoy doing that part.'

Just then the food arrived. Meadow thanked Frankie and Bear glanced up briefly to say thank you to her too as she placed all their dishes on the table before he turned his attention back to the photos again. 'These are amazing. I'm so happy you followed your dream.'

'Thank you.'

She picked up one of the tiger prawns and put it on her plate, licking off the garlic butter that was still on her fingers. Bear passed the phone back. 'Thank you for sharing that with me.'

'My pleasure. So what's your thing that no one else knows?'

Bear frowned for a moment as he picked up a chicken wing. He chewed thoughtfully.

'Come on, I told you mine,' Meadow said.

'I... write stories.'

Meadow felt her eyes widen. 'You were always so good

at writing stories when we were kids. I remember you won a prize in class for one of them.'

'It's not something I've ever grown out of. It's something I love, every spare second I get I'm scribbling down ideas or writing a scene.'

'What kinds of stories do you write? Crime, horror?'

'Children's books, ones with dragons and mermaids and ordinary children leading extraordinary lives.'

'I'd love to read them.'

Bear shook his head. 'It's not something I really want other people to read.'

'But isn't that the whole point of writing a story, for other people to enjoy?'

'No, it makes me cringe to think of other people reading my stories. What if they aren't very good?'

'But what if they are?'

Bear shook his head.

'What's the worst that can happen if I read it?'

'You hate it.'

'I couldn't possibly hate it. I might look at it and think that the story has holes in it or the characterisation needs to be stronger or it doesn't flow as well as other books I've read, but I couldn't hate it because it's written by you.'

'But you might think less of me,' Bear said.

'Bear, I promise you, there is nothing you could do that would make me think less of you. You're my favourite person in the whole world.'

A slow smile spread across his face.

'Writing a book, with a proper beginning, middle and end is really hard so you've already impressed me. And if you can't face sending it to me, you could still send it to an agent or a publisher.'

'I'm not sure it's good enough for that.'

'But you won't know until you try. My friend is an author so I know a little about how things work. If you submit to an agent or a publisher and they like it but don't feel it's ready for publication then they may send you some advice, things for you to change. If they really like it, they'll even work with you to make it perfect. But you can't let the rejections get you down. Books, films, TV programmes are very subjective. What one person loves, another will hate. It'd be a very boring world if we all loved the same things. Getting a deal is about the book being seen by the right person at the right time. And things have changed in publishing now. Self-publishing is equally as valid as having a publisher. You'd have to market it, but you know marketing from running the ads for Wishing Wood. You could just tailor the ads to sell your books instead. But I know you could make a huge success of it.'

'You haven't read the book yet, it could be shite.'

'But I know you. You are an incredible man, Bear Brookfield. You're the sort of man who can do anything once you put your mind to it. But if we're going to date,' she gestured to their little fake arrangement. 'Then you need to learn to share all of yourself, not keep some parts locked away.'

Bear smiled and nodded. 'OK, I promise I'll think about it.'

'Good. Now shall we try the calamari?'

'OK, I'll cut a bit off and we can try it together,' Bear said. He sliced a chunk off and then cut that into two pieces. He skewered one piece on his fork and held it across the table for her to eat, which felt a bit intimate. She leaned forward and carefully bit it off the fork.

'Mmm, it's a lot more tender than I thought,' Meadow said. 'Tastes a bit like chicken.'

She picked up the other piece with her fork and held it over the table for Bear to eat. His eyes locked with hers as he took it off the fork and then he chewed it, clearly considering it.

'That does taste good.'

She watched him lick his lips, which made a kick of desire jolt through her. She was definitely going to enjoy this date.

CHAPTER SIXTEEN

Meadow licked her spoon after eating the most delicious crème brûlée. The date had been wonderful. Bear had held her hand for most of the evening, he'd been attentive, full of compliments, shared his food and been just utterly lovely. Under the guise of being on a date, she felt like she had discussed things she had never spoken about before tonight. They'd talked honestly and it felt like no subject was off the table.

'Thank you for tonight,' Meadow said. 'It's been the best first date I've ever been on. Any woman would be lucky to have you in their life. You're the most incredible man. Kind, funny, generous, brilliantly clever.'

'That's kind of you to say, but there's a big difference between what we have, this wonderful close friendship, and that kind of love where you want to be with that person forever, as we told Star this morning.'

'I don't know about that. I was chatting to Leah today. Her and Charlie have recently got married, she's expecting his baby in a few months.'

He blinked in surprise. 'Wow, they've been friends forever.'

'Yes, and when Star asked her if she loved Charlie with carousel love or rollercoaster love, she said it was both. That she loved Charlie as a friend, that loyal, unwavering kind of love, the love of his companionship, but she loved him with that pure unadulterated joy of rollercoaster love too. I think friendship is a wonderful start to a relationship. I imagine their relationship will last forever because they have such strong foundations to build on.'

He stared at her as he finished off his coconut ice cream.

'Do you ever wonder why we never got together?' Bear said. 'When we were younger it felt like we were going that way and then suddenly we weren't.'

She groaned. 'I know why.'

'You do?'

'Because I was a silly, immature girl who made some terrible decisions. I regret the way I acted after our kiss, the things I said and did. Everything that happened between our kiss and me finding out I was pregnant around six weeks later, I regret it all. Those weeks after the kiss changed the course of my life forever and while I can never ever regret having Star, the circumstances around her conception, I regret that more than anything. I regret that my actions hurt you, that was never my intention. I regret that my immaturity meant that we never spoke about it at the time and that made things so much worse. So yeah, I have a few regrets about that time.'

Plus the secret made all the worse by eight years of

hiding it from him. She regretted that too in many ways though she knew she could never tell him.

'Wow! I never knew you felt like that.'

'Why would you? You just saw my stupid actions and took them at face value.'

'I don't hold anything against you. I was pissed at the time but we were both kids, we both did some stupid things in our time, but that was a long time ago,' Bear said.

'And I'm very happy with the life I have now. I live in a spectacular treehouse with my best friend and my daughter so I really can't complain, but if I was to live my life all over, there would be quite a few things I'd do differently.'

'The benefits of age and wisdom.'

'You make me sound decrepit. I'm only four months older than you,' Meadow said.

He grinned.

Suddenly the music that was playing in the background changed and Ed Sheeran's 'Perfect' came on.

'Oh I love this song,' Meadow said.

'Well then we should end our date with a dance.'

She looked around at all the other diners eating or finishing their meals. 'What, here?'

But Bear was already standing up and offering out his hand and she took it before she could change her mind. She got to her feet and there was a moment or two while they awkwardly shuffled together, not knowing where was appropriate to put their hands, before Bear settled with his hand on her back, she put her hand on his shoulder and he held her other hand and they started moving slowly around. She looked up at him and knew that nothing had ever felt so right as this moment, where she was standing in his arms. He moved his hand ever so slightly up her back, just above her dress, and the feel of his skin against hers was complete heaven. His eyes were on hers the whole time and the rest of the world just faded away and for a moment she let herself imagine that this was real, the two of them here like this. His lips were just a few inches away from hers and she knew if she leaned up slightly she could kiss him although she was too scared of the reaction to actually do it.

'I'm sorry your date was rubbish,' Bear said.

'I'm not. Not one bit, because if it had been OK and I'd sat there and tolerated it for a few hours, I wouldn't have had this spectacular first date instead.'

He smiled. 'I'd have to agree. I've never been so happy to have a crappy date before because it's led me to being here with you.'

She stared up at him for a moment.

'Do you think we can ever go back, to how it was before?' Meadow said.

He shook his head. 'No, but we can move forward and maybe in some way that's better. We're older and wiser, we know what we want, less likely to make bad decisions.'

She glanced down to his lips for a brief second, willing herself to be brave enough to take that step, wondering if kissing him would be a good decision or a bad one. What would happen if she did and he didn't feel the same way? It would ruin their friendship and she never wanted to lose him, he meant the world to her. She would enjoy tonight for what it was, two best friends out for a lovely night, even if her heart was desperate for more.

CHAPTER SEVENTEEN

Meadow let out a little sigh as Bear pulled up in the car park of Wishing Wood. The date was officially over. She'd had a lovely night chatting and laughing with him. It couldn't have gone better. Apart from the fact it wasn't real.

Meadow undid her seatbelt and made to get out.

'Hang on, stay there,' Bear said, getting out.

She watched in confusion as he ran round to her side of the car and then smiled when he opened the door for her.

'Now I know Connected Hearts say you shouldn't give your date your address but would you let me walk you back home?' Bear asked.

She grinned. 'I'd love that. Besides, you look very trustworthy.'

He slipped his hand into hers and they walked together along the paths lit by golden lanterns. The sea glittered under a starlit sky and she smiled as she watched a small fishing boat head out to sea. All the treehouses were lit up with fairy lights as they made their way through the trees to Wisteria Cottage, making it look like an enchanted fairy village, but they arrived at her house all too soon.

She turned to face him. 'I have had a lovely date with you tonight, thank you.'

'I enjoyed it too,' Bear said.

'So… no sex on our first date,' she teased.

Bear's eyes widened and then he laughed. 'I have too much respect for you to sleep with you on our first date. Maybe we'll save that for our fifth.'

She smirked. 'OK.'

'Goodnight Meadow,' Bear said and placed a kiss on her cheek, lingering there for slightly longer than necessary.

Then he turned and walked away through the trees and she couldn't help staring after him with a big smile on her face.

She climbed the steps to Heath's treehouse and he smiled at her when she let herself in. He was sitting on the sofa reading and she sat down next to him, cuddling into his side. He slipped an arm round her shoulders and kissed her forehead. 'Don't think I don't know that you're only after my nuts.'

Meadow giggled and took a small handful of honey roasted cashew nuts from the bowl on his lap.

'Look at the smile on your face, did you have a good night?' Heath said.

'I did. It was… almost perfect.'

It would have been perfect if it had been real but it had still been the best night she'd had in a very long time.

'Oh, I'm so pleased. Are you seeing him again?'

'I think I'll be seeing him very soon,' Meadow said,

touching her cheek where she could still feel Bear's lips on her skin. 'Is Star OK?'

'She's fine.'

'I'm going to go and give her a kiss goodnight and then I'm going to bed myself.'

She got up and walked up the stairs to Star's room, which was completely different to her room in Meadow's treehouse. This one had sea creatures swimming across the walls; dolphins, sharks, turtles, seahorses. It looked wonderful. Over in Meadow's treehouse Star's room was adorned with stars, moons, planets, comets and had a skylight with a telescope pointing at the real night sky.

Star was asleep, her arm wrapped round an oversized narwhal.

Meadow stroked her head and placed a kiss on her cheek. 'Goodnight sweetheart.'

Star stirred and smiled sleepily when she saw Meadow.

'I love you Mummy,' Star said.

Meadow's heart melted. 'I love you too.'

Star closed her eyes and drifted back off to sleep.

Meadow left her in bed and went back downstairs, giving Heath a wave as she walked out. He waved back. She walked across the rope bridge to her own treehouse, got undressed and cleaned her teeth before climbing into her own bed with a huge smile on her face. Her real date with Josh had been a disaster but she still couldn't help but smile over how the night had gone.

She checked her phone before she lay down and saw she had an email from Bear. She frowned in confusion because normally he'd text or WhatsApp her if he wanted to say something. She opened it and her heart leapt when she realised he'd sent her one of his stories. Her heart swelled with love for him. That he had trusted her with this was such a big deal.

She read the message that came with it.

As you said, if we're going to date, then I have to share all of me, not keep some parts locked away, so here it is, The Lost Crystals, the first book in my series. Hope you enjoy it.

Bear x

She smiled. She forwarded the file to her Kindle and then lay back to read the first chapter.

CHAPTER EIGHTEEN

Bear walked into the restaurant the next morning and straightaway his eyes found Meadow, over by the counter chatting to Alex, the chef, as she and Star helped themselves to breakfast.

He grabbed himself a coffee from the machine at the back and went and sat down opposite Heath. There was no sign of River and Indigo yet.

'Hey,' Heath said. 'Meadow said her date went really well last night. How did yours go?'

Bear frowned in confusion. 'She said that?'

'She said it was perfect and she hoped to see him again soon.'

Bear couldn't help the huge smile that spread across his face at hearing that. He'd known she'd enjoyed herself but to hear that she'd described it as perfect was lovely to hear.

Just then Meadow and Star came to the table.

'Heath said you had a great time last night,' Bear said, being careful not to mention the word 'date' in front of Star.

Meadow blushed and it filled his heart to see. She focussed on her breakfast. 'I had a spectacular night last night.'

Bear couldn't take his eyes off her. Was something going on here? Was she finally having feelings for him after all these years? Surely not.

'How was your night out?' Heath asked Bear, again dancing around the dating topic.

Meadow looked up at him and their eyes locked. 'My night was wonderful,' Bear said.

Meadow smiled and turned her attention back to her breakfast.

Heath looked between the two of them. 'But you two were in the same place last night. Did you two not talk to each other about your new friends after?'

'Umm… my meeting with my friend finished before Bear's so not really,' Meadow said.

'So when are you seeing your friend again?' Heath said.

'Tonight.' Meadow popped a piece of banana into her mouth and looked up at Bear, a challenge in her eyes.

'Is that so?' Bear said.

'There's a group event to meet a whole bunch of new friends. He said he'd be there.'

'Did he?' Bear said.

'Oh yes, we made a deal.'

'Well, in that case I better come along too, have a chat with this friend, see if his intentions are honourable.'

Meadow grinned. 'I can assure you he is the perfect person to be my *friend.*'

Star looked up from the book she was reading as if she

knew this conversation about making friends was going in a weird direction.

'If he's so perfect, why are you meeting other friends?' Heath asked, stealing a walnut from Star's plate.

'Hey!' Star said, indignantly.

Heath immediately slid a strawberry off his plate onto his daughter's and she seemed happy to accept this exchange.

'Wait, I didn't see the strawberries up there,' Star said.

'I think they had run out,' Meadow said. 'Why don't you go and ask Alex if there are any more?'

Star got up and ran back over to the counter, chatting to Lucien, one of their housekeepers, as he got his breakfast.

Meadow waited for Star to be out of hearing distance before she spoke. 'I haven't ever been on a date before. I went out with a few boys when I was seventeen but that normally involved sitting on a park bench or hanging around together outside the local supermarket. I never went out on any proper dates. And while last night was… amazing, and I'm looking forward to seeing him again later, I'm not entirely sure he wants a relationship, I think he was just being nice. And I do think I should meet other people too, just for balance. Besides, I've signed up to do these five dating events with Mix n Match where they practically guarantee to find your perfect match at the end. I'm interested to see how that plays out.'

'I'm interested to see that too. It's a bold claim,' Bear said. 'I still think internet dating will win.'

'Well, internet dating has zero points so far,' Meadow said.

'You said last night went really well?' Heath said, looking thoroughly confused.

'It did. Last night wasn't an internet date.'

'Now I am confused,' Heath said.

But thankfully they were saved from any more awkward questions by the arrival of River, Indigo and Tierra.

Indigo sat down. 'Hey, how did it go last night? You look tired,' she waggled her eyebrows mischievously. 'Was it a late night?'

'I was up late reading a brilliant book.' Meadow's eyes locked with Bear's again and his heart leapt. She'd read his book? 'I was only going to read one chapter but it was so good, I ended up reading nine. I was up until two which is why I look so tired. I can't remember the last time a book kept me awake halfway through the night.'

'Which book is this?' River said.

'It's my friend's. It's not out yet. I was given an early copy. It's called *The Lost Crystals* and it is incredible.'

His heart soared. She liked his book. He suddenly felt ten feet tall.

'So if you were busy reading last night, does that mean that your... meeting wasn't that successful?' Indigo asked.

'No, I read after. My *meeting* was utterly lovely but I do have a group event tonight, which I'm looking forward to.'

As Star returned to the table the subject quickly moved on so the little girl didn't realise what they were talking about.

Bear couldn't take his eyes off Meadow. He felt like something had happened last night to move them forward.

Maybe tonight, at the group event, he needed to pull out all the stops so there was no doubt at all of what he wanted.

CHAPTER NINETEEN

'So far, three out of four food stations were visited by someone or something,' Star said, consulting her clipboard as they walked through the trees to the next food station.

Bear helped her over the little brook that bubbled and curved through the middle of the woods. He waved at Emma and Jason Lovegrove who looked like they were on their way to the beach, poor Jason weighed down with a hundred different beach accessories.

'The nuts didn't seem that popular but maybe that's because they don't smell as strongly as the fruit and meat we left out so the animals weren't able to find them,' Star said. 'So far all the meat has been eaten so we know something is out here eating it, or several somethings.'

'I think it's likely that there's several somethings,' Bear said. 'In a wood this size there could be all sorts of animals and many animals live in groups so there could be more than one of each of these animals. I think, if the webcams arrive, we should just set them up tonight with the food stations and just see what we capture. I have five coming so we put them up – if we get no action on one or two of them for the next few nights, we can always move them. I think by putting out more cat or dog food, that will be attractive enough to any carnivores or omnivores that live in the woods.'

'I agree.'

They fell into silence for a moment and Bear got the distinct impression Star wanted to say something.

'Bear, is Mummy going out to meet all these new friends so she can find a man to marry and have babies with?'

God, she was so astute.

He cleared his throat. 'What makes you think that?'

'Because Leah and Charlie were friends before they got married and he gave her his baby. And Mummy and Daddy were friends before they got married and had me and I think that's what really really good friends do. And I think Mummy wants to find a friend who she can marry and have a baby with but it's hard to find the right friend because you have to have rollercoaster love with them not carousel love. Mummy and Daddy have carousel love not rollercoaster love but Leah says she loves Charlie with both rollercoaster and carousel and I think Mummy needs to find someone like that. And this morning at breakfast Mummy was talking about this new friend she met last night and she had those moony eyes she has when she loves something, not Daddy but Chris Hemsworth or The Rock or Jason Momoa, she loves them. Or you. She looks at you with moony eyes when you're not looking and then pretends she isn't when you look at her. And she had the same moony eyes you did when you saw Mummy in her pretty dress before she went out last night. And I think you and Mummy have rollercoaster *and* carousel love for each other and you want to get married to each other and have a baby. But she doesn't want to tell you she loves you with rollercoaster love and you don't want to tell her so now you are both looking for other friends when you are clearly looking in the wrong place.'

Bear had no words at all. He had always wondered if Meadow had feelings for him that went way beyond friendship. Had she been wondering the same thing about him all these years too and neither of them were brave enough to act on it? Despite it having been clear from the very beginning that Heath and Meadow had never had any kind of real relationship, with Meadow even pushing Heath to date other people, Bear had never wanted to pursue anything with her because she'd been married to his brother and that felt like a crappy thing to do. But now they were divorced, was it time to have that conversation once and for all? The irony of having a little girl with all her seven years of wisdom having to point out the obvious rather than the adults seeing it for themselves was not lost on him.

'Why won't you tell Mummy you love her with rollercoaster love?' Star asked.

He let out a heavy sigh. 'I think love is a bit complicated, the rollercoaster kind. If Charlie had told Leah that he loved her with rollercoaster love and she didn't feel the same way, then it would have been awkward between them and they might have felt they couldn't be friends after that.'

Star looked at him incredulously. 'That's stupid. You said carousel love is constant and always there no matter what you do. If Charlie and Leah couldn't be friends because he loved her more than she loved him then I don't think they were really friends to start with.'

Bear nodded. 'Good point.'

'So you'll tell her then?' Star said, simply, as if it was that easy. Maybe it was.

'I will tell her, I promise, but it may take me a few days to tell her in the right way. Will you promise not to say anything to her until I do? I think this kind of thing is better coming from me than you.'

Star clearly thought about this for a moment then drew a cross over her heart. 'I promise.'

She spotted the other feeding station and ran on through the trees as if this big heavy conversation hadn't just happened.

'Look, this plate is empty too,' Star said, excitedly, running towards it, but Bear suddenly caught her arm and held her back.

'Hang on, there's a paw print on the ground,' he said, pointing at the perfect print in the mud immediately in front of the plate.

'There is!' she gasped, crouching down to look at it. 'What animal could it be?'

'Well, it's fairly big so I'm guessing a badger,' Bear said, taking his phone out of his pocket and looking up various paw prints. 'No, actually the badger print is more hand-like with the narrower toe pads and much wider overall, see it's very different to this.'

Star looked at his phone and the paw print and nodded.

'But the fox print is much smaller than this, the pads are smaller and the surface area of the print is much smaller.'

'What else could it be?' Star said.

Bear thought for a moment about all the possible animals it could be without saying out loud what he was thinking, which was that this particular paw print looked like it belonged to a very large dog... or a wolf. He scanned through various UK animal prints on his phone, almost everything else besides a fox and a badger had much smaller prints. Suddenly he had an idea.

'It could be an otter,' Bear said. 'We have them in Bosherston Lakes, which isn't far from here. I've never seen an otter in the woods but that's not to say they haven't wandered a bit further afield from their usual stomping ground.'

He felt like he was now clutching at straws. The otters at Bosherston liked lakes and rivers, he couldn't imagine they would suddenly decide to swim in the sea instead, that felt like a very different habitat than what they were used to. And then what, one day, as they were floating past one of the beaches they decided to go for a wander in the woods? It was getting more and more unrealistic the longer he thought about it.

He found an otter print on his phone and held it up next to the paw print on the ground. 'What do you think?' Bear said, hopefully, but even he could see the prints were markedly different.

Star screwed up her little face. 'That's not an otter print.'

'No, I don't suppose it is.'

They were silent for a moment as they stared at it.

'Could it be a wolf print?' Star asked, reverentially, as if asking if it was a unicorn's.

He didn't want to dampen her enthusiasm but he refused to believe there was an actual wolf wandering around the woods.

'Maybe it was just a pet dog owned by one of our guests,' Bear said, because that was much more likely.

Star let out a tiny sigh of disappointment. 'You're probably right but if the thing that has eaten all our food turns out to be a pet dog, I won't be happy.'

'No, I'm sure that's not the case. But there's only one way to find out, we set up the webcams and see what we capture. I'm hoping they arrive today but if not they'll definitely be here tomorrow.' He noticed she still looked a little bit sad that the paw print wasn't a wolf's. 'Listen, if the wolf is out here, we'll capture him on the camera. We'll put food out again to attract him tonight and that way he'll definitely be back when we set up the webcams tonight or tomorrow and we'll see him if he comes.'

Star nodded, the smile back on her face, and he vowed to himself that when the camera invariably picked up foxes, badgers, pet dogs and no wolves, he would find the nearest zoo or wildlife park with wolves and take Star to see them.

CHAPTER TWENTY

'So tell me all about your date last night,' Indigo said as she walked into the office and sat down.

Meadow smiled. Bear was still checking out all the food stations with Star so she was free to talk.

'My date was a complete disaster, he turned up with his mum and she was awful. I got out of there as quick as I could.'

'Hang on, this morning you said it was utterly lovely.'

'The utterly lovely part was after I had escaped out of the bathroom window. Bear took me on a date to show me what my first date should have been like. We went to a restaurant, we held hands, we talked non-stop all night and at the end of our meal he even danced with me. It couldn't have been more perfect.'

'Aww. Bear is just so lovely, isn't he?' Indigo said.

'He is. I'm not sure any man is going to live up to that. He set the bar very high.'

'Do you think you might want to date Bear for real if he was such a perfect date?' Indigo fished.

Meadow grinned. 'What is it with the Brookfield family trying to matchmake me with Bear? I've already had Amelia pushing me towards him.'

'I'm not part of the Brookfield family, not officially. So I'm saying this as your friend, if last night was so perfect, you have to ask yourself why.'

'Because Bear pulled out all the stops to make it special for me.'

'And why would he do that?'

'Because he's my friend.'

'Heath is your friend. If he did that for you to introduce you to the dating world, would you be sitting there with such a huge grin on your face when you're telling me about it?'

'No, that would be weird,' Meadow said, thinking about what it would be like to hold Heath's hand or to dance with him in the way that Bear danced with her.

'And why would it be weird?' Indigo said.

'Because we've never been anything other than friends. There is nothing romantic about my relationship with Heath.'

'But there is about your relationship with Bear,' Indigo said.

Meadow cursed. She had walked straight into that one.

'OK, I might have a bit of a soft spot for Bear,' she said, downplaying the huge space in her heart that was taken up solely by him. 'It doesn't mean he feels the same way.'

'But why would he go to all that effort if he doesn't? I can't see Heath or River doing that for you and they both adore you.'

Meadow thought about this for a moment. The night

before she had to keep reminding herself that it hadn't been real, especially when they'd been so close to kissing while they were dancing. What if it had been a lot more real than she'd thought?

Just then Amelia arrived, somehow making the little blue shorts and diamante wellies she was wearing look fabulously glamorous, as always. She was tying up her sheet of silvery hair in an extravagant and effortless plait ready for her day of playing in the woods or on the beach with Star.

'Star and Bear are just finishing checking the food stations they left out last night in the woods,' Meadow said. 'They are trying to find the best places to put up some webcams. They'll be back in a minute.'

'That's OK, I'm not in any rush,' Amelia said, a sly grin on her face. 'How was your first date last night?'

Meadow glanced at Indigo, hoping to convey in the briefest of looks not to mention anything about Bear. But she trusted her, especially after Indigo had been at the receiving end of Amelia's nosiness when she and River first got together.

'Awful,' Meadow said. 'He brought his mum along and she was very disapproving of me being a divorced mum. I got out of there after only a few minutes of hell.'

Amelia seemed delighted with this. 'See, I told you. Bear would never have done something like that.'

'I'm sure he wouldn't,' Meadow said. 'I'm attending a speed-dating event tonight, so hopefully I might meet some nice men there.'

Amelia's face fell. 'I don't really like the sound of that.'

'You said I should date other men.'

'Well I suppose so but—'

'How is your search for a man going?' Meadow quickly tried to divert her.

Indigo's face lit up. 'Are you looking for a man, Amelia?'

'I'm... not sure,' Amelia said and Meadow had the pleasure of seeing her squirm uncomfortably.

'We could set you up with an online dating profile,' Meadow said.

'I've seen one for over-sixties, silver dating I think it's called,' Indigo said, tapping a few keys on her computer. 'Here it is, we could do this now.'

'Oh look, here come Star and Bear,' Amelia said, hurriedly. 'I'll go and meet them. And maybe I'll have a little word with Bear about all this nonsense. If you won't ask him out, maybe I can get him to see sense.'

'By all means,' Meadow said. 'And by the time you come back your dating profile will be fully set up with photos and if anyone messages you, I'll be more than happy to hand out your number.'

Amelia hesitated.

'Unless you want to call a truce on interfering in each other's love life?' Meadow said.

Meadow could see Amelia was torn. Amelia was clearly tempted to let Meadow set up a dating profile purely so she could still interfere with Bear and Meadow's love life. In the end she let out a heavy sigh.

'OK, OK. A truce. At least for now. I'll go and take your daughter down to the beach.'

'And that truce includes her too, I don't want any of your meddling to reach her ears,' Meadow said.

Amelia nodded reluctantly and moved out the reception area to meet her great-granddaughter.

'You know that won't be the end of it,' Indigo said.

'I know, but at least it might give me a few days' respite.'

They looked out the office to see Amelia talking to Bear.

'I wouldn't count on it,' Indigo said.

CHAPTER TWENTY-ONE

Bear was sitting on the floor of the chapel a while later, wiring an electric socket. As rustic and simple as the wedding venue was supposed to be, River had recognised there would probably be a need for music or somewhere to plug in a laptop or a projector if the couples wanted to share some photos, so today's job was to add several sockets around the room. Bear sighed as he dropped one of the small screws to secure the front panel and it rolled across the floor and disappeared beneath the floorboards. Fortunately, he had some more.

'You OK over there?' Heath said as he secured a plank of wood in the opposite corner. 'There are lots of sighs of frustration coming from your direction.'

Bear's mind really wasn't on the task. His thoughts kept drifting to the spectacular date he'd shared with Meadow the night before and how excited she'd been that morning when she'd been talking about it. He'd been thinking about the promise he'd made Star about telling Meadow how he felt and the words he wanted to use. He couldn't really concentrate on the sockets.

'Just things not going to plan,' Bear said.

'Life never goes to plan. But sometimes it's the unplanned things which turn out to be the best.'

Bear looked over at him. 'Christ, that's a bit philosophical for half past twelve on a Wednesday afternoon. I just dropped my screw down the gap in the floorboards, I wasn't lamenting the twists and turns of my life.'

'Ah, just me then,' Heath said.

Bear frowned. 'You all right?'

'It was just something Meadow said a few days ago, it got me thinking about where my life would be now if it hadn't been for Star. One moment in time and my life changed forever. Star is the best thing that ever happened to me.'

Bear grabbed another screw from his toolbox. Presumably, that one moment in time was when Heath and Meadow had slept together. Bear could only assume there'd been alcohol involved as neither of them had ever showed any interest in each other before. It had been a huge shock to find out that Meadow was pregnant with Heath's baby.

'I don't think any of this would have been here if it hadn't been for her,' Heath said.

'You and River had plans to build this place before Star was on her way.'

'They were pipe dreams. Me and River lacked any kind of motivation to get off our arses and do it. I was a mess and alcohol was my friend. I don't think my life would have turned out too great if Star hadn't come along.' Heath paused. 'What about you? I love my life and I wouldn't change it for the world but I always think this life can't be enough for you. Wiring an electric socket, putting up a few light fittings, setting up some Facebook ads, it's all a bit mundane for a man of your brains, isn't it?'

'I like working here, I love being part of all this, even if my contribution is the small mundane things.'

'I didn't mean—' Heath started.

'I know you didn't.'

'I love you working here too. And your contribution is equally important if not more important than me and River throwing up a few wooden houses. All of it would be worthless if we didn't have people to fill them. You're responsible for that. You're responsible for us being fully booked for the rest of the year with your ads and marketing. So don't dismiss what you do here. I just wondered if it was enough for you, whether you ever needed more?'

Bear looked at him in confusion. 'Where has all this come from?'

Heath sat back against the wall. 'I was helping Meadow set up her dating profile the other day, I was on your computer and I saw the story you were working on. I didn't read it, well just the first few lines to realise what it was. I figured if you wanted me to read it, you'd have given it to me so I respect your privacy on that. But you were always writing stories when you were little and, if you're still doing that now, I wondered if that was something you wanted to pursue rather than being our resident sparky?'

Bear leaned back against the wall too, watching a bright orange butterfly flutter across the ceiling, thudding gently against the reflections of light from the open windows.

'When I was little I wrote stories about normal little boys who found out they had extraordinary powers. They were always tasked with some great quest. They were important. I was not. Those stories were a way for me to escape from my own world where I felt… insignificant.'

'Christ Bear, why would you think you were insignificant?'

'Having both parents walk out on us when we were little doesn't do great things for our self-worth. You and River found solace in the bottom of the bottle, I found my peace in stories where I could control the outcome, where little boys had families that loved them.'

'Bear… shit… I had no idea. We should have done more for you, we should have been there—'

'I don't blame you two, not at all,' Bear said. 'We all had our own demons to slay. And you two were always there for me, even if our parents weren't.'

Heath cleared his throat. 'You are loved. I know I don't say it enough, but you are.'

Bear grinned. 'I know. But that's why this place is enough for me, because we're a team. You, me, River, Meadow and now Indigo, we're a family and it didn't feel like we had that growing up. Now we have this… gang and I love it.'

'But you still write the stories?'

'When I was older, I thought that if my stories were a good way for me to escape from my world maybe one day they might help other children to escape when they read them. So I kept writing them. And when Star was around five or six and I was reading her stories, the characters who had the biggest adventures were always boys. Most of the books she reads now, Harry Potter, Percy Jackson, Alex Rider, they are always boys saving the world and I wanted her to see that girls can have adventures too. That she can have big dreams as well. So the main character of the series I'm writing now is a girl called Starlight.'

'You wrote a story for Star?' Heath's voice was rough when he spoke.

Bear shrugged. 'Yeah. Not that she's seen it. No one has. Well, until I sent the first book in the series to Meadow last night. We were chatting and I told her that I write stories. She wanted to see them.'

'That was the story she was excited about this morning at breakfast?'

'Yes. It seems she likes it.'

'I'd like to read it too.'

Bear swallowed a lump in his throat. 'OK.'

'And I'd really like Star to read it. She will get such a big kick out of this story that was written for her.'

'I'd like that too.'

'Are you going to do anything with these books, send them to a publisher or an agent?'

'I don't know.'

'But you said you wrote them for children who needed to escape, you wrote them for girls who needed to see girls as the heroes of their stories. Why wouldn't you want to share your stories?'

Bear stood up, caught the butterfly gently in his hands and released it out the window. He turned back to face Heath. 'I don't have many memories of Mum and Dad, we hardly saw Dad at all after they left, Mum was there for a few days two or three times a year. But the one memory I have of Mum that is more vivid than anything else is showing her the story I had won a prize for at school and telling her I wanted to be an author when I grew up. She read the story, it was only a page long, and she laughed and told me I'd never be an author if I wrote like that. She told me I had to aim higher because being an author was never going to pay the bills. Then she screwed it up and threw it in the bin. I haven't shown anyone my work since, well, until last night.'

Heath stared at him in horror. 'Bloody hell. I knew they were bad parents, I just didn't realise quite how bad they were.' He paused. 'Did you know she was an author too?'

Bear sat down on the windowsill. 'I didn't know that.'

'She was never published. She sent her stories out to publishers and agents and got rejection after rejection. Her sister, Annie, used to look after us fairly often and she had no problems telling me what our mum was doing with her life. She was always writing, always sending it out in the hope of getting some validation, but she never did. Apparently she was quite bitter and angry about it all. I imagine she took that bitterness out on you when you told her your dream. But you should never ever let anyone stamp on your dreams like that. Or let her experience hold you back. We make our own path in life. You wrote those stories to encourage Star to go after her dreams, to have big adventures. You need to go after your own.'

Bear thought about what Meadow had said to him the night before, it gave him such confidence to hear what she thought about him. He nodded. 'I think you're probably right.'

CHAPTER TWENTY-TWO

Bear was just finishing off the last electrical socket and then he had to go and get ready for the speed-dating event later that night. River was busy working near the entrance on the archway that would become the chapel doors. Heath had already gone to spend some time with Star.

Bear's phone beeped with an email notification and when he pulled it out of his pocket he saw he had a new message from Twilight. He logged in to his profile on Connected Hearts to read it.

How was your date last night?

He thought about how to answer that question. He'd had a lovely time with Meadow but technically that hadn't been his date.

Not good. How was yours?

She replied almost instantly. **I bet it wasn't as bad as mine. So I was wondering if you wanted to go for a drink or dinner some time?**

His heart ached for her, he knew that must have taken a

lot of courage to ask him that if she hadn't asked out someone before.

He thought about it for a moment because his gut was to say yes, he wanted to get to know Twilight better, but at the same time he wanted to see how things were going to play out with Meadow.

Last night on their fake date they had just clicked and of course he knew that was because they were such good friends but there seemed to be something else going on, maybe something deeper. She'd talked about how she regretted her actions after their kiss, and he really needed to talk to her about that and find out why, because if she regretted pushing him away did that mean she wanted a second chance with him? Was she waiting to see if he wanted that too before she made her move?

And then this morning over breakfast, she'd talked about their date as if it had been real and how much she liked the man she had dated the night before. Well, that sure as hell wasn't Josh. Even Star had spotted her moony eyes, as she called it. Bear had promised Star he would tell Meadow how he felt too. Maybe tonight at the dating event, he might get the chance to talk to her. He wanted this second chance with Meadow more than anything. He didn't want to start something with Twilight and then have to finish with her if something happened with Meadow, that wasn't fair on Twilight when she was venturing out on the dating circuit for the first time.

He cringed as he wrote out his answer, hating himself just a little bit for lying to her.

I'm afraid I'm away with work now for the next five or six days at least. But the second I get back, I'd be very

happy to take you out for dinner. Maybe I should set you a riddle for you to work out which restaurant I'll be taking you to.

He would give it a week to see if all these dates would lead to something finally happening with Meadow and if not he would take Twilight out but at least this way he wasn't going to hurt Twilight.

She quickly replied. **I would love that. I'm up for the challenge. You might have to give me the clues the night before so I have time to work it out, otherwise I might be very late for dinner.**

He smiled. **I can absolutely do that.**

Are we still OK to chat while you're away or will you be too busy?

He thought about it. It felt a bit crappy to keep his options open with Twilight but if nothing was going to happen with Meadow maybe it was time to get over her once and for all, to move on with someone like Twilight. There would be no harm in chatting to her in the meantime. He could be a friend to her if nothing else and it sounded like she needed a bit of a sounding board with these dates she was going on, he could do that for her.

It will be great to chat, work doesn't take up a lot of my time and I'll always find time for you.

OK, I'll speak to you later. X

He smiled as he put his phone in his pocket.

'So how did your date go last night?' River asked, taking off his toolbelt and wiping his hands.

'It wasn't a proper date, I was just there to support Meadow on her first ever date.'

'And how did that go? She seemed happy enough this

morning.'

'Not good but… I took her out after and showed her how it should have been done.'

River grinned. 'So that's why she was happy, she had a lovely evening with you.'

'I… tried to make it special for her. I want to encourage her to aim high when she goes out with different men. I want someone for her who is attentive, respectful and kind, someone who will hold her hand, dance with her, really take the time to listen. She shouldn't settle for an OK date. She should be swept off her feet.'

River laughed and shook his head. 'I'm not sure if that was remarkably clever thinking or just naïvely brilliant.'

'What do you mean?'

'No man she dates is going to live up to that.'

'Then she needs to choose better men.'

'Or the man who has already given her all that.'

Bear sighed. 'I suppose there was an element of that. There were times last night where the date felt so real. When we danced there was a moment where I thought we might kiss and it looked like she really wanted that too. I need to talk to her. We have the speed-dating event tonight, maybe I'll get a chance to talk to her then.'

'Maybe if you speak at a hundred miles an hour. That kind of conversation might be better in private.'

'Well, I'm sure there'll be time before and after the speed dating, but we'll probably get ten minutes or so with each date, won't we? How else are you supposed to get to know someone if it's less than that?'

'I guess. I've never done it,' River said. 'Is that going to be enough to tell Meadow how you feel?'

'It will have to be.'

CHAPTER TWENTY-THREE

'Three minutes?' Bear said, as he read the leaflet explaining how their evening was going to go.

Meadow couldn't help giggling at his incredulous expression.

'How do you get to know someone in three minutes?' Bear said, clearly outraged.

'I think you can tell a lot about someone in three minutes,' she said as she looked around the bookshop where the event was taking place. Right now people were just milling about chatting, new arrivals were registering their details with the organiser. 'I think attraction is fairly instant and then I think you can click with someone on an intellectual or chemistry level fairly quickly too. According to scientists it takes between ninety seconds and four minutes for you to tell if you like someone.'

'You can't dive deep in three minutes?'

'But this is technically a first date with someone, you never dive deep on a first date,' Meadow said.

Or at least that's what the websites had said when she'd looked for advice on dating and specifically speed dating.

'This way we get to meet as many people as possible in one night so we have more of a chance of meeting the one,' she said.

'I guarantee you're not going to find your soul mate after spending three minutes with them,' Bear said.

'No, but you might find someone you might like to know more.'

By the look on his face, he clearly didn't agree.

'Ladies and gentlemen, may I have your attention please,' called Imogen, the lady who seemed to be in charge tonight. The quiet buzz of chatter died down as everyone listened. 'Thank you all for coming and a huge thank you to the wonderful Red Dragon Bookshop for letting us use their fabulous shop this evening.'

There was a polite round of applause.

'Over the course of the five events you will have the opportunity to meet and chat with different people and if you feel you want to get to know these people more outside of the Mix n Match events, of course you are free to do so. Mix n Match will also be matching you based on different criteria. I thought we'd start the evening off slightly differently. I'm going to give you fifteen minutes to look around the shop and choose a book that best represents you. It could be your favourite book or a book you'd like to read. Maybe you might choose a book that's about your favourite country or topic or just one that has an appealing title. Bring it with you as you meet your potential dates. Then if the conversation gets stilted or awkward you can share your books to try to show the other person who you are.'

'Oooh, interesting,' Meadow said, quietly, and there were other murmurs of appreciation from the other candidates.

'Now, that I can get on board with,' Bear said.

'It's a shame I can't share *The Lost Crystals* with my dates,' Meadow said. 'It's a brilliant book and it would show my dates the kind of thing I like to read.'

He turned to her with a grin. 'Do you really like it?'

'I love it and I promise I'm not just saying that because you're my friend. It grabbed me and didn't let go. You have a wonderful talent. It's a shame to keep it locked away.'

'I thought about what you said actually and I've decided to submit it to a few publishers and agents.'

'You have?' Meadow was delighted for him.

'We'll see what the response is,' Bear said.

Imogen started speaking again. 'I will ring the bell in fifteen minutes and, women, I'd like you to take a seat at your corresponding numbered table, but on the inside of the circle, facing outwards,' she gestured to the circle of tables on the floor below them. 'Once the women are seated I'll ask the men to sit down on the outside of the table again at your corresponding number. It doesn't matter where you start because you will get a chance to meet all your potential matches tonight. Once everyone is seated, I will ring the bell to start your three minutes and ring the bell again once the three minutes are up. At that point, men, you will move to the next table on your left. You'll have a few moments to move and make a few very quick notes about your match before I ring the bell again to start your next date. At the end of the night, if anyone took your fancy you can let me know and if they also like the look of you, which would therefore make you a match, then we will share your contact details with each other. We won't share your details with anyone unless you let me know you are interested in meeting that person.'

There were nods around the room and a few people speaking quietly.

'Now as you know, this is no ordinary speed-dating event,' Imogen went on. 'Something you might have noticed when you were asked to give a saliva swab when you arrived here tonight, which I'll explain more about later or you can read the pamphlet you were given when you arrived which explains everything. There are lots of ways we connect to people that go beyond just what someone looks like. Love is a range of positive emotions and this can be triggered by very different things. Body language, eye contact, smell are all things we respond to. That attraction can be seen in increased levels of adrenaline, dopamine and serotonin.'

Meadow nodded as Imogen spoke. This was clearly a woman who knew her stuff.

'So tonight we will be measuring your heart rate and breathing, as that is a good indication of attraction and an increase of adrenaline. If any of you have ever been in hospital there's a good chance you were given an oximeter to wear on your finger which measures your pulse and the levels of oxygen in your blood. The smart watches we gave you tonight to wear around your wrist are very similar but they are also linked up with our computers so we can record how your heart rate changes when you meet a new date. We will then feed that data into our famous Mix n Match computer program and it will find the person you responded to the most. If they also responded to you, then you will be matched. So you have two chances to match with someone tonight, the person who you are interested in after meeting them and the person our computer program matches you to based on your body's responses to each other.'

There were more murmurs of interest as people looked around the room at their potential matches.

'OK, then. I'll give you fifteen minutes from now to find a book and if at any point during that time you have any questions or concerns, please do come over and talk to me,' Imogen said.

Everyone suddenly spread out like they were on a treasure hunt as they quickly scanned the shelves to find the perfect book that would represent them.

Bear strode off towards the non-fiction section, which wasn't a surprise. Meadow moved over to the fiction, scanning the titles for something that could help to sum her up. She loved romance books but she knew a lot of men were quite dismissive of that genre for painting an unrealistic picture, and she didn't want any potential men to be put off by her rose-tinted, over-the-top view on romance. She had an interest in history, the Romans, the Tudors, Ancient Egypt and Greece but would that really tell her dates anything about her? She couldn't exactly discuss the nitty-gritty of history and some of her favourite historical facts in just three minutes.

She noticed that some of the men and women were already starting to take their seats after having chosen their book. She glanced around to see if she could spot Bear and to her surprise he was at the till buying one of the books. That wasn't part of the night's arrangements. Imogen had made it sound like they were merely borrowing a book from the bookshelf. No one else was buying a book either.

'You have five minutes left,' Imogen called.

Meadow scanned the shelves frantically. This was a lot harder than she'd first thought. She walked out of the fiction section and into the non-fiction and that's when she spotted it. A great big, colour hardback called *Hedgerows and Woodlands*, the accompanying book for the latest nature programme she loved to watch on TV with Star and Bear. She quickly picked it up and then went downstairs to find her seat.

She sat down, drumming her fingers against the table nervously, eyeing the men as they filed by to find their seat. Would any of these be her match?

Bear walked past and she felt that wonderful flutter in her belly as she watched him. He flashed her a wink and she smiled and then he glanced down to her hands, her fingers still going crazy on the table, and he doubled back.

He bent down to whisper in her ear. 'Just relax and be yourself. The real you is pretty bloody spectacular so make sure they see that.'

She smiled as he walked off and sat himself down around eight tables away. She watched him, so at ease with himself. Well, at least on the surface. He had some insecurities himself if he had been so against people reading his stories.

'OK, time is up, can you all take your seats,' Imogen said.

Meadow found herself looking over at the woman who was now sitting down opposite Bear. She was very pretty and giggly. Was that the kind of woman he went for? In fact, she had no idea what kind of woman Bear liked. He had gone out on lots of dates over the years but, as far as she knew, he'd never had any kind of serious relationship. He was leaning forward to shake hands with her and Meadow felt a small kick of jealousy that Bear looked interested.

'Hello.'

Meadow looked up at a tall, gangly-looking man folding himself into the seat opposite her. He had a nice smile.

'Hi,' Meadow said.

'I'm Harris.'

'Meadow, pleased to meet you.'

'This is a strange way of meeting, isn't it?' Harris said. 'Three minutes to impress someone.'

'I think three minutes gives us a good baseline. I think attraction, which is what they are measuring with these,' Meadow gestured with her smart watch. 'Is pretty instant.'

'Oh, so you've already made your mind up whether you want to see me again,' Harris said, frowning.

'I, erm…'

'So I don't need to bother talking at all, you'll just take one look at me and decide yes or no,' he said, while people were still taking their seats around them. 'That's very shallow.'

Meadow blinked in surprise at how badly this mini date was already going and they hadn't even officially started yet. 'I think, as Imogen said, there are lots of things that go into an attraction, a smile, a nice comment, eye contact, body language. It's not just about looks.'

Harris folded his arms and Meadow didn't need to be an expert in body language to understand that.

'But it's mainly about looks,' he said with disdain.

'Your looks haven't put me off but this whole negative attitude has,' Meadow said.

'Well I certainly wouldn't pick you either,' Harris snapped.

'Ladies and gentlemen, here is the bell to start your first date. You have three minutes starting from now,' Imogen called, ringing the bell.

Meadow and Harris stared at each other. Harris opened up his book and started reading it, clearly having no interest in even chatting to Meadow. God, this was embarrassing. She glanced around and everyone was chatting enthusiastically with their dates.

Meadow cleared her throat. 'Sorry, I think we got off on the wrong foot, can we start again?'

Harris turned sideways in his seat, facing away from her, and raised the book so he wouldn't even have to look at her.

Meadow glanced at the couple at the next table and they were both staring at Harris in shock. She looked around the room, some people were politely chatting, others seemed to be getting on like a house on fire, but no one else was sitting in silence, impatiently waiting for the three minutes to be up. She looked over at Bear and he was laughing at something his date was saying. It would be kind of ironic if Bear found someone at a speed-dating event, something he was so against, and

Meadow didn't, even though she'd been the one pushing its merits.

The three minutes with Harris were the longest three minutes of her life and they both let out a huge sigh of relief when the bell rang to indicate time was up. Harris was quick to scramble out of his seat and stood impatiently at the next table while the couple said their goodbyes.

The man got out of his seat and moved on but as Harris was about to sit down the woman stopped him.

'I have no interest in talking to you at all after seeing the way you treated her,' the woman said, indicating Meadow.

'Oh, for fuck's sake,' Harris snapped and to Meadow's surprise he turned and stormed out.

'Bloody hell,' the woman said, watching him go.

'I'm so sorry,' Meadow said. 'I didn't mean to ruin your date as well.'

'Christ no, you did me a favour. I definitely don't need to waste my time on cockwombles like that.'

Meadow laughed. 'I'm Meadow.'

'I'm Heather.'

'But now you have no one to talk to,' Meadow said.

Heather held up her book. 'But I have this. Infinitely better.'

A man slipped into the seat opposite Meadow, looking almost fearful. 'I'm not sure what you did to make the last man walk out of the whole event after spending three minutes with you. Am I safe to sit down?'

'Yes, you're fine,' Meadow said, with a sigh. 'We had a little disagreement about...' she decided not to tell him she had been talking to Harris about instant attraction, in case he felt the same way Harris did, 'about the merits of speed dating. I don't think Harris was a fan.'

The man nodded but she could see he was on edge. This mini date was clearly not going to go well either. 'I'm Meadow.'

'Dan.'

The bell rang to indicate the start of their date and Meadow leaned forward to try to engage with him. 'What book did you bring with you?'

Dan held up a book on trains.

'Oh, trains. That's interesting,' she tried to sound enthusiastic.

'I love trains. I have a model railway in my loft.'

Meadow wondered if this was the same man she had matched with on Connected Hearts a few days before. She hadn't reached out to him then but maybe fate was giving her a second chance.

Bear had said it was good for men to have a hobby. And she didn't have to share everything with the person she'd end up with. Most of them probably wouldn't understand her passion for making dresses either. She would be open-minded about this.

'What is it about trains that you like?' Meadow asked.

His eyes lit up. 'I've always loved them, even when I was a small boy. I used to live next to the train tracks and we'd get freight trains rattle through all hours of the day. Big, powerful beasts. They have this air of adventure and mystery about them. Once they left me, they'd wind round a corner and disappear into the trees ending up god knows where, carrying their mysterious loads. It's terribly exciting. I believe the steam locomotives are the single greatest invention we have ever seen and it's my mission to travel around the world on every remaining steam train. But I loved the power of the diesel trains too and now the speed of the electric trains is something wondrous to behold.'

Dan carried on talking about his love of trains and different trains he'd been on for the full three minutes, barely pausing to draw breath. The bell rang and he enthusiastically shook her hand before moving on to poor Heather.

Another man slipped into the seat opposite and Meadow plastered on a big smile as the bell rang for the start of their date.

'Hi, I'm Meadow.'

'I'm Steve.'

'And what book did you bring with you?'

Her heart sank as he held up a book about pigeons.

CHAPTER TWENTY-FOUR

The bell rang to indicate her latest mini date had ended and Meadow's heart leapt when she realised her next mini date was with Bear.

'Hey, how's it going?' Bear asked, giving her a warm smile as he sat down.

'Well, the first man walked out of the whole event after three minutes with me. The second *loved* trains more than life itself. The third man had that same love for pigeons. Patrick, he was the fifth I think, maybe the sixth. He seemed nice.'

Bear pulled a face. 'We need someone better for you than just *nice*. You need to find someone who makes your heart race, someone amazing and brilliant who you're excited to meet again.'

Meadow sighed because there had only ever been one man who made her feel like that.

He reached across the table and took her hand. 'You need to be with someone who will hold your hand on a date, someone who will listen to you, encourage you in your dreams, someone who will dance with you to your favourite song.'

Her heart thundered against her chest. She swallowed, remembering her perfect date the night before. 'I would like that very much.'

He stared at her, then glanced at his watch, cursing under his breath.

'What book did you choose?' Bear said.

Meadow blinked at the sudden U-turn in the conversation. Although he was the first person to ask about her book. She showed him the accompanying book from the TV series *Hedgerows and Woodlands* and he laughed as he showed her the exact same book.

'I love nature but growing up in Wishing Wood you kind of take it all for granted sometimes,' Bear said. 'I love watching this programme with you and Star. It was so interesting and seeing Star's passion and enthusiasm for it made it all the more enjoyable and made me look at our wildlife with new eyes.'

Meadow's heart filled for him. He had chosen that book because he had watched it with her and Star.

'Same. I love that show,' she said. 'I could watch it a hundred times over and not get bored. I thought this book was a good way to show my passion for the world we live in and particular the wildlife. Did I see you buy another book? A black and white one?'

'Yes,' Bear rummaged in his bag. 'I bought you this.'

He placed a copy of *How to Make a Dress* by Jenny Packham in front of her and Meadow let out a little gasp.

'It's not an instruction manual or anything like that, I know you're more than capable of making your own dress.

It's kind of part memoir and an exploration of dresses through the ages. It talks about her inspirations and her experiences,' Bear said.

Meadow nodded. 'I know this book, I've wanted to read this book. How did you know?'

'You said that Jenny Packham was your guru so I figured you might like this.'

Meadow stared at it, her breath catching in her throat. 'This is... wonderful, thank you.'

Bear shrugged like it wasn't a big deal but it was. One throwaway comment she'd made the night before and he'd listened and remembered. This was such a thoughtful gift.

Suddenly the bell rang to indicate their three minutes were up and Meadow wanted to wail. She wanted longer with him.

Bear got up and made to move on but Meadow suddenly leapt up and threw her arms around him. He froze for a second and then wrapped his arms around her, holding her tight.

'Thank you, this is a beautiful gift, you have no idea what this means to me,' Meadow said.

She looked up at him and realised their lips were mere inches away from each other. He stared down at her and then he bent his head and gave her a lingering kiss on the cheek, burning her skin with his lips. 'You're very welcome.'

They heard the sound of the bell ringing to indicate the next date had started but they were still staring at each other.

There was the sound of someone clearing their throat and they looked round to see Meadow's next date sitting at the table patiently – or rather impatiently – waiting for her.

Bear gently pulled away and went to sit opposite Heather and Meadow quickly sat down. Her next date looked a bit confused by the huge demonstration of affection he'd just witnessed. She plastered on a big smile and started chatting to him but all she could think about was this beautiful book Bear had bought her for no other reason than to make her smile. And she also couldn't stop thinking about how it felt to be held in his arms, the kiss that still warmed her cheek.

Nothing was ever going to compare to the feelings she felt for him. She might as well give up and go home now because Amelia was right, she was never going to find anyone who made her feel like this.

CHAPTER TWENTY-FIVE

Bear stood up as the last date ended, giving Debbie a warm smile before wandering off to find Meadow. The evening hadn't exactly been a huge success in terms of finding his soul mate. There had been a small handful of women he thought he might want to see again but no one who had made his heart race, no one he was excited about seeing what would develop between them. By the look on Meadow's face it seemed she hadn't had the best night either. Three minutes really wasn't long enough to build any kind of relationship with someone.

He touched Meadow's back to let her know he was there and her face lit up in a big smile when she saw him.

'How did your night go?' she asked.

'It was... fun,' Bear said.

'Anyone take your fancy?'

'I don't think so. Maybe a few women who were nice but it didn't feel like the time was long enough to see if we had anything worth pursuing.'

'I know what you mean,' Meadow said.

'Are you going to tell the host you were interested in anyone?' Bear said, the part of him that wanted to keep her for himself fighting with the part that wanted her to be happy.

'I don't think so.'

'No one that made your heart race?' Bear said.

She paused before answering this time. 'No.'

'Ladies and gentlemen, can I have your attention,' Imogen called. 'Thank you for taking part tonight in our first dating event. I hope you met some wonderful people. Be sure to come and tell me if there's anyone you'd like to see again and, if they want to see you again, your details will be shared with each other tomorrow.

'Now let's get on to the exciting part. The results of the smart watches. Some of you had some very interesting chemical reactions to each other tonight. If you had a reaction to someone as picked up by our watches and they also had a reaction to you then you will be matched shortly and your details will be automatically shared. Your watches will buzz and show you the number of the person you are matched with so you can go and find them and have a chat. Some of you have had a reaction to more than one person so the results for those people who matched with multiple people will be staggered. For the rest of you who didn't match with anyone on a chemical level, feel free to stay as long as you want and have a proper chat with the other participants. Now before you go, don't forget to give a saliva sample, if you haven't already done so, so you can be genetically matched at our labs, the results of which we will share at one of the later events. And I'm happy to answer any questions. For now, I'll leave you to chat and look out for any chemical matches on your watches.'

People started chatting and moving around the room.

'Shall we go?' Bear said. 'I'm starving.'

'Me too.'

They started to move towards the exit when suddenly Bear's watch buzzed with a match. He glanced down at it to see that it flashed number seventeen. Meadow. And to prove it Meadow's watch also flashed with his number. They looked at each other.

'That's just because we know each other, right? It's picked up our friendship and confused it for something else,' Meadow said.

Bear swallowed. Because he was damn sure that for him the watch had picked up on his inappropriate feelings for his best friend – but what had it picked up in her?

'I guess so, what else could it be?'

She stared at him, looking as if she wanted to say something. But suddenly his watch was buzzing again, this time with a new number. He glanced at it in confusion to see number eighteen now showing. Meadow's next-door neighbour, Heather. A nice girl but the only reason his heart was racing when he was with her was because he was still thinking about that almost kiss with Meadow after she had hugged him.

'Oh look, you matched with someone else, that's nice,' Meadow's voice was strangled.

'No, I, erm… that's a mistake,' Bear said.

But suddenly Heather was coming towards him with a huge smile on her face.

'Hello you.' Heather leaned up and kissed him on the

cheek. 'I knew I had a reaction to you, I mean look at you, I bet every woman in the room had a reaction to you. But I didn't think you had a reaction to me. I'm so flattered.'

'I, erm...' Bear said, because he had nothing else he could say.

'I never get matched with anyone at these kinds of events, I think it's my height, men don't like women who are taller than them, but you're one of the few men I've met who is taller than me. And you were attracted to me. I'm so happy right now, I can't even tell you,' Heather went on.

He watched Meadow discreetly slip away, leaving them alone, and though Heather was grinning at him inanely, he couldn't have felt more miserable.

CHAPTER TWENTY-SIX

Meadow took off her smart watch and handed it back to Imogen while everyone else was still milling around chatting to people or getting matched.

'Did you have fun?' Imogen asked.

'It was nice to meet so many different people,' Meadow said, tactfully.

Imogen checked the number on the badge Meadow was wearing. 'Ah, number seventeen, your chemistry with number twenty-five was off the charts.'

'Yes well, I wanted to talk to you about that. Me and Bear, number twenty-five, we're friends. I mean, he's my best friend, I've known him all my life. So that would have skewed the results, right?'

Imogen frowned and shook her head. 'No, these monitors don't pick up that kind of connection. We have trialled these on family members, friends, even enemies, and while hate or anger or friendship can provoke a chemical reaction, it doesn't have the same results as a physical attraction.' She paused for a moment while she consulted her tablet, bringing up both Meadow and Bear's charts for the time they had their date.

Imogen looked around to make sure no one could hear. 'You love him, don't you? You felt a strong affection for him, that I can see, and desire and passion too, but these kinds of results are only ever present when someone is head over heels in love with someone else. Your history explains it, because you would never feel this kind of love for someone you've just met no matter how much you were attracted to them. And based on his readings he has the same feelings for you. I have been doing this matchmaking for five years now and studied it and researched it for many more years before that and I've never seen this kind of love before, not even in couples who have been married for years. I have no idea why you two aren't together, whether there are other complications in your life that are keeping you apart, but trust me when I say: you two belong together.'

Meadow stared at her, feeling like she had been punched in the gut with that news. Bear loved her? Surely not.

She turned round to look at him to see he was happily chatting to Heather. How could he love her and be matched to someone else?

'Ah yes, he also matched with someone else,' Imogen said and Meadow turned round to look at her. 'Number eighteen. That's… interesting. And more than a bit weird.'

'How do you mean?'

'Let me get up his chart for the whole evening,' Imogen said. She studied it for a moment. 'Ah, the wonders of technology, it's amazing until it cocks up.' She turned the tablet round to show Meadow. 'These red lines are connected to the bell, the start and stop times of each date. And a tiny gap in between each date while people are moving around. You can see here that throughout the evening his heart rate remained steady for every date apart from here, number seventeen, when it suddenly gets a lot higher. The bell rang here to end your date and then it spikes exponentially in this tiny gap between the dates. Although he was with number eighteen from this point onwards his heart rate is still recovering from what happened here, at this spike. What happened at the very end of your date, after the bell rang?'

'He, umm... he bought me a book, something really personal to me, and I hugged him to say thank you and then... there was a moment where I thought we were going to kiss.'

'That's what caused this massive spike, he clearly thought you were going to kiss, too. Then his date with number eighteen started here but his heart is still recovering from that near kiss. This is why the program matched him with number eighteen as well, it doesn't take into account what happened prior to his date with number eighteen starting, it just recognises that his heart rate was elevated during their date. And hers was too, not surprising, he's a good-looking lad. But I certainly wouldn't get too upset about him matching with someone else. If I were you, I'd go over there and kiss him, lay claim on him once and for all.'

Meadow laughed and turned to look at him again. 'I think we need to talk about all this first, before we jump ahead to any kisses. This, us, just wasn't on my radar because I never realised he felt the same way I did. I'm guessing he never realised how I feel either.'

'Well, it's certainly something you need to talk about sooner rather than later,' Imogen said as they watched Heather put her hand on Bear's arm and Bear laugh loudly at something she said. 'Before it's too late.'

CHAPTER TWENTY-SEVEN

Meadow sat down opposite Bear at breakfast the next day as he was working away on his laptop. Star was busy chatting happily to Alex and Lucien at the counter and Meadow was hoping to talk to Bear, although she knew her time was short. He had still been speaking to Heather when she'd left the dating event the night before so they hadn't had a chance to talk about them matching.

He looked up and closed his laptop, pushing it to one side. 'You OK? You left early last night.'

'Well, there didn't seem any point in hanging around. I only matched with you and I certainly didn't want to be in the way of you and Heather getting to know each other.'

She hoped she didn't sound jealous, she wanted Bear to be happy, but she couldn't help feeling confused that he had matched with her because he supposedly loved her but had spent over half an hour talking to someone else. It felt like they really needed to discuss this, unless Imogen and her amazing computer program was wrong and it was simply a platonic connection that had been recorded the night before. But if so how did it explain the spike of his heart rate when they nearly kissed?

He frowned. 'You could never be in the way.'

'Heather seems nice.'

'She is… but…' he trailed off.

Meadow glanced over at Star. They probably had less than a minute before she came over to join them. Nowhere near enough. Now wasn't the time.

'Are you working on your story?'

Bear looked at the laptop. 'Yes, I always like to write in the mornings.'

'Did you tell Heather about your book?'

God, she did sound jealous and she hated that.

'No, of course not.'

'I'm sorry, I'm sounding like such a cow, I want you to be happy, I really do. I just thought… last night—'

'Alex has seen the wolf too,' Star said excitedly as she arrived at the table with her breakfast. 'Round the back of the kitchen. Only Alex thinks it might just be a dog. She gave it some leftovers and it ate them and then ran off when she tried to get close.'

Bear stared at Meadow for a second before turning his attention to Star. 'I've had an email to say the webcams are arriving today, so we'll hopefully capture some footage of this thing tonight and see for ourselves.'

'I'm so excited. The Wolf of Wishing Wood and we'll finally get to see him,' Star said. 'I've been reading all about wolves and they are such amazing animals. Very clever and they live in packs of brothers, sisters, mums, dads, aunts and uncles, just like we do. We live in a pack too.'

Meadow smiled at that idea.

'Sometimes members of the pack mate for life, that's like getting married but never getting a divorce,' Star said.

'Those wolves must love each other a lot,' Meadow said.

'Yes.' Star ate a grape. 'Mummy, do you think you will get married one day and mate for life?'

'Oh,' Meadow glanced at Bear. 'It would need to be someone really special to want to be with them for the rest of my life.'

'Like a best friend,' Star said innocently.

Meadow watched Bear smirk at her obvious match-making tactics.

'I think being really good friends with someone is an excellent start to any relationship, just like Charlie and Leah. Now, what tattoo are you going to get today at Dwelling?' Meadow said.

Star had seen the henna tattoos and was desperate to get one.

'A wolf,' Star said.

Meadow smiled. Of course she was.

CHAPTER TWENTY-EIGHT

Meadow walked into the wedding chapel treehouse with Bear and Indigo. Bear had asked them to come and have a look at it and listen to some proposed ideas he had for changes to the plan. River and Heath were already in there working away.

'Wow, this place looks great,' Meadow said, looking around. There were large arched windows down the sides letting in a ton of natural light and the whole place had a simple, rustic feel that would look so elegant when dressed with white flowers and candles or fairy lights.

'Well, it's not finished yet,' River said. 'But Bear had some ideas.'

'I wondered how you felt about leaving the roof as it is,' Bear said. 'Put up a glass ceiling in that section to protect the guests from the rain but not have the closed-in roof that you'd originally planned. It lets in all that wonderful light and River suggested we could put up white blinds we could pull across to mute the light if it was a really sunny day.'

Meadow looked up. The way the sunlight was pouring through the roof was beautiful, little motes of dust sparkled in the air and the emerald green of the treetops made it look like an enchanted glade.

'I think that could totally work,' Indigo said.

'I do too. It's lovely right now, we'd lose a lot of this light if we were to finish the roof as planned,' Meadow said.

'Tell them about the stained-glass window,' Heath said.

'We can't change that,' Meadow said. 'We have the most beautiful design picked out.'

Bear took her hand and tugged her gently to the large open space at the end that would hold the stained-glass window. 'Look at that view, the sea, the trees, the golden sands. No pretty stained-glass window in the world could compete with that.'

She looked out at the leaves dancing in the golden light of the sun, the azure-blue sea that looked like a sheet of glass today. Bear was right, it was exceptional and living here it was easy to sometimes take it all for granted.

'My worry is that without the roof and the stained-glass window to dull some of this light the wedding photos might be too bright,' Indigo said. 'We don't want the bride and groom silhouetted against the window. Let's take some photos and see what they turn out like. You two stand together there in front of the window.' She directed them as she pulled out her phone. 'Stand closer, look like you're in love with each other.'

Meadow shuffled closer to Bear, so close she could feel his warmth, smell his amazing scent. She looked up at him as Indigo fired off a few shots.

'You can re-enact the wedding you two had when you were kids,' Heath said.

Meadow smiled at that memory. 'How did you know about that?'

'Keep looking at Bear,' Indigo said.

'I told him,' Bear said. 'When he told me that as a child it was your dream to get married in these woods. I said, we'd already done that.'

'That feels like a lifetime ago,' Meadow said. 'Yet I remember it so vividly.'

'Me too.'

She stared up at him, at his soft, gentle eyes, and smiled.

'These photos actually look great,' Indigo said. 'They showcase the view perfectly and the light is wonderful for capturing the happy couple. I'm happy with this if you are, Meadow?'

'What do you think?' Bear said. 'Is this what you imagined for your dream wedding?'

Meadow didn't take her eyes off him. 'This is exactly how I imagined it.'

CHAPTER TWENTY-NINE

Bear was sitting in reception with Indigo. Meadow and Star had gone off to Dwelling now the festival had started properly. Star wanted to get a henna tattoo and make a flower crown so Meadow had taken her there.

He idly logged in to Connected Hearts to see he had another message from Twilight.

Dating is hard. Having the courage to tell someone you have feelings for them, handing them your heart on a plate. I don't know how anyone does it.

He smiled. She'd met someone. It said something about his relationship with Twilight that he was genuinely happy for her rather than being disappointed he had missed his chance.

He composed his reply.

That part is difficult. Trust me, I know how hard that is. What if they don't feel the same? And once those feelings are out there, you can never take it back. But I think we get so caught up sometimes in the 'what if they

don't' worries, without considering how wonderful it would be if they did. Maybe it's worth the risk.

He waited to see if she would reply and after a few moments he saw the three little dots to indicate she was writing a message.

I know you're right.

He could see she was still writing, so he waited.

I suppose I worry because I never had any good role models when it came to a long and happy marriage. My dad hated my mum. I would often look at the horrible way my dad treated my mum and wonder why they ever got married. How could he ever have loved her if he could treat her so badly when I was growing up? He hated me too, I think they both did, and I sometimes wonder if it was me that ruined their life, and whether I'm just not that lovable. And I worry about putting my heart out there and never having my love reciprocated, or worse that the man I fall in love with and marry will one day hate me as much as my dad hated my mum. Sometimes I wonder whether it's easier to protect my heart, never give it away in the first place, then I can never get hurt.

He sighed. He knew that feeling all too well, his own parents had walked out on him and his brothers when he was very young. Being parents was not something they had wanted to be. He had spent years questioning if there was something wrong with him to make his parents walk away in the first place.

She sent another message. **God, I'm sorry, that's a whole shitload of baggage to dump at your feet.**

He quickly sent a reply. **We all have baggage. I didn't**

have any kind of relationship with my parents either. I barely even remember them and I grew up thinking I just wasn't good enough. I can totally relate to how you're feeling. But while we are a product of our past, we can't let that ruin our future. Our parents' attitude towards us is not a reflection of who we are but who they were.

She replied instantly. **You are very wise. Oh I better go, my daughter has just fallen in love with an iguana, I might have to distract her before iguanas get added to the long list of pets she wants. I'll message you again later. Xx**

He quickly sent a reply. **Good luck with that. Chat soon. X**

'How's all the dating going?' Indigo said, noticing he was on the Connected Hearts website.

Bear thought about how to answer that question. His date, if you could call it that, with Josh's sister had obviously been a disaster. The women he had met at the speed-dating event the night before had been nice, but certainly no one he could ever imagine forever with. Maybe that wasn't fair as he'd only chatted with them for three minutes, but still he wasn't excited about any of them. But on the other hand, what was happening with Meadow, the possibilities of something developing between them, he was very excited about that.

'Meadow said you two matched last night,' Indigo prompted.

'We did. I'm not sure if that was because the computer program picked up on our friendship or something more,' Bear said.

'Is it something more for you?' Indigo fished.

Bear grinned. He certainly wasn't going to discuss that with Indigo.

'Listen, you were really supportive when I turned up here pregnant at the start of my relationship with River, so let me return the favour. I see you two together and I don't care how close you are, or how long you've known each other, the chemistry between you both is so much more than friendship. You know that. You tell her how you feel for her and I promise she will say it right back.'

Bear looked back at his conversation with Twilight. He knew he needed to talk to Meadow and take his own advice to Twilight, because being with Meadow was definitely worth the risk.

CHAPTER THIRTY

Meadow was walking around Dwelling, admiring the different stalls and little workshops there. Star was running on ahead, wanting to see everything at once and then reporting back what she'd found.

There was a man teaching children how to make clay finger pots and coil pots, while another workshop was demonstrating how to make flower garlands and crowns, something Star was desperate to have a go at, plus there was also a lady teaching people how to play the harp. It was all very mellow and happy. There were a number of different stalls displaying things like wellies in a multitude of patterns and designs, beautiful handmade jewellery, and crocheted and embroidered bags, which Meadow loved. Felix, one of their garden and maintenance staff, was selling t-shirts, caps and mugs with the Wishing Wood logo on. It was something he had approached her about a few months back and, as merchandise was not something they had done yet, she was happy for him to trial it. They looked good. Alex, their chef, had a stall with a range of delicious savoury bites and Lucien, one of their housekeeping crew, was helping her. Meadow was pretty sure something was going on between them, the number of times she'd seen them together lately. Greta, another of the garden and maintenance team, was selling wooden pan pipes and wind chimes with her husband. There was a definite community feel about the place.

Leah was selling some clothes she had made and she had agreed to showcase some of Meadow's clothes too. The last few weeks, Meadow had been busily stitching, cutting, embroidering a range of different clothes, mostly children's outfits but also a couple of dresses too. She hadn't been over to Leah's stand yet because the thought of her designs being on display made her nervous and excited all at once. When she sold items on Etsy people either bought ready-made items or put in a custom order but she never got to meet the customers face to face. Watching people look at the clothes she had made, discussing whether to buy them or not or dismissing them as not something they wanted was scary and she wasn't sure she was ready for that.

Just then Amelia fell in at her side. 'This is great, isn't it? The festival gets better and better every year.'

'It really does,' Meadow said, watching as Amelia waved at an elderly gentleman with a ridiculously curly moustache. He was wearing a rather fabulous gold waistcoat with green leaves embroidered up the sides. 'See anything you like here?' she asked innocently.

'I bought these wonderful wellies,' Amelia said, pulling them out from the bag she was carrying. They were painted in metallic tones of blue, green and turquoise and on each side was a wonderful narwhal.

'They are brilliant. Star would love them herself. I'll have to see if they do them in her size. But I meant have you met any men?' Meadow gestured to the man Amelia had waved at who was unable to tear his eyes off Amelia.

'Edwin is wonderful,' Amelia said, blushing as he winked at her. 'I took your advice by the way.'

'What advice?'

'I set myself up on a dating website last night.'

'You did?' Meadow felt a little disappointed. That had been the thing she had held over Amelia in order to call a truce between them. 'I thought you didn't want to do that, you seemed dead against it yesterday.'

'No, not against it, I just wanted it to be on my terms. I didn't want you and Indigo answering questions for me on my dating profile, putting up photos that I hadn't approved and handing out my number to any Tom, Dick or Harry. So I did it myself and, I have to say, I have sixty-eight matches already, which is rather exciting.'

'That's great.' Meadow tried to find the excitement for her but all she could see was now the door was open for Amelia to continue interfering in her love life again.

'I'm still honouring the truce, if that's what you're worried about,' Amelia said as they walked past the stalls.

'You are?' Meadow watched as Star stood hypnotised by a harpist and the beautiful music that was drifting around them.

'It made me quite stressed thinking of you and Indigo interfering in my love life, setting me up with a man I had no interest in. And I realise that I'm guilty of causing you the same stress. I'm not saying I'm not going to keep asking you for updates, I'm desperate to see my grandson happy with you and for you to be happily married to the right Brookfield brother, but I'm not going to do or say anything to interfere any more. Love is a powerful thing, a magnet that pulls people together. I have no doubt that you and Bear will find your way to each other eventually, without interference from this meddling old bat.'

Meadow stared at her in surprise, she had no words at all. She hadn't been expecting that. Eventually she found her voice. 'You're not an old bat.'

Amelia smiled. 'But I am meddling?'

Meadow tipped her head. 'Sometimes.'

'So, this is not me interfering, I'm not going to pass any comment or words of advice, but do you have any updates for me?'

Meadow smiled and decided to throw her a morsel. 'We both attended a speed-dating event last night. We had to wear these wristbands that monitored our hearts and breathing to find out if we were a match on that physical level, and me and Bear did match.'

Amelia's face lit up into a big grin and Meadow knew it was taking every ounce of willpower she had not to say a word about that.

Amelia cleared her throat. 'That's good. Now, are we going to have a look at the clothes stall that is selling your clothes? I notice you've been assiduously avoiding that all morning.'

'How did you know they were mine?'

'Leah told me when I went over there to look at them.

Come on, if I can't interfere in your love life, I can at least interfere with this. Star, this way.'

Amelia practically frogmarched Meadow to Leah's stall. Star ran on ahead to chat with Leah. Meadow had given Leah five women's dresses to sell and twelve pairs of children's dungarees in various prints and sizes. As they approached, she could only see one of her dresses on display and three dungarees. She felt a little disappointed in that, she totally understood that Leah had her own clothes to sell but she had worked hard to get the stock ready for the Dwelling event and to think they might be stuck in a box somewhere at the back of the stall out of sight was a bit disheartening.

Leah waved at Meadow.

'How's it going?' Meadow asked.

'Good, really good,' Leah said. 'We've had a very successful morning.'

'Are people interested in Meadow's clothes?' Amelia asked bluntly, asking the question Meadow was desperate to but wasn't quite brave enough to do so.

'Yes, very,' Leah said, happily. 'What you can see is what is left. Everything else has sold out. People loved the dungarees and there was even a small fight that broke out over one of your dresses, the purple one. I took the number of the losing party and said I'd get you to call her so you can make another one for her.'

Meadow felt the smile filling her face. 'Really?'

'Yes. I have your money here. I'll give it to you tonight as I'm pretty sure, the way things are going, you will sell everything you gave me by the end of the day.'

'That's wonderful. I wasn't sure my clothes would

appeal, thought they might be a bit too flashy for something as simple and chilled-out as Dwelling.'

'Us women love to get dressed up, no matter what the occasion. And the dungarees are so cute, who could resist?'

Meadow couldn't help feeling a huge sense of pride. Her dream of being a fashion designer had come true and, despite her little Etsy page, this was the first time it had felt real. She might not be making dresses for the rich and famous, but she was doing it and no one could take that away from her. She thought about Bear and how they'd matched the night before. Now all she had to do was work on making her other dream come true.

CHAPTER THIRTY-ONE

Bear walked into the Dwelling area and it was clear to see the festival was well under way. There were food stalls selling sweets, cakes, and savoury items that smelt amazing. There were people playing music everywhere he looked, guitars mostly, but there were a few other unusual instruments too; a harp, an accordion and some pan pipes were all being put to good use. There was a man showing a small group how to weave willow into baskets. A woman was demonstrating to another group how to whittle wood and there was a generally happy relaxed vibe about the place.

He spotted Heath walking around the festival, holding Star's hand. Star had a flower crown on her head and was sporting a very impressive wolf tattoo on her shoulder. She waved at him when she saw him and he went over to see them.

'Love the tattoo, Star,' Bear said. It really was very good.

'Thanks, but it's not real. It will wash off in a few weeks.'

'Probably for the best. I'm not sure your school would be very happy if you go back in September with a big wolf on your shoulder.'

Star giggled.

'I got a very exciting email last night,' Heath said to Bear.

Bear smiled, knowing Heath was talking about the story Bear had sent him.

'I started reading it and honestly I was hooked. If you're happy for me to do so, I could send it to Star's Kindle too.'

'What's this?' Star said.

Bear smiled. 'Well, I've written a book, for children around your age. It has a girl in it called Starlight who goes on some amazing adventures.'

Her eyes widened. 'You wrote a book about me?'

'It was inspired by you, a girl who is brilliant and brave. And maybe it will encourage you to go on your own adventures,' Bear said.

'I want to read it.'

'You will. Your dad will send it to your Kindle and then you can read it for yourself,' Bear said.

'That's so exciting.'

'You'll love it,' Heath said.

'I... umm, also sent it to three agents and a publisher this morning, just to put the feelers out,' Bear said, hardly believing he'd done it.

'If they don't snap you up it's their loss,' Heath said.

'Well, let's see what they say first, there's probably a lot of room for improvement.'

'Not from what I read last night. I thought it was brilliant.'

Bear couldn't help smiling at his words. It felt good to finally share his hard work and to hear words of encouragement after all this time.

'Bear, have you seen the iguana over there?' Star said. 'He's so cute, and he's wearing a little hat. The man let me hold him and he's really heavy. You must go and see him.'

Bear frowned. 'An iguana?'

'Yes, his name is Cucumber. Daddy, can we go and see the clay pots now?'

'Oh yes, I want to try my hand at those myself.'

Star waved goodbye to Bear as she dragged Heath off to another stand.

Bear looked around and sure enough he could see a man with an iguana curled round his shoulder. What were the chances of that? Either Twilight, being a local girl, had brought her daughter to Dwelling and had been messaging him when he was only a few metres away in the office at the front of the field or… Or Twilight was actually Meadow and she had lied to him about her Connected Hearts name, knowing full well he would have teased her for the connection to that bloody film. God, now he thought about it, there were so many similarities between Twilight and Meadow. The fact that they both had a daughter, they both loved riddles, they both hadn't dated for a very long time. Their relationship with their parents. Christ, had he really been talking to Meadow all this time?

He grabbed his phone and brought up the Connected Hearts app, then he did a search for Iris Starfish. Her profile came up straightaway and he gave a little sigh of relief. His heart sank though when he saw that he and Iris Starfish were a twelve percent match. Twelve! They couldn't be more different. All this time he had been completely in love with her and they had nothing in common. That couldn't be right. Or maybe it was and the old saying of opposites attract really did ring true. It was hard to accept that he wouldn't even have looked at Iris with such a low match percentage, he would have just passed her by.

He read through her profile and none of her answers to the questions seemed to chime with the person he knew, but he was aware that a few typed answers to stock questions wasn't the best way to reveal someone's character.

He decided to send her a quick message to see.

Hi, this is Bear.

He watched her online light come on as she read the message and then he watched the three little dots move as she wrote her reply.

Hi Bear. As we are such a low match, I'm sure you can understand that I don't want to take this conversation any further. Goodbye.

Bear's mouth fell open. How rude. He glanced around the field to see if he could spot Meadow and, sure enough, he saw her sticking her phone back in her pocket, a big grin on her face. She was messing with him and it made him laugh.

He wandered over to talk to her. She was looking at what appeared to be a wedding dress with a very natural vibe, perfect for an event such as Dwelling. It was quite a simple straight style but it was covered in embroidered flowers.

'Hey,' Bear said and he felt warm inside when her whole face lit up at seeing him.

'Hi.'

'So you're looking at wedding dresses now for the dream wedding?'

She laughed. 'I was looking at the embroidery actually. It's so pretty. I've never really thought what my wedding dress would look like but I definitely didn't think about something like this. But now I've fallen in love with it.'

'Wouldn't you make your own wedding dress?'

'I suppose I could. Not having a boyfriend or a fiancé it's not something I've ever thought of. My embroidery is good but it's not like this. This would take forever to achieve.'

'From the photos you showed me the other night, your embroidery skills could easily compete with this. Though I'm sure you're right about how long it would take.'

She turned to face him. 'While we're alone talking about my dream wedding, I wanted to talk to you.'

'I wanted to talk to you too… about last night and our first kiss.'

CHAPTER THIRTY-TWO

Meadow stared at him, her breath catching in her throat. She'd known they had to talk about how they'd matched the night before but she hadn't been expecting a conversation about their first kiss. She looked around. It felt wrong to be talking about something so personal in a field full of people.

'Come on, let's talk over here,' she said, walking under the shade of a huge oak tree at the side of the field, away from everyone else. The sapphire-blue sea sparkled beneath them. She turned to face him.

Bear took a big breath. 'Last night, when we matched, I've been thinking about it ever since and why it happened and if you... Because I...' he trailed off and shook his head.

Her heart was racing. Was he trying to tell her that he had feelings for her too?

'Let's clear something up first,' he said. 'On our date the other night, you said your immaturity prevented you from talking about our first kiss. Well now we're older, wiser, maybe we should talk about it rather than dancing around talking about our feelings. You said you regretted your actions after we kissed.'

Meadow swallowed. 'I do. If I could do it all again, I would never have acted the way I did.'

'So you don't regret the kiss?'

'Not for one second.'

'But you pushed me away, told me the kiss didn't mean anything.'

'Because I was an idiot.'

He let out a heavy breath, clearly not understanding. 'Was it because of your dad?'

She shook her head. 'Dad has left me with a deep mistrust of men, but I always trusted you,' she sighed. She hadn't wanted it to all come tumbling out but if they stood any chance of moving forward she had to be honest with him. She could never tell him the truth about Heath but she could certainly tell him why she had pushed him away.

'Promise you won't hate me?' Meadow said.

'I could never ever hate you,' Bear said.

She bit her lip. 'The morning after we had kissed, I bumped into Heath and he told me about your apprenticeship offer with Strawberry. I didn't want you to stay because of me and miss out on an amazing experience so I tried to make out like the kiss was nothing when it had been everything. I dated other boys so you'd think you had nothing to stay here for.'

His eyes widened. 'Jesus Christ, Meadow. I could never have gone, we couldn't afford it. The money they were offering wouldn't have even covered a shoebox in London. We were left some money when our parents died but most of that had been used to pay off debts and to help River go to university to study architecture so he could build Wishing Wood. When the offer came in, River offered to sell the place to get the money for me or try and get a loan but I didn't actually want to leave home, not because of you, but because… I was settled here, happy.'

He pushed his hand through his hair. 'After our parents walked out on us when we were young and we were raised by a multitude of relatives, life felt uncertain, unpredictable. And then when River was old enough to look after us himself it suddenly felt like we were in charge of our own lives for a change, we had each other to rely on rather than some relative who'd been lumbered with us. River had big plans for Wishing Wood and although I didn't know anything about carpentry or building houses like he and Heath did, I was excited about being such a big part of my own future, of being in control of my own life. It was flattering to be offered the apprenticeship from Strawberry but I didn't want it. And if you'd talked to me about it instead of making that decision for me, you'd have known that.'

Oh god, she had suspected he hadn't wanted it after she had started dating other boys and Bear had still turned it down. She knew then she'd made a mistake.

'I'm sorry, I was young and silly and I look back at that time and cringe. I was trying to do the right thing for you. If it helps I was utterly miserable because I was completely head over heels in love with you.'

He stared at her in shock. 'You were in love with me?'

Christ, she hadn't meant to say that but she nodded. 'Yes.'

'And you never thought to tell me that?'

'I was going to. I was going to apologise for being a twat and tell you I loved you but then I found out you were sleeping with Milly Atherton so I figured you probably didn't care.'

He frowned in confusion. 'I never slept with Milly Atherton.'

'No you did. I was gutted. Of all the people to sleep with, you chose the girl who had made my life a living hell throughout school.'

'I never slept with her. I never even kissed her. Why the hell would I? She was an absolute bitch.'

Meadow felt sick, her heart suddenly roaring in her ears. No, this couldn't be right. Henry, the boy she had been sort of dating, told her Bear had been sleeping with Milly Atherton. She hadn't wanted to believe it then but her friends, Sally and Fliss, had backed it up. They'd said they'd seen him not half an hour before butt naked on the beach with Milly, clearly having the best sex of his entire life. Apparently he was shouting out Milly's name, telling her he loved her. Her friends had laughed at her for being in love with Bear when he was busy sleeping with someone else and she'd felt small and insignificant, like their kiss really hadn't mattered at all. But the whole thing had been a lie.

'Is that why you slept with Heath, to get back at me for sleeping with Milly?' Bear said, incredulously. 'Stick two fingers up at me by sleeping with my own brother? Christ, that takes pettiness to a new low.'

'No, that wasn't what happened,' Meadow said, desperate to tell him the truth about Heath but she knew she couldn't.

'Then why did you sleep with him?'

She shook her head.

'I don't even know what to do with this information right now,' Bear said. 'Our lives could have been so different.'

Meadow felt a bitter wave of disappointment crash over her. How could she have been so stupid? He was right, it could have been so different and now it felt like it was too late.

Bear took a step away from her, pushing both hands through his hair.

'I need to put the webcams up before it gets dark,' he said. 'I'll catch you later.'

Meadow watched him walk away and felt her heart break all over again.

CHAPTER THIRTY-THREE

It was getting late and Bear was fed up. Some of the webcams had taken a lot longer to put up than he'd thought and he still wasn't sure what to make of what Meadow had told him earlier.

But he had promised her he would be at the dating event tonight, even if he was going to be late.

He made his way back towards his lodge just as Amelia was heading back to her car. She was the last person he wanted to talk to but she had already seen him.

'What's going on with you and Meadow?' Amelia said, getting straight to the point. She seemed pissed and he wondered what Meadow had been telling her.

'Nothing is going on,' he muttered, trying to walk past her.

'Well I beg to differ, I saw Meadow earlier and it was very obvious she'd been crying.'

Bear felt a pang of guilt like a kick to the stomach.

'And you're stomping around here with a dark cloud

hanging over your head and a face like thunder, something has happened.'

Bear stopped and sighed, looking out over the sea painted with rose and cranberry as the sun dipped below the horizon.

'Look, I know I promised Meadow that I wouldn't interfere with whatever it is that is going on between you two but I can't sit back and let you make stupid mistakes,' Amelia said.

'We had words about something that happened a long time ago.'

'About Meadow getting pregnant?'

He turned to look at her. 'Well, I guess that was a small part of it. But a lot of things went wrong around that time, there were a lot of misunderstandings, things we needed to talk about. I'm annoyed she made decisions for me without even discussing it with me.'

'Bear Brookfield, you listen to me,' Amelia said. 'I don't know what went on between you two eight years ago and, despite my desperation to be kept up to date on all the gossip, I don't need to know. You know why, because it's in the past. No amount of getting angry, frustrated, upset or disappointed is going to change what happened. And you were both children. I look back at the person I was in my twenties and I cringe at what a selfish idiot I was. You two were younger than that. The benefit of age, wisdom and maturity is a wonderful thing, so is the gift of hindsight. Life is too short for regrets. We can't dwell on the past when you need to focus on the things that will make you happy in the future. You and your brothers had a crappy childhood and I wish I had known what was happening so

I could've done something about it. But neither of you have let that past ruin your lives. You refused to let it define you. The three of you are better men because you were determined to move on from that. Don't let this thing that happened between you and Meadow eight years ago be the thing that drives you apart. Let it go. Be the better man.'

He stared over the sea again, the rose pink turning to deep purple as the night clouds moved in. He knew she was right. He had overreacted. He remembered what he'd said to Twilight about not judging her on her past and how he was more interested in who she was now, not the person she was in the past. The same should hold true for Meadow. He was in love with the woman Meadow was now and knowing what had happened eight years ago didn't change that so why had he got so upset?

'If the lack of communication was the thing that caused so much upset eight years ago then that's the thing you need to fix now,' Amelia said. 'Talk to her, be honest with her. Then maybe you can move forward.'

He sighed. 'Thanks for the pep talk but I really need to go.'

He moved off towards his lodge. Amelia was right, he had to talk to Meadow. But right then he had no idea what to say.

CHAPTER THIRTY-FOUR

Meadow stood in a large room with around sixty other men and women who were all milling around talking in small groups. She felt completely out of her depth. Although she was always quite happy meeting and talking to the customers at Wishing Wood, initiating conversations face to face with potential matches was always a bit daunting. The speed dating hadn't felt so bad because she had to talk to the men who arrived at her table, but going up to one of them and starting a conversation felt a lot harder. She'd tried chatting to a few women since she'd arrived here tonight, as that always felt easier, but as all the women here were looking for a man, they weren't interested in wasting their time talking to another woman.

There were some different men there tonight than at the speed-dating event the night before. She knew Mix n Match were running two groups of people for their events, so each event would take place on two different days. That way there wouldn't be too many people at one event and people would get to meet different potential matches at each event too.

Her heart wasn't in this at all tonight. There was a lot of wine being poured at the back of the room. She wasn't great with wine, she always got very drunk, very quickly. She was tempted just to go home and forget the whole evening. She felt so sad right now. She had hurt Bear again with her revelations about what happened after the kiss. She didn't know whether it would be better or worse for him to hear the real truth of how Star was conceived, although she could never tell him. Right now, he hated her and she didn't blame him. He hadn't even bothered to turn up for the dating event tonight, despite promising he would. She hadn't seen him for the rest of the day and, when she went to his house earlier, he either hadn't been in or was refusing to answer the door.

Imogen, the lady in charge of the Mix n Match dating events, took to a small stage area and tapped the microphone to get everyone's attention.

'Ladies and gentlemen, thank you for coming to our Mix n Match dating event,' she said. 'Tonight is what is known as a group dating event. Simply put, you can spend the night mingling with as many different people as possible to see if you feel a connection with any of them. And to get the conversation going, tonight is also a wine-tasting night. In a moment, ladies, you will line up on one side of the long table at the back and, gents, you will line up along the other side. You can try as many of the wine samples as you'd like by moving up and down the table and feel free to discuss the wine with the men or women opposite you. What you like or don't like about the wine, how it tastes, how it smells, what it makes you feel. And of course you can talk about other things as well.'

Everyone started looking round at the long wine table. That was a lot of wine to try. Thankfully, the wine samples were in small shot glasses so it literally was a taste.

'Now this is not just a wine and mingle night,' Imogen went on. 'Mix n Match go much deeper than that. Tonight we will be looking specifically at body language. You can tell a lot about someone from their body language, the way they move and interact, even tiny things could be a big sign of attraction. Our body language is stronger than any words and some of it is very subtle. Men, if the ladies touch their hair or lick their lips when they talk to you, then chances are they are attracted to you. Eye contact is another big one from both sexes. Dilated pupils are not something you can control but if our pupils grow wider then we're excited about something or someone. Touch is the biggest way to show you're attracted to someone. We touch things we like, clothes we see in a shop, jewellery, people are no different. Facial expressions, other gestures and smiles are also important parts of showing you are interested.'

Meadow thought about this. While she agreed with most of what Imogen was saying, some of these things could be faked.

'Now fortunately, you don't have to be experts in body language or even have to be aware of it tonight. Our sophisticated computer program will do all of that for you. When you came in, you were given those tiny cameras that fit over your ears. The camera will pick up everything from the person you are talking to, just as their camera will pick up your reaction to them. All the information will be fed back to the computer and if it sees a mutual attraction, as in both of you are giving off body language to say you are attracted, the computer will match you and send a signal to those wristbands you were given. If your wristband beeps or vibrates while you're talking to someone, it means you are both attracted to each other, which might make the conversation easier. Feel free to move over to the sofas to continue talking to someone you've been matched with and see if you have anything in common beyond that initial attraction. Of course, the attraction might grow the more you talk and get to know someone, so don't be put off if your wristbands don't beep or vibrate straightaway. If you have any questions, please do come up and ask. Although a lot of the questions will be answered in your leaflet. Enjoy your night.'

Everyone started moving off towards the wine table and Meadow followed. Staff were directing men to one side and women to the other. She moved to an open space at the table and looked down at the tiny shot glasses in front of her filled with what looked like a rosé. There was a card next to it explaining what the wine was, and the different flavours to expect. She glanced up at the man opposite her who was staring at her intently, not blinking. Christ, someone was trying hard on the eye contact part. It was actually a little creepy. Not wanting to engage in conversation with him, she focussed on the wine, taking a small sip from the shot glass, and then another. It tasted good, kind of fruity like strawberries, although she was no expert when it came to wine.

'What do you think?' Creepy guy was still staring at her with wide unblinking eyes.

'It's nice, fresh and fruity. Not dry. What did you think?'

'I don't drink wine.'

'Ah, this isn't ideal for you then.'

'I can still talk to pretty ladies. You're very pretty.'

She forced a smile and hoped the cameras would be able to tell it was fake. 'Thank you. I'm going to go and try some more wine, it was nice to meet you.' Meadow finished her shot and threw it into the small bin in the middle of the table and then moved off much further down the table to the next available space.

The next wine looked to be sparkling which she liked, so she picked it up and took a big sip. She looked over at the man opposite and at least he looked fairly normal. Nice-looking too.

He leaned over to hold out his hand. 'Hi, I'm Max.'

'Meadow.'

'That's a lovely name.'

She smiled. 'Thank you.'

'I feel like we're in some futuristic film with these cameras strapped to our heads. I feel a bit like The Borg.'

'I'm sorry, I don't know what that is,' Meadow said.

The light faded from his eyes as if she had just told him Santa didn't exist.

'Oh, really? Surely everyone has heard of The Borg.' He put on a robotic voice. '"You will be assimilated. Resistance is futile."'

She shook her head. 'Sorry.'

Max finished his shot of wine and moved on without

even saying goodbye. For all her cheerleading of face to face meetings, this was not going well.

She finished her shot and was just about to move on when someone took Max's place opposite. He was a good-looking man, although his smile was just teetering on cocky rather than happy. To be polite she picked up another shot of wine and took a sip. 'Hello, I'm Meadow.'

'Isaac.'

'And what is it you do, Isaac?' Meadow asked.

'I deal with hedge funds.'

Meadow wasn't entirely sure what that was either, other than it was some kind of investment thing, but she didn't want to disappoint him like she had with Max so she just smiled politely and waited for him to ask what she did. He didn't.

'I love this wine-tasting idea,' Isaac said. 'There'll be a lot of drunk women by the end of the night. And a lot of men getting laid.'

A shudder of revulsion went down her spine. 'That's disgusting.'

He shrugged. 'It's a fact. Women get a lot easier when they're pissed.'

Meadow pulled a face and moved on down the table. That was too close to home for her.

She stopped at another gap and picked up a shot of red wine. She'd heard the expression that you shouldn't mix your drinks, was that the same for different kinds of wine too? She took a sip. Stupidly she'd not had anything to eat tonight, as she'd been so upset over what happened with Bear she hadn't felt like eating. With no food to soak up the alcohol she was going to get drunk very quickly. Maybe she needed to pace herself. She could chat without drinking every time she moved on.

'Hello,' the man opposite said. 'I'm Oliver.'

'Hi Oliver, I'm Meadow. What do you do?'

'I'm an accountant.'

'Oh, that sounds like fun,' she tried and failed miserably to sound enthusiastic about it.

He grinned. 'It totally isn't, it's very boring but it pays the bills and I was always good with numbers. How about you?'

'I work at the treehouse resort up the road.'

His face lit up. 'I drive past there all the time, it looks magical. I bet the guests love staying there.'

'It is and they do, I love where I work, I feel very lucky.'

This felt nice, normal. Oliver didn't seem like a creep or a disgusting shitbag at all. She took another sip of her wine as she felt herself relax a bit. Maybe this wouldn't be so bad after all.

CHAPTER THIRTY-FIVE

Bear stepped inside the large hall where the group dating was going on. People were standing around in small groups or sitting on sofas chatting, there was a large number of people chatting by the long table at the back of the room, all drinking what appeared to be shots. Everyone had thin pencil-shaped poles hooked over their ears, making them look like they were about to do a concert, and they were wearing microphones.

He couldn't spot Meadow and he really needed to talk to her.

He moved further into the room and was immediately accosted by the lady who had been in charge the previous night.

'Hello, I'm Imogen. It's Bear, isn't it? Are you here for the dating event?'

'Umm, yes.' Bear was quite surprised that she remembered his name from the night before.

'Oh, you're a little late, I think most of the wine has

already been drunk, but that's OK, I'm sure you can mingle and chat.'

'Great, thanks,' Bear said, turning to walk away.

'Sorry, we have to register you for tonight's event just in case you match with someone. If you come over here,' Imogen gestured to the table by the doorway.

'Oh, I really need to talk to someone.'

'It will just take a few minutes,' she said.

Bear sighed and followed her to the table.

'Firstly, here is your camera, it hooks over your ear like this,' Imogen said.

'What do I need a camera for?'

'So our computer software can pick up any positive body language towards you. If you have positive body language to the woman you're talking to as well, then our software will consider you a match and this wristband will beep and vibrate to let you know you've been matched. It explains it all here in this leaflet, what kind of body language our cameras will be looking for, what it means. It's nothing really for you to worry about, just enjoy the evening. Let me just add you to our system.'

Bear gave his details as quickly as he could, his eyes scanning the room for Meadow. Was she even here?

'Are you looking for Meadow?' Imogen asked.

Bear looked at her. 'Yes, how did you know?'

'Because your chemistry last night at the speed dating was off the charts.'

'Because we're friends?'

'Because you love each other,' Imogen said, simply. Bear stared at her, his heart thundering in his chest. 'She's over there by the sofas.'

He quickly moved through the room, scanning it for Meadow. He spotted her sitting on a sofa chatting quite passionately to Oliver. Bear had worked alongside Oliver on the lifeboat crew and played rugby with him a few times in a local team. He was a good man and, while he didn't seem to be into Meadow with the way he was leaning back in his chair listening to her, he wasn't desperately looking around the room for a way out either. Oliver was a laid-back man and quite happy talking to anyone – whether they were a fifteen-year-old boy or an eighty-three-year-old woman, he had time for them all.

Bear walked over, 'Meadow, I—'

She looked up at him and her face lit up. 'Bear, you came!'

She got up and hugged him, and he wrapped his arms around her, holding her tight. He caught Oliver's eye over her head. 'Sorry to interrupt, Oliver, this is important.'

Oliver shrugged. 'By all means. We've just been talking about women's football and why they aren't paid the same as men. In fact, we've covered many women's sports tonight, where the media, the sponsors and the organisers don't treat women with the same respect as men. It's been quite an interesting conversation. I haven't matched with anyone, but I have become a feminist so it's been a good night.'

Bear smirked but suddenly realised that Meadow was crying into his chest.

He pulled back to look at her. 'Hey, what's wrong?'

'You hate me.'

'No honey, I promise that would be impossible,' he wiped her tears gently from her cheeks. 'You were trying to do the right thing for me and yes it was misguided and unneeded but you loved me and you wanted me to be happy even if that wasn't with you, that's incredibly selfless. And I wasn't honest with you either. I was in love with you then too.'

That had been a lot easier to say than he thought it would be. Probably because he was hiding behind the past tense. He hadn't admitted he still loved her now. Although he fully intended to do that tonight, too.

She stared at him. 'You were in love with me?'

'Yes and I didn't tell you so we're even on that score.'

Tears filled her eyes again. 'I've made such a mess of things.'

He so rarely saw Meadow cry. When Star was born and she'd been in an incubator, she'd cried quite a bit then. Sometimes he'd watch an emotional film with her and she'd shed a few tears but nothing like this. He looked around as a big cheer went up at the back of the room as some man downed a shot.

'Meadow, have you been drinking?' he asked gently.

'Just a few shots of wine,' she said, holding up her fingers to show a very small amount.

'And maybe a few more,' Oliver said. 'She was quite sad for the first part of the night, until the alcohol kicked in.'

And that had been Bear's fault for his stupid overreaction to what she'd done eight years before when she had been only a child herself.

He turned his attention back to Meadow and bent his head to meet her eyes. Sure enough she was looking a bit dazed, her eyes glazed over.

Suddenly both their wristbands started beeping and vibrating.

He looked down at them in confusion. Meadow let out a hollow laugh. 'It thinks we're a match, it doesn't know we're friends, so it assumes we're attracted to each other.'

She looked really sad about this too.

'I don't know, these computer programs are pretty sophisticated,' Oliver said. 'They can tell the difference between friendship, family and sexual attraction.'

Bear looked at him.

'It's all in the leaflet,' Oliver said, waving it in the air.

Bear sighed. He was damned sure Meadow's camera had picked up his attraction to her. He wasn't sure what his camera was picking up when Meadow was looking so miserable.

He swept a hair from her face. 'How about we go home?'

She nodded.

He grabbed her bag and jacket and put an arm round her to guide her out. 'Thanks Oliver.'

Oliver waved them off and then turned his attention back to the leaflet.

Bear escorted Meadow to the table near the entrance and handed back their cameras and wristbands which were still frantically beeping.

Imogen looked at him with a smile. 'You matched again, how funny,' she said dryly.

'I think these are broken,' Meadow said.

'Come on,' Bear said, helping her towards the door, she was a bit wobbly on her feet.

There was a cocky-looking man who oozed overconfidence, standing near to the door with a woman who looked a little worse for wear herself. The man looked at Meadow and let out a guffaw.

'Oh, look who it is, Miss Judgemental. She told me I was disgusting when I said alcohol was going to make it a lot easier to get laid tonight, and here she is going home with a man.'

'Shows what you know, you turd, this is my best friend and he would never sleep with me, never,' Meadow said.

Bear quickly ushered her out.

'That sounded a lot better in my head,' Meadow said, quietly, as he draped her jacket round her shoulders.

'Oh no, you definitely told him. Although what you said wasn't exactly true. How was your night?'

'A bit rubbish if I'm honest. Meeting people face to face didn't really work. One man stopped talking to me and walked away because I didn't know what a borg was.'

'The Borg? It's an alien race from *Star Trek*.'

'Well how am I supposed to know that? I've never seen it.'

'Some of the Trekkies take themselves very seriously. There are whole conventions dedicated to the series and movies, people dress up and everything. Obviously to that man it was very important to him you liked *Star Trek*. Although I have to admit, that does seem a bit petty.'

'Would you be turned off by a woman if she didn't like *Star Wars* and Luke Skywalker and Darth Vader, or if she didn't know who Princess Leia was?'

'I'm impressed you remember those names, since you slept through most of the movies.'

'Well, I took some of it in. I could see you wanted me to like it, so I tried.'

His heart swelled with love for her. 'Well no, it doesn't bother me if you don't like *Star Wars*. Just like it doesn't bother you that I don't like twinkling vampires.'

She smiled. 'You'll always tease me about that film, won't you?'

'Yes, always.'

They carried on walking, his arm round her shoulders, guiding her and keeping her upright.

'What did you mean when you said it wasn't true?' Meadow asked. 'When I told Isaac you wouldn't ever sleep with me. You said that wasn't true.'

'Maybe that's a conversation for tomorrow,' Bear said.

She was silent for a moment. 'I always imagined what it would be like to sleep with you,' she said.

He nearly missed his step himself then. 'You did?'

'I always imagined you'd be the first person I'd make love to. I wanted it to be you, so badly. And the worst thing was I was going to find you to tell you I loved you and this guy I was seeing and Sally and Fliss told me they'd just seen you having sex with Milly Atherton on the beach, how you'd been clearly having the best sex of your entire life and had been telling her you loved her and I believed it. And then when I did have sex, I cried after because it wasn't you. Because you loved someone else who wasn't me. And everything was a lie. Everything. You never slept with her and you did love me.'

Bear felt the anger boil up in him, she had been betrayed by people she trusted. The whole of her life changed in an instant because of one silly lie. And he knew why too, Fliss had asked him out and he'd turned her down. This was Fliss getting her own back on him and being spiteful to Meadow at the same time, it had clearly been a win-win.

They reached his car but Bear turned her to face him. 'Meadow, I wanted you to be my first too. First and last actually. I was head over heels in love with you and I have no doubt at all, if we had made love back then, it would have been incredible.'

'Oh,' she said softly, tears filling her eyes again.

He cupped her face and wiped the tears away. 'I would have kissed you everywhere and I mean *everywhere* until you were screaming out my name. Then I would have made love to you very slowly and very carefully, taking my time, holding you close, telling you how much I loved you and only you.'

'I would have liked that very much,' Meadow said, her voice barely a whisper.

He was starting to believe that Imogen was right and Meadow did have feelings for him, but she was drunk, he couldn't really trust her overemotional state right now. 'I would have, too, and when you're sober we're going to have a proper conversation about whether that's something you would still like to do now.'

Her eyes widened. 'Make love to you?'

'Give ourselves a second chance at having a proper relationship, and yes making love to you would absolutely be part of that.'

She swallowed. 'I… yes… I'd want that more than anything.'

He nodded, his heart filling with hope. 'Let's talk about this tomorrow.'

He helped her get in his car and then moved round to sit in the driver's side. He started the car and focussed on driving, taking the corners carefully until he stopped at some traffic lights. He turned to face her and smiled when he saw she was leaning against the window, fast asleep.

She probably wouldn't remember any of their conversation in the morning.

He pulled into the driveway of Wishing Wood and parked as close as he could to Wisteria Cottage, Meadow's house.

He got out and walked round to Meadow's side and carefully opened the door and she lurched awake as she nearly fell out.

'God sorry, didn't mean to fall asleep. Wine always makes me sleepy,' she muttered.

She climbed out the car and wobbled a bit. Bear bent down and scooped her up into his arms. She wound her arms round his shoulders, nuzzling into his neck which was the most incredible feeling in the world.

'Bear, what are you doing?'

'Taking you to bed.'

She giggled against his throat. 'My lucky night after all.'

He smiled as he went up the steps to Wisteria Cottage and let himself into Meadow's treehouse and then climbed the stairs up to her bedroom. He laid her down carefully on the bed and he could see she was already dozing off again.

He took off her shoes and then covered her with her

duvet. He leaned over and kissed her on the forehead. 'Goodnight Meadow.'

He moved to go out the room.

'I love you, you know,' Meadow said, quietly.

He smiled at the drunken declaration of love. 'I love you too.'

She smiled, rolled over, snuggled into her pillow and fell asleep.

Bear went downstairs and walked across the rope bridge to Heath's treehouse.

Heath looked up from where he was lying on the sofa, watching TV. 'Hey, you're back early.'

'Meadow's a little drunk, I've just put her to bed.'

Heath laughed. 'Oh, she doesn't do well on alcohol, she rarely drinks it. I've just this second put Star to bed, we stayed up to watch a movie together. I'll grab her and take her over to Meadow's so I can keep an eye on her.'

'OK, good, I think she'll be fine, but she's definitely a bit wobbly.'

Heath stood up and stretched. 'Did *you* have a good night?'

'Well, I wasn't really there long, the webcams took a lot longer than I thought they would to set up.' That and he'd spent a lot of time thinking. 'But me and Meadow apparently matched, according to their fandangled computer software.'

'That's not a surprise, you two are closer than some married couples. It was bound to pick up on that.' He moved to the stairs and gave Bear a wave. 'I'll see you tomorrow.'

Bear nodded and walked out, retrieving the leaflet from

his pocket. The leaflet was very clear, the software was trained not to pick up on family or platonic love. The body language in those cases was very different to that when you were near someone you were attracted to. After their chat tonight he was more convinced than ever that Meadow had feelings for him too. He wasn't going to wait any longer, first thing tomorrow he was going to talk to her, tell her how he felt. And then he'd find out once and for all if she wanted the same thing.

CHAPTER THIRTY-SIX

Bear sat back from his computer after writing a complicated fight scene with a dragon. It had turned out quite well. He was really enjoying this book.

He checked his phone and saw he had a message from Twilight. He smiled and opened it.

Hi... I'm a bit drunk.

He smiled and wrote back. **Did you have a good night?**

Her reply was instant. **Not really. I went to this dating event where we mingled with lots of different men and I was hooked up to a camera so it could look at body language of the men I was talking to see if any of them were attracted to me.**

God, this was too much of a coincidence. There were far too many similarities here between the two of them. But if it was Meadow, then who the hell was Iris Starfish? If Twilight was a local girl looking for love then it was quite plausible that she was attending these dating events at the same time Meadow was.

He sent a reply. **Did you match with anyone?**

No. Well apart from one person but he doesn't count.

He frowned and was just about to ask why that person didn't count when she sent another message.

There was one guy there who was clearly only interested in sex. Is that all men think about? When I meet men and we're sitting in a pub chatting, are they just nodding politely and really thinking, when can I get this woman into bed?

Crap, she'd had a rubbish night by the sound of it. He had to answer that carefully. **I think men do think about sex a lot more than women but any decent man would take the time to really listen to you, to enjoy your company and conversation for you, not for what may or may not happen at the end of the night.**

She was quick to reply. **When you go on dates, are you hoping for sex at the end of it?**

He thought how to answer that question. **Not any more. I've been on several dates where for the women the end goal was sex and that's always fun but I'm looking for something more now. Maybe I've grown up but sex with a woman I barely know doesn't appeal to me any more. I'm looking for someone I can spend forever with. I think when I find that person, of course sex is going to be a part of our relationship, being intimate with someone is a way to show them you love them, but it's not the end goal.**

There was a long gap this time before he could see she was writing a message back. Finally, her reply pinged through.

When I started online dating, I didn't really think about sex. I just wanted to find someone to love but of

course sex is going to be part of that. I don't feel I have anything to offer in that department.

What do you mean? Bear asked.

Oh you will laugh at me now. I'm sure what I'm about to tell you will guarantee you want nothing more to do with me but you should know what you're letting yourself in for before it goes any further. I've only had sex once in my life.

He felt his eyebrows shoot up. **That doesn't scare me away. Was your first time an unpleasant experience? Has it put you off doing it again?**

Her reply came through quite quickly. **My first time was pretty crappy. I was so young and when I look back at that time I cringe about what happened. I wouldn't say it's put me off, I know sex can be so much better than that, but I suppose it has put me off dating. I've been busy raising my daughter for the last eight years so there hasn't been a ton of opportunity but I certainly didn't put myself out there to try to find a man. I know this sounds silly and naïve but the next time I have sex I want it to be with someone I love and trust.**

He frowned. He hated that her first experience of sex had been so bad. **I totally understand wanting to be with someone you trust. Want to tell me about what happened that first time?**

OK but you can't judge me on it. I was young and immature.

Bear smiled. **I promise.**

So when I was seventeen I was completely in love with my best friend, let's call him Bob. Bob was super smart, into computers and programming and the kind-

est, most wonderful man I've ever met. He was destined for amazing things, I knew one day he would be jetting off to work in some big computer company on the other side of the world. Well one day we kissed and it was the perfect kiss. But the next day I heard he'd been offered an apprenticeship with Strawberry. The big computer software company. So when he asked me out on a date I turned him down because I didn't want him to miss out on such an amazing opportunity. He would have been in London and California, it was such a big deal for him. To prove I wasn't interested I went out on dates with a few other boys. I hoped he would take the apprenticeship but he never did. He stayed here and then, almost as if he was trying to get back at me for dating these other boys, he started going out on dates with other girls. It was all very silly and immature but we were only children at the time.

Bear stared at the screen in horror because suddenly it was very obvious that Twilight was actually Meadow. Christ he was so stupid. The fact that Twilight had a seven-, nearly eight-year-old daughter, her love of riddles, being at the festival yesterday and seeing the iguana. He'd made the connection then but talked himself out of it when he'd found Iris Starfish on Connected Hearts. Maybe she'd tried Iris Starfish first as her username and as that name was already taken she opted for Twilight Rose but lied about it because she knew he'd tease her.

She was still writing. He'd almost forgotten she was telling him about her first crappy sexual experience. He wasn't sure he wanted to hear this now. Because if

Meadow had only one sexual experience and she got pregnant with Star it meant her crappy sex was with Heath.

I was dating some guy, let's call him Harry. He was desperate to get me into bed. I wasn't interested in that at all. One night, he told me that Bob had slept with Milly Atherton. I hated her with a passion. She was always such a cow to me at school, made my life a living hell. To think that Bob, my best friend, had slept with her purely to get back at me was gutting. I didn't believe it but then my two best friends Sally and Fliss backed him up, they said they'd seen Bob and Milly having sex with their own eyes. I felt so insignificant.

He stared at the screen in shock. Was Harry really Heath? Had Heath been the one to lie to her that he'd slept with Milly Atherton? This was getting worse by the second. And he knew what it was to feel insignificant and unimportant. He hated that she'd felt that way.

I was so upset and me and Harry had been drinking and he said he wanted to make love to me. I'd so wanted my first time to be with Bob because I knew it would be beautiful. But sitting in Harry's bedroom I suddenly felt so silly for thinking that sex would be this big romantic moment between two people who love each other. Everyone else was having sex like it was no big deal and when Harry started kissing me I just thought, why the hell not. He started undressing me and I let him. He asked me if it was my first time and I said that it was. He laughed and said he'd never had sex with a virgin before. I felt so stupid for waiting for Bob when he was off sleeping with another woman, and Milly Atherton of all people. Harry told me he'd done it lots of times

and he'd make me feel good. Well I'm not sure where he learnt about sex, but he squeezed my breasts like he was honking one of those old-fashioned horns. He asked me if it felt good and I felt like there must be something wrong with me because all those other girls he'd been with must like it and I was the pathetic seventeen-year-old virgin, so I just told him yes, it was nice. He had a really small penis. I had nothing to compare it to but even I knew that it was small. He told me that sex might hurt as it was my first time and thank god he was so small because it didn't. He was thrusting on top of me so fast like he was taking part in some kind of race. He asked me if it felt good and the whole thing was just so bad I would have laughed if I hadn't been so miserable. I was still so upset with myself for sleeping with someone who wasn't Bob when I loved him so much that I was close to tears. Thankfully it was over very quickly, less than thirty seconds and he was done. He rolled over and fell asleep and I got out of there as fast as I could. That was my first time. It wasn't exactly a shining example. I went home and cried because sex was so disappointing after that big build-up in my mind, because I'd done it with someone I didn't have any feelings for and mostly because it hadn't been with Bob.

Bear was shaking with an uncontrolled rage. No, there was no way Heath would have done that to Meadow, lied to get her into bed, got her drunk, laughed at her for being a virgin, made her feel pathetic and stupid for not having sex before. He had no idea what Heath was like in bed and had no desire to know, but he could not imagine his brother pounding away at Meadow like she was a piece of meat and not caring when she was visibly upset.

His fingers were shaking as he typed out a response. **And there was no one else after that?**

No. Not because I was scared off by it. I found out a few weeks later I was pregnant and things just changed so much, so quickly. There was never really any time for dating after that.

He stood up and paced away from the computer. He had to talk to Heath because none of this made any sense. But he had to give her a response first. She'd poured her heart out to him, told him some really personal stuff. He moved back to his laptop, trying to calm himself down to give her a proper reply.

You are not insignificant or pathetic or stupid. I'm so sorry that was your first time and that you were made to feel that way. It should have been so different to that. Harry sounds like an absolute dick and he definitely didn't deserve you.

No he didn't and I wish I had been mature enough to recognise that. The worst thing is, I found out today that Bob never slept with Milly Atherton. My whole life changed in an instant because of that lie and I ruined the best thing that ever happened to me.

He wanted to give her some words of comfort, put her mind at ease that he would always be there for her no matter what, that he still loved her after all this time and what happened in the past didn't change how he felt, but she had no idea she was talking to him and he couldn't think straight with the anger he was feeling right now.

She sent another message. **Oh I know I'm going to**

regret telling you all this in the morning. I'm going back to sleep now. Night. X

He watched the little light that meant she was online go grey to show she'd gone. He stood up on shaky legs and walked out of his house, walking automatically to Meadow's treehouse. He climbed the stairs, feeling numb. He could see Heath lying on Meadow's sofa, reading a book. Bear opened the door, which was still unlocked and Heath looked up, flashing him a small smile.

'She's OK, fast asleep. I checked on her half an hour ago.'

'I need to talk to you. Outside,' Bear said, stepping back.

'It sounds like you want me to step outside for a fight,' Heath laughed.

'I'm hoping it doesn't come to that,' Bear said.

Heath's face fell and he followed Bear outside onto the rope bridge.

'This sounds serious,' he said.

'It is.'

Heath stared at him. 'Come on, let's go to my treehouse so we can talk.'

He crossed the rope bridge and let them both into his treehouse, closing the door behind him.

Bear paced across the lounge.

'Come on, for god's sake, out with it,' Heath said.

'OK, I've just been texting Meadow and she told me about her first time having sex.'

Heath visibly paled and Bear felt his fists clench by his side. It couldn't be true.

'She told you that?'

'Yes, she said the man she slept with lied to her to get

her into bed, got her drunk and laughed at her for being a virgin. She said she was so upset because she really wanted to be with someone else and he didn't seem to care. She also told me that she's never had sex since.'

Heath stared at him in horror.

'Now there have been plenty of times that I thought you were a bit of a twat but I can't believe that the man she told me about who had so little respect for her is you. But the alternative is that Star isn't yours and I can't get my head around that either.'

Heath was silent for the longest time but eventually he spoke. 'Star is mine—'

'You piece of shit.'

Heath held his hand up. 'Star is my daughter, in every way that matters… except biologically.'

CHAPTER THIRTY-SEVEN

Bear stared at him in shock.

'Star isn't yours?'

'She is mine. I might not have provided the sperm but that doesn't mean she isn't my daughter.'

'So you two... never...'

'Me and Meadow have never slept together. We're friends. It's never been more than that between us. She came to me terrified. She'd found out she was pregnant, the arsehole who had donated the sperm had told her to get rid of it and her *wonderful* parents had kicked her out. She was seventeen, no job, no home. What was I supposed to do? I offered to marry her, raise the baby as my own, and she said yes. And there has not been one single day since then that I regretted that decision. I have an amazing daughter I am utterly in love with and I raised her with my best friend, life doesn't get much better than that.'

Bear sat down on the sofa.

'Promise me, this won't impact on your relationship

with Star. She is still your niece. That hasn't changed,' Heath said, urgently.

'Of course it won't. From the second I held her a few minutes after she was born I fell in love with her too.'

They were both quiet. The magnitude of this secret was huge.

'I take it she doesn't know either?'

Heath shook his head. 'We swore we'd never tell anyone. Maybe we'll tell her when she's older. I don't know. I'm surprised Meadow told you.'

Bear sighed. 'She... doesn't know she told me. She thinks I'm someone else?'

Heath's eyes widened. 'What?'

'I didn't know. I met this woman online, we've been chatting for a few days but Connected Hearts don't allow photos and our profiles are under different names. She's Twilight Rose and I'm AstralSurfer. She told me she was Iris Starfish so when I started chatting to Twilight, I had no idea it was her.'

'Oh yes, that name was taken. Good job really, I said it sounded like a porn star name.'

'Anyway, you must have woken her up when you went to check on her because she started messaging me and she's still very drunk. She told me she had a crappy night and how men are only interested in sex and then the whole sorry story came tumbling out. It was only when she started talking about it that I realised that I was actually talking to Meadow.'

'Crap. She will be horrified that she's told you.'

Bear shoved his hand through his hair.

'Did she ever tell you the reason she ended up sleeping with that shitbag?' Bear asked.

'There was a boy she had a crush on who slept with some girl she hated.'

'I'm the boy and, no, I didn't. He lied to her, told her I'd slept with Milly Atherton. I never even dated the girl, let alone slept with her.'

'Jesus.'

Bear quickly gave a rundown of their kiss and why she had pushed him away when he'd asked her out.

'So you liked her too?' Heath asked.

'Loved. Still do.'

Heath stared at him. 'Bear, I had no idea. You must have hated me for marrying her.'

'I did. But you didn't know I had feelings for her and now to find out why you married her, well my respect for you has just gone through the roof.'

Heath sat down on the sofa opposite. 'What a mess. All of that angst and upset was for no reason.'

'I just wish she'd been honest with me. I don't know if we'd still be together now or whether we'd have lasted a few weeks, but it would have saved a lot of heartache.'

'I can't say I wish for the same. If none of that had happened, I would never have had Star.'

Bear sighed.

'Meadow is going to wake up tomorrow and be absolutely horrified that she told you all that,' Heath said. 'Firstly that she told anyone at all and then to find out it was you, it will kill her. She was so adamant that you, River and Amelia should never find out. She was worried you would think she was deceitful and wouldn't accept her and Star into our family so readily.'

'That's rubbish, Meadow has always been part of our family, even before we kissed and she got pregnant. This doesn't change anything.'

'I know that. But she will be mortified that you know. I think she'll feel she's let me down too. Maybe she'll be OK that she's told this faceless person who isn't connected to our family as long as she doesn't find out that you know. Maybe you don't tell her who you are.'

'You want me to lie to her?' Bear said. 'We've been chatting online for the last few days, how can I continue talking to her and not tell her who I am?'

'I don't want her to get hurt over this.'

Bear thought about it for a moment because he couldn't stand for her to get hurt over it either. She'd carried this secret for eight years, it was clearly important to her. 'I could delete the conversation. Pretend it didn't happen. She's always on the dating site when she's on reception. Chances are she's logged in to the site automatically. I know her password to log in to her computer. I could go there now and delete the whole exchange.'

Heath clearly considered it. 'I don't know if she's drunk enough to forget a whole conversation and it's a pretty big conversation too. She will be pissed to know we've gone into her dating profile and messed around with things.'

'I'm not sure we have an alternative.'

'OK, we'll give it a go, but I think, after that, you fade away. Stop talking to her and she'll never know it was you,' Heath said.

'I can't do that. I need to come clean about who I am.'

Heath sighed. 'OK, but leave it a few days to make sure any memory of that conversation has gone away. If she sees the conversation gone and believes that she didn't write it, then maybe you can tell her then.'

Bear sighed. This felt so dishonest but he would do anything to stop her getting hurt.

'OK, looks like I've got a conversation to delete.' He stood up.

'What are you going to do about Meadow? Will you tell her how you feel?' Heath said.

'Yes, I think so. I was going to do that tonight but then I got there and found she was drunk, so it didn't feel like the best time. I'd decided to tell her tomorrow morning but it feels a bit weird to lie to her about who I am and what I know and then tell her I love her. I'm pretty sure she feels the same way, but I'm not totally sure. The lady in charge of these dating events said we have matched twice now because we love each other. I know we both loved each other back when we were in our teens but I have no idea if those feelings still stand for her or not.'

'She's never said anything that makes you think she has feelings for you?'

'Sometimes I think she does have feelings for me and sometimes she'll say something to make me dismiss it. We spoke tonight about how we both wish we were each other's first time. And I told her when she was sober we would talk about whether she wanted to give us a second chance and she said she did but she was so drunk she could have agreed to anything and she won't remember any of it in the morning. Star thinks we both love each other but I'm not sure if that's just Star seeing what she wants to see.'

'My daughter is very perceptive,' Heath smiled.

'I've wanted to tell her so many times but me and Meadow have a great friendship, I don't want to ruin that by making things awkward between us if she doesn't feel the same. We see each other every day, work alongside each other, have meals together. I'd rather have her in my life as a friend than not at all.'

'No, I can understand it might make things a bit weird. But if it was me and I had been in love with the same woman for eight years or more, I'd want to know. With her being married to me and you seeing that we weren't in a loving relationship, there must have been a part of you always wondering if you'd get another chance with her. You need to know, because if she doesn't feel the same way, maybe you can finally move on once and for all.'

Bear nodded, Heath was right. 'I do wonder if all these dating events we're going on might bring it all to a head. The first date she went on the other night that she really enjoyed, that was with me.'

Heath's eyes widened. 'It was?'

'The guy she was meeting turned up with his mum who was very disapproving of Meadow getting pregnant so young. The woman I was meeting was his sister, who also wanted to check Meadow out for her brother. We got out of there as quick as we could and, as that was technically her first ever date, I decided to show her how it should be done and we went on a date of our own.'

'Bear, she came back in here after that date floating on air. Whatever you did, you ticked every single box for her. Maybe you hold off on that conversation until you two have finished all the dating events. Maybe during the course of these events, you prove to her that you're the man she's looking for. Leave her with no doubt who she should be dating without saying a word. And if things still remain the same after you've finished, tell her then.'

Bear thought about it. Maybe that was the way. He didn't relish the thought of telling her and possibly getting rejected. He could hold off for a bit longer, give Meadow time to see him as more than just her best friend, but also a man she could date and be happy with.

'Thanks for the talk,' he said, and then paused, clapping his brother on the back. 'You did a wonderful thing'

'I did the right thing and it worked out wonderfully.'

'Thank you for taking care of her, I dread to think what would have happened to her and Star if you hadn't.'

'It was my pleasure, genuinely. They saved me too.'

Bear walked out, his brain a mess of thoughts and emotions he couldn't even name. Today had been a lot to take in and he felt suddenly exhausted from it all, but sleep would be a very long way off tonight.

CHAPTER THIRTY-EIGHT

Meadow woke the next day, her head banging. The room was too bright and it took a few moments of opening squinted eyes to get used to it. She rolled onto her back and watched the sun dance across the ceiling through the leaves surrounding the window.

She thought back to the previous night and groaned. Why had she drunk so much wine? The tiny shots were so deceiving, she presumed she was only drinking a small amount but she had knocked back quite a few of them.

She thought back to the men she'd met. All of them weird. She had been so relieved to find Oliver was normal and nice to talk to that she had accosted him and spent the rest of the night chatting to him, rather than having to talk to any other strange men. She let out a little gasp. And then Bear had arrived and taken her home. Had he been there all the time, talking to lots of women? No, she would have seen him. Had Oliver perhaps called him to come and get her because she was getting more and more drunk? God that was embarrassing. She tried to remember what they'd discussed after Bear had arrived. He'd been really lovely so obviously he'd forgiven her for their silly argument the previous day.

She hated that she had let him down so badly all those years before, taking the decision to leave out of his hands, hurting him in the process, and it had all been for nothing. She had so wanted to tell him the truth about what happened the night Star was conceived. It wouldn't make any difference to the fact she had pushed him away so he would take the apprenticeship, but she wanted him to know that she hadn't slept with his brother to get back at him for sleeping with Milly Atherton. She hadn't even slept with Henry for that reason, she had been drunk and so sad and Henry had taken advantage of that.

She frowned as she suddenly remembered telling that sorry story the night before. Her heart leapt. Had she told Bear? Or Oliver. She wracked her brain, willing it to clear. No, she had written it in a text.

She gasped. Had she told AstralSurfer?

She quickly grabbed her phone and brought up the Connected Hearts app. She clicked into her conversation with him, her heart racing, hoping that she hadn't. She stared at the screen, the last message she had sent him had been about the iguana. She frowned in confusion; she remembered writing out the big, long story in her message, keen to get it off her chest to someone even if she couldn't tell Bear. She distinctly remembered that he had commented on it, said he was sorry that her first time had been like that. But there was nothing there. Had she dreamt the whole thing? Had she told someone else?

She clicked through all of her messages on the app to

other people but, apart from a few offers to meet some men, and some dick pics from other men, there was nothing.

She opened up her text messages to Bear to see if she had inadvertently told him but that was clear too.

She didn't understand any of this. After she had started talking to Oliver, it had all got a bit blurry after that. She vaguely remembered Bear taking her home, but the conversation she'd had about what had happened eight years before was getting clearer and clearer.

She clicked back into the conversation with Astral-Surfer and sent him a message.

Morning. I got a bit drunk last night at one of these dating events. I remember having a conversation with you, telling you some really personal stuff. Did I completely imagine that? Or did I make a twat of myself and you've somehow deleted those messages to spare me the blushes?

She waited for his response.

She hated the thought that she had blurted that secret out to a complete stranger. She had never told anyone. Only she and Heath knew the truth and she wanted it to stay that way.

His reply popped through.

Hi Twilight. We didn't speak at all last night. And if I did want to delete our conversation, I could only delete my part, not yours. Your blushes are spared. Maybe you dreamt it. Did you have a good night?

She sighed with relief. Maybe she had dreamt it. She always had very vivid strange dreams when she'd been drinking. She typed out her reply.

It was pretty rubbish. I'm not sure face to face meetings with strangers is my strong point. I didn't really have anything in common with them. At least with online dating we are already matched for our likes and dislikes. She paused before she typed. **You're the only one I've felt a connection with so far.**

She watched the screen to see his reply but the little three dots to show he was typing didn't appear. Oh god, she hoped she hadn't scared him off. Why was it all so complicated? The three dots appeared and then vanished again. He was clearly trying to think how to respond to that.

Finally his reply popped through. **I really like you too.**

She stared at the reply. Was that it? That's what he had spent so long writing? Maybe he wasn't good with words, not the emotional kind anyway.

She decided to try and skip past the part where she had awkwardly told him she felt a connection. **I have another dating event tonight. We'll be sniffing people to find our soul mate, I'm not really sure how that will go down.**

He replied. **I'm not sure that would be my kind of thing either.**

She smiled. **You sound like my friend. He's not keen either.**

Your friend sounds wise. I think I'd like him.

She wrote a reply. **When are you back from your work trip? I'm looking forward to meeting you.**

She imagined him checking his diary, trying to fit her in.

Not yet.

And that image quickly faded away.

OK, I should go, I'll chat to you later, Meadow wrote.

Sorry. I'm just a bit stressed with work. I'll chat to you properly later. Xx

She watched his online light go out and stared at the phone for a moment before climbing out of bed and heading for the shower.

CHAPTER THIRTY-NINE

Bear logged out of his Connected Hearts app and threw his phone down on the bed. He hated this. He felt like he had to watch everything he said so he didn't reveal who he was or what he knew. And now he had lied to her by telling her they hadn't spoken the night before, that he hadn't deleted her conversation and he was still away with work. He hated that too. No good was going to come of this.

He should have told her who he was last night as soon as he realised and not let this conversation go any further, or at the very least he should have told her this morning when she was sober enough to be able to deal with it. Now the longer he dragged this out by not telling her, the worse it would be when he did come out with the truth. What if she told him some more personal stuff in the meantime, she would be mortified to find out that she had been talking to him. Even taking the secret about Star out of the equation, she had already been really honest with him, talking about some things she wouldn't have talked about if she'd known who he was.

Was it best for him to just stop messaging her, let AstralSurfer fade away? Then he would no longer have to lie, because he wouldn't be saying anything. But that would hurt her too and he didn't want her to go scuttling back inside her shell just as she was venturing out of it.

He sighed, it was such a mess.

He hadn't slept well the night before, the huge secret about Star weighing heavily on his mind. Not the fact that Star wasn't Heath's but why hadn't Meadow told him? She hadn't trusted in him not to react badly, that was the crux of it. They were best friends and she had supposedly loved him and she had been scared he wouldn't accept her or Star into the family. Even when he had held her hand as she had given birth, when he hadn't left her side through the next few weeks while Star had been in intensive care, she still hadn't told him then.

If he was honest with himself, the biggest thing that was bugging him about all of this was that she had gone to Heath when she found out she was pregnant, not him. She hadn't trusted him to raise her baby with her. He knew he'd only been sixteen at the time, and Heath had been nineteen, but he would have raised her little girl like his own, just like Heath did. But he supposed she wouldn't have come to him if she'd thought he was in love with Milly.

But even now, eight years later, she still hadn't felt like she could share that secret with him. Could they really move forward in a relationship if she didn't trust him?

He eyed the phone on the bed. And if he was forced to lie to her maybe he didn't deserve that trust.

He sighed. He didn't have time to dwell on this now. He'd promised Star they would look at the webcam footage from the night before that morning.

He finished getting dressed and headed down to breakfast.

CHAPTER FORTY

'OK, let's have a look, shall we?' Bear said, clicking open the video files he'd downloaded from the cameras.

Star opened up her notepad and clicked her pen, ready to take notes. He smiled at her enthusiasm.

They were sitting in the reception area, Indigo was on the phone to a customer and Meadow was chatting to Sharon Ecclestone, one of their guests, about the horseshoe bats and the best place to see them. For the first time in a very long time, it had been awkward between him and Meadow at breakfast. Although he knew that awkwardness had come from him. He just didn't know what to say to her. After the night before, after what they'd talked about after the dating event, he should be taking her for a walk on Pear Tree Beach and telling her he loved her. But her secret and his lies felt like they were overshadowing all of that. Of course his feelings for her hadn't changed but he had lied to her this morning and it didn't feel like the best time to tell her how he felt. Maybe Heath was right and he'd wait a few days for it all to die down. He caught her eye as Sharon left and Meadow gave him a little smile. They still hadn't cleared the air properly after his silly overreaction the day before, well not that she would remember. He smiled back, a million different things he wanted to say flashing through his head, but he couldn't find the words for any of them.

'So the cameras have motion detectors so they recorded when anything moved?' Star asked, snapping his attention back to the videos.

'Sort of. These cameras use something called infrared, which detects a moving heat pattern which animals have. Otherwise the cameras might pick up every time a leaf was blowing in the wind. This way we know that all the motion files we're about to watch should be an animal. Although we might pick up some of the human occupants as well, making their way back to the treehouses.'

Star giggled. 'Well, humans are animals too.'

'That's true.'

He watched as Meadow stepped outside to talk to one of the guests who had checked in the day before, giving directions to the beaches and other nearby sights. Why was he so hyperaware of everything she was doing today? Her words from the night before flashed into his mind. How she had often thought about what it would be like to sleep with him. How she wanted him to be her first, how she had cried after she'd slept with that shitbag because she wished she'd slept with him instead. Their lives would have been so different if she had. Although he couldn't regret the existence of the brilliant little girl sitting next to him.

He clicked open the first file and after a few seconds a hedgehog came into view, snuffling at the fruit they'd left out and sniffing at the camera. Beside him Star gasped with delight.

'He's so cute.'

'He is, very. Or it could be a she.'

'How can we tell the difference?' Star asked.

Bear fiddled with his watch as he thought. That could be an awkward conversation about male and female body parts. He decided to play it safe. 'In a lot of species, especially mammals, the males tend to be bigger than the females. But a young male might be smaller than an older female so that rule doesn't always apply. Something like a lion is very obvious because the males have that big mane but the females don't, and with some animals, like birds, the male and females have different markings, but with a lot of animals it's very hard to tell the difference. But if we start to see this hedgehog regularly and others too we'll be able to tell the difference with the shape of its nose or the colour of its fur or other characteristics. Want to give this one a name, something that is not male or female?'

Star watched the hog eat the food they'd left out. 'Strawberry.'

'Good name.'

They watched Strawberry move around the screen for a while and Star made a note of which camera it was, what time and what Strawberry was doing. To their surprise, as Strawberry feasted on a nut, it was joined by another, much smaller hedgehog.

'Oh, do you think that's Strawberry's baby?' Star asked.

'It could be. Hedgehogs tend to be solitary creatures so, if this smaller one is hanging around, Strawberry could be its mum.'

'I'll call that one Peanut.'

Bear nodded. The video clip came to an end and they watched the next one. This one was much shorter than Strawberry's clip but Star gave a squeal of delight as a fat badger waddled across the screen.

'We're very lucky to see one of those,' Bear said. 'They are very shy.'

Indigo leaned back in her seat to have a look too while chatting to the customer on the phone.

'They live in groups, don't they?' Star asked.

'They do but they don't always get on with the members of their group, just like any family really, which is why some badgers might forage for food alone.'

'Does that mean we won't see any others here?' Star asked.

'It depends. We might have seen that badger because the camera is really close to their sett, so we may see many more. But badgers can travel around a mile from their sett, sometimes more to get food, so we'll have to wait and see if we get more glimpses of this badger or others here.'

Star carefully made a note in her notebook. 'I'm going to call that one Dash because it dashed across the screen.'

'Great name.'

They watched the last clip for that camera to see a tiny fieldmouse come and eat a raspberry before scurrying away. Star called that Tails because it had a really long tail.

They moved onto the first clip of camera two where they had left out some cat food. Bear pressed play and then immediately sat up to stare at the screen more carefully.

'Bear, is that—'

The clip didn't last long just a few seconds before the

animal was gone and Bear immediately replayed it and then pressed pause when it was in the middle of the screen.

'That's... a wolf, isn't it?' Star said, her voice holding a tremor of nerves and excitement.

Bear wanted to say that it wasn't, that maybe it was a fox or a dog because of course it couldn't be a wolf, but he couldn't say those words. The animal on the screen *was* a wolf, there was no denying that.

CHAPTER FORTY-ONE

'See, I told you,' Heath said, a huge grin on his face. 'No one would believe me but that's pretty hard evidence to ignore.'

Bear watched his brother with a smug smile on his face as he waited on hold for his friend to come back to him. Kristofer was a local vet but as luck would have it he'd also spent six years working with wolves on a special nature reserve in Canada. If anyone would be able to identify the animal it would be him. There were three clips with the wolf from two different cameras so Bear had sent them over to him. In the meantime, Meadow and Indigo were desperately ringing round every zoo and wildlife park in the whole of Wales and some in England to see if any of them were missing a wolf.

Star was sitting on Amelia's lap with wide eyes as she took in all the activity. He thought she might be scared but she was visibly buzzing with excitement, practically bouncing in her seat.

'I think we need to alert all our guests to the potential dangers,' River said. 'Some of them have small dogs with them, can you imagine the horror if the wolf eats one of the pet dogs?'

'Let's not panic just yet,' Bear said. 'Let's just wait to see what Kristofer says. I've watched these clips a hundred times and the face is more gentle and floppy than astute and sharp. I think we're looking at a stray dog.'

'That's exactly what it is.' Kristofer had obviously come back on the line. 'I can see why you would think wolf because the likeness is uncanny but there are a number of characteristics which are different. The nose is shorter, and he had a bit of a goofy expression when he was running. Wolves have a narrow frame and longer legs, this dog is wider, stockier. Wolves are shy, not boisterous, and this dog seemed to be having the time of its life running through the trees. Wolves have bigger heads too and, while it's hard to tell with these clips shot at night, wolves have yellow eyes and this animal did not have those.'

Bear breathed a sigh of relief.

'I think what we're looking at here is a husky-shepherd-malamute cross. It might even have some Northern Inuit dog in him too. There has been an increasing trend, especially in foreign countries, to breed dogs that resemble wolves, with little thought to what those dogs will turn out like. My guess is that this dog is around a year old and he got too big and loopy for his owners to be able to cope with him and so they dumped him. But I highly doubt he is going to make off with any small children anytime soon. I would try to catch him, put some food out, gain his trust and then bring him in. We can scan him to see if he's microchipped and go from there.'

'OK, will do. Thanks Kristofer.'

'My pleasure. I'm looking forward to meeting him.'

Bear hung up. 'OK, panic over, Kristofer is one hundred percent positive it's a stray dog.' He explained the differences that Kristofer had pointed out and that he thought he might be a husky cross. 'He's one year old so still a puppy really. I think now we know he's out there he should be fairly easy to catch but I don't think it's anything to worry about.'

Meadow put the phone down. 'And none of the parks or zoos I've contacted are missing a wolf. It does make more sense that it's a stray dog rather than an actual wolf.'

Heath sighed theatrically at having his wolf discovery dashed but nodded. 'It does make more sense and if the wolf expert says they look really similar I do feel validated.'

Meadow smiled and rolled her eyes. 'You hate being wrong.'

'No, I just love it when I'm right,' Heath said.

'I'm kinda glad it isn't a wolf,' Star said.

'I am too,' Amelia said. 'I like a bit of excitement in my life, but I don't think I'd want to meet a real wolf while walking through the woods.'

'I am a bit disappointed though,' Star said. 'I've never seen a wolf before.'

'There is a wolf sanctuary near Shropshire,' Meadow said. 'Maybe we can visit one day.'

'I'd love that,' Star said.

'In the meantime, we need to catch this dog,' Bear said. 'Me and Meadow have a thing tonight but it should be finished fairly early. How about we do a little camp out after to see if we can meet him? Star, do you want to join me?'

Star looked eagerly at Meadow and Heath. 'Can I?'

They glanced at each other and Meadow nodded. 'Of course you can. You might also see some of these other creatures too, if you're really quiet.'

Star clapped her hands together excitedly.

'Well, I better dig out our old camping gear,' Bear said.

'I'll have to see what supplies I've got,' Meadow said. 'I haven't been camping for ages.'

'Why don't you join them?' Amelia said, innocently, taking the words right from Bear's mouth.

'You can join us if you like,' Bear said, ignoring the exchange of looks from River and Indigo and the big smirks from Heath and Amelia.

'I'd love to.'

Bear grinned. 'Sounds like a plan.'

CHAPTER FORTY-TWO

Bear pulled on a shirt ready for the dating event that night and started buttoning it up, thinking, as always, about Meadow, the secret and his relationship with her as Twilight and AstralSurfer. She didn't have many friends, she had grown up being best friends with him, River and Heath and some of her girl friends had been jealous of that, especially in the teenage years. It seemed like she felt she could confide in AstralSurfer and he didn't want to take that away from her by ignoring her or pushing her away.

She had told him stuff about her dad that he hadn't known. Meadow had never really spoken about her parents growing up, apart from how strict they were with her and that her dad had a bad temper. He'd known that her parents had kicked her out when they found out she was pregnant so he was aware their relationship had never been great, but he hadn't known that her dad had hated her mum or that her parents had made her feel they hated her. To grow up with that must have been so difficult and it explained her wariness of relationships.

But knowing a lot of this personal stuff made it even more difficult to come clean about who he was. She had told AstralSurfer, not him.

He had to find a way to tell her the truth and the longer he left it the worse it was, although he did think Heath was probably right and he should leave it at least a few more days to let the worry of telling him the secret about Star fade away.

He picked up his phone and sent Twilight a message.

Hi, sorry about earlier, I was in the middle of a breakfast meeting and was trying to be discreet about messaging you.

He cringed at how easy the lie came, but it was a tiny lie and it was only so she didn't get hurt by her drunken ramblings.

He sent another message. **I just wanted to wish you luck tonight with your smelly dating event.**

Her little online light came on and then he saw she was typing a reply back.

I just laughed out loud at that. Hopefully it won't be too pongy. I just hope my friend won't chicken out of coming, he's really against it.

Well, it is a bit of a weird way to meet people, but I'm sure he'll come, for comedy value if nothing else, Bear wrote.

Twilight sent a reply. **I think he'll enjoy it. He smells amazing, I think the women will be around him like bees round honey.**

He smiled at that, then rubbed his hand across his chin as he thought about her comment. **I did a bit of research into the science behind pheromone dating after you told** me what you were doing tonight. If you're attracted to someone's scent, you're attracted to them too. So why aren't you two together if he smells so good?

I don't think a lifelong relationship can really be built on smell alone. But honestly, we have a long and complicated history. Not romantically, apart from one incredible kiss when we were in our teens, but lately I've felt like we were growing closer and that maybe something might happen. We matched at the speed dating the other night but he also matched with someone else. The organiser of the event said he matched with her because his heart was still racing after his date with me, so I was excited. But we had a silly row yesterday about something I did in the past and I don't think he will ever forgive me for it. Well two things actually, at least as far as he's concerned. He thinks I slept with his brother to get back at him for some silly argument and I didn't. I did sleep with someone but not to get back at him, just because I was really sad and very drunk, which is a pathetic excuse but I was young. Anyway, while I think we'll always be friends, I think the chance of anything ever happening romantically between us has long gone.

He sat down on the bed. He hated that she was carrying this guilt. He'd been chatting to her all day but there had been an awkwardness, she'd clearly put it down to their stupid row the day before as she didn't know he was party to her biggest secret. He needed to make sure she knew he didn't hold a grudge, especially now he'd discovered the truth about Heath. He read her message again.

It sounds like you'd quite like something to happen romantically.

There was no reply although her online light was still on. Maybe she didn't want to admit it, especially to a man she was hoping to date at some point. Or maybe she didn't want anything to happen. Maybe she was as confused as he was about the mixed messages flying between them over the last few days.

He sent another message. **I told you before that I'm more interested in the person you are now rather than what you did in the past. And I'm sure your friend feels the same.**

He paused before sending another message.

Maybe you should find out once and for all tonight if he has feelings for you. You should let him smell you at the pheromone event, see if he's attracted to you too. I don't think it's ever too late if you love each other.

There was still no reply. He looked at his watch, maybe she'd already gone but not logged out of the conversation. Then he saw her writing a reply.

That's some good advice. Thank you. I'll let you know how it goes. Xx

Then her online light went out and suddenly he was looking forward to tonight a lot more. He could finally tell her how he felt without saying a word.

CHAPTER FORTY-THREE

'I can't believe I'm doing this,' Bear muttered. 'Spending the evening sniffing three-day-old t-shirts is not how I would choose to spend my time. I feel quite repulsed by the whole thing.'

'You don't have to sniff the t-shirts. You can sniff the women, if they give their permission of course,' Meadow said, looking around. Tonight's event was in a wonderful hotel overlooking the sea. They were in a large room that had big windows and patio doors that filled the room with the spectacular view of the sea.

'You want me to walk around and sniff a load of women's armpits?' Bear said.

'No, necks apparently, that's the best place to get a good whiff,' Meadow said and then laughed as Bear couldn't have looked any less enthusiastic.

'Ladies and gentlemen,' Imogen said, catching everyone's attention. 'Thank you for coming to our Mix n Match event. Tonight we are going to be focussing on scent. Everyone has a unique scent and our pheromones are probably more important than appearance when it comes to attracting someone. You might tell yourself you have a type, that you only go for redheads or blondes, but one day you meet someone who doesn't fit with your normal type, and you are attracted to them and you don't know why. It probably has more to do with their scent than anything else. Scientists have studied this attraction extensively and certain pheromones stimulate desire and arousal.'

There were giggles and raised eyebrows around the room.

'Now there is one pheromone called androsterone which makes men attractive to women. Women also produce this attractive pheromone but in nowhere near the levels that men do. But ten percent of men produce an excessive amount of this pheromone and these men are considered to be the sexiest men in the world. Forget your Chris Hemsworths, Paul Rudds, or Idris Elbas, who *People* magazine have voted as the world's sexiest men in the last few years, even an average-looking man would be considered sexier and more desirable if they have this pheromone in abundance. But apart from our androsterone-excessive men, who tend to be sexually attractive to all women, our scents will appeal and repel different people. All of you will have very different reactions to the t-shirts you're going to smell tonight. Some men might find t-shirt number one appealing and others will not and that's the beauty of this kind of event. There is a scent for everybody.'

Meadow gave Bear an encouraging nudge. He still didn't look happy.

'So this is how tonight will work. All of you were asked

to sleep in the same white t-shirt for the last three nights and bring it with you tonight. We've put the men's t-shirts in the rather stereotypical blue bags and the women in pink. All the bags will have a barcode on and we've given you all a scanner, similarly to what you use at the supermarkets. You can sniff the t-shirts and, if it appeals to you, you can use your scanner to scan the barcode. If the same person is attracted to your scent as well then your wristbands will vibrate and show the number of the person you are matched with. We'll also email you the details of who you match with, too. Now if sniffing bags and t-shirts isn't your thing, you can ask if the men or women around you would be happy to be sniffed directly. The necks are the best places to have a sniff of your potential matches. But please ask permission before you do this. Hope you enjoy your night.'

'Right, shall we get sniffing?' Meadow said, moving over to the long table where there were t-shirts in blue bags on one half and t-shirts in pink bags on the other.

'This is not my kind of thing,' Bear said. 'I'd rather be camping in the woods right now looking for wolves than doing this.'

'Do you not believe that scent plays a big part in who we do or do not find attractive?'

'I have never gone on a date with someone because they smell nice.'

'How do you know? According to the leaflet they handed out tonight, pheromones are not something we can really detect, at least consciously. You could have been subconsciously attracted to someone purely because their pheromones and yours speak to each other.'

Bear looked sceptical.

She decided to take AstralSurfer's advice.

'OK, smell me,' Meadow said. 'Tell me what it makes you feel.'

'I'm not sniffing you like a dog,' Bear said.

'I'm not asking you to sniff my bum, I'm asking you to sniff my neck.' She scooped her hair away from her neck and wrapped it round the other side, exposing the side of her neck to him.

Bear sighed and then bent his head, breathing her in just below her ear and causing a punch of desire to slam into her stomach. This was so intimate and that thought hadn't occurred to her when she had offered it. She just wanted to see if he liked her scent as much as she liked his.

He shifted his hand to her waist, as he took in her scent, and the heat of him burned into her hip. He moved a bit closer and for the briefest of seconds his lips grazed against her skin in no more than a whisper. Her breath hitched at the touch of his mouth.

After the longest moment, he stepped back and his eyes were dark.

She stared at him and cleared her throat. 'Was it nice?'

He shook his head. 'That was definitely not *nice.* That was something else entirely. But you have just proved me completely wrong. There is something to be said about scent, after all.'

He moved down to the pink end of the table. She stared after him for a moment feeling thoroughly confused. Then she followed him.

'Did you like my scent?'

He turned to look at her and his cheeks were still

flushed. 'Meadow, I... OK, if you want a simple answer, then yes I liked your scent. A lot more than I imagined I would. Come on, let's do this. Your daughter is waiting to go camping.'

She paused, feeling suddenly bold. 'Can I smell you?'

A small smile appeared on his lips. 'Go on then.'

She stepped closer and, to her surprise, he suddenly lifted her so she could reach his neck more easily, her feet dangling off the floor.

'You could have just bent down,' Meadow laughed, but the laugh died on her lips as he slid his arms round her back holding her tighter against him. The warmth of his body was wonderful, his hard muscles pressed into hers. The look on his face showed that he hadn't really thought about this sudden intimacy before he'd picked her up. She slid her hands round the back of his neck, holding onto him for support as she moved closer to take a sniff. The scent of him she recognised instantly. She knew she'd be able to pick that scent out of a line-up of hundreds of men. It was comforting, warm but sexy as hell, it made her stomach clench with desire and need. She moved closer on the pretext of sniffing somewhere different when really she couldn't get enough of him.

'Are you done?' Bear asked, his words tickling the back of her neck.

'Not even close,' Meadow said without thinking and then laughed at the honest brazenness of her words. 'I, umm... need to be thorough.'

Bear, it seemed, was quite happy to hold her. In fact, as she continued to smell him, she felt him move his face so he could smell her again and it made goosebumps explode over her body. She'd read several articles about sex over the years, keen to know how different her first time should have been, but not one of them had ever mentioned how smelling each other could be such a turn-on. Maybe it was just the proximity of his lips next to her skin, so close it was almost like he was kissing her, coupled with his body against hers, the feel of his arms around her, his wonderful scent that was everywhere. She was in absolute heaven and they still had all their clothes on.

Bear moved back slightly to look at her. 'We're getting a few looks.'

Her eyes cast down to his lips for the briefest of seconds and then she glanced around the room. Almost every single person in the room was staring at them, some in horror, some in amusement or surprise.

Meadow felt her cheeks flame red. She had almost completely forgotten they were in a room filled with people.

'OK, you can put me down now.'

Bear placed her gently down on the floor and she took a step back, both of them staring at each other.

'Well, that looks like fun,' a woman with wild curly blonde hair came up to them. 'If that's what we're doing, can I have a go now?'

She lifted her arms like a child wanting to be picked up and Bear took a step back. 'No, sorry, I, umm... excuse me.'

He turned and walked out the patio doors onto the terrace, leaning on the wall as he looked out onto the view.

'That's a bad sign. If a man who had just been sniffing me walked out the room that quickly, I'd be worried about my body odour,' the woman said. 'He's clearly gone out for some fresh air.'

Meadow couldn't even find it in her to be pissed off by that comment, she was too busy committing every touch, every feeling about that wonderful moment to memory. She could still smell him on her clothes, on her skin. Her heart was racing, she could barely catch her breath, and from the way Bear had been looking at her once he'd put her down, he felt the same way too. A huge part of her wanted to go after him, to talk about this, but she would respect the fact that he needed space right now.

Meadow flashed the woman a polite smile and moved off down to the end where the blue bags were currently being sniffed.

One woman was staring at her as she approached. 'Wow, that might have been the sexiest thing I've ever seen. I felt like I was watching a porn film. The way he was holding you with his hands splayed out across your back, the way he was closing his eyes as he was sniffing you. That was as hot as hell,' the woman fanned herself. 'Please tell me you've just met and you had this instant love at first sight connection?'

Meadow smiled. 'I'm afraid not. We're best friends.'

'There was nothing friendly about that. He definitely doesn't see you as a friend. Trust me on that.'

Meadow was starting to think that might be true and that filled her heart.

She turned her attention to sniffing some of the shirts. Some were nice or OK, some were deeply unpleasant but none of them made her think of dragging the owner straight off to the bedroom to have her wicked way with him.

Although the instructions were to wear a white t-shirt, there were a few coloured shirts, presumably because those men didn't own a white t-shirt. She'd seen Bear bring a very pale blue one and she started casually looking through the bags trying to find it. She suddenly spotted one and she picked it up and opened it, taking a whiff of the soft fabric. The resulting kick of desire that slammed into her stomach confirmed it was his. God, this shirt was a hell of a lot more potent than just his skin, presumably because he showered on a regular basis, whereas this shirt had been worn for at least three nights. It smelt divine. She could sniff this all night and never get bored.

She glanced around to see Bear had returned to the pink end of the table and was smelling the different shirts at quite a speed. She quickly scanned the barcode on Bear's shirt and returned it to the bag.

'Is that his?' The curly-haired blonde woman was back and practically snatched the t-shirt out of her hand so she could take a sniff. 'Good lord, I want a piece of that.' The woman went in for a bigger, deeper sniff and then rolled her eyes to the sky as if she was completely turned on it by it. 'Christ that's magnificent.' She scanned the barcode with her scanner before taking another sniff.

'Let me have a go,' another woman joined them.

'And me,' said a different woman.

'I want to smell this man myself,' said the woman who had spoken to her when she'd arrived down the blue end of the table.

Meadow took a step back to accommodate the women

who were starting to gather round them. Suddenly everyone wanted to sniff Bear's t-shirt.

She glanced round in time to see Bear scan one of the women's t-shirts, then he put the bag back on the table and walked away. Had he really sniffed all the bags already? How many had he scanned?

He spotted her hanging back and moved over towards her.

'What's going on?' Bear gestured to the small frenzy that was happening at the table.

'Umm... some poor guy's t-shirt is being mauled like a piece of meat thrown into the lion's den. Maybe he's one of the ten percent of super-high androsterone people.'

Bear looked over and his eyes widened as he realised it was his shirt.

He turned back to her. 'Look, I'm kind of done here. I'm happy to stay if you want to stay a bit longer, but I'm keen to get back for Star. I don't want to let her down.'

Meadow smiled with complete love for him. 'I'm done here too.'

They walked back towards the entrance table where they had collected their wristbands and scanners but, before they got there, their wristbands beeped to say they had been matched. Her heart leapt. Bear had chosen her too.

'I've been matched to number fourteen,' Meadow said, looking up at the number fourteen label on his shirt.

Bear smiled. 'And I've been matched to number eight.'

Meadow grinned.

'Do you want to stay and see if you matched to anyone else?' Bear asked.

'I only scanned one t-shirt.'

'I did too.'

They stood staring at each other for a moment. Then Bear took her hand as if it was the most natural thing in the world and led her back to the table. They handed over their scanners and wristbands to a stunned Imogen.

'You two matched again?' she asked in surprise.

'It was meant to be,' Bear said and then led Meadow outside.

CHAPTER FORTY-FOUR

They didn't really talk much on the short drive on the way back but Meadow was excited about what might happen between them. Standing there sniffing each other had been really hot and she knew he had felt the same. This was the first time she had seen any real evidence that he was attracted to her and she couldn't stop smiling about it. She glanced across at him and saw he was smiling too.

They pulled up outside Bear's house and got out and walked back past the reception area towards the tree-houses, but suddenly a man came running out of the trees, and she recognised him as Jason Lovegrove, one of the guests. He looked absolutely petrified. Meadow wondered if he'd seen the wolf.

'Do you work here?' Jason asked.

'Yes we do,' Meadow said. 'Is everything OK?'

'My wife has just gone into labour.'

'OK, stay calm.' She glanced at Bear who was already pulling his phone out of his pocket to call an ambulance. 'We'll call the paramedics and they'll be here soon to help.'

'No, you don't understand, she's only thirty-five weeks. My son can't come yet, he won't be big enough.'

Meadow's heart dropped, feeling the panic she had experienced when Star had insisted on coming early, worrying if her baby would survive.

She heard Bear relaying the added complication to the emergency services.

'OK, let's go back and see your wife. Which treehouse are you in?' Meadow said, trying to stay calm.

'Honeysuckle.'

'Right, Bear is going to wait here for the emergency services and he will bring them right over and get the ambulance as close as possible. I'm going to come with you and make your wife as comfortable as possible.'

Bear nodded and she quickly followed Jason back to his treehouse. 'My daughter was born at thirty weeks and she was perfectly formed, albeit a little small, but everything was working as it should be and she was fine. She'll be eight in a few months. I'm sure your son will be fine too.'

'God I hope so. We tried so hard to conceive and in the end we went down the IVF route. This was our fourth attempt at getting pregnant. Everything has been smooth sailing up until now.'

'I'm sure you have nothing to worry about. Have you chosen a name?'

'We liked Quinn.'

'Quinn is a great name.'

They rushed up the steps into Honeysuckle Cottage and then up the stairs to the bedroom. Jason rushed to his wife's side and took her hand as she puffed her way through a contraction.

'It's OK, Emma, I'm here, help is on the way.'

'He can't come now,' Emma said. 'He needs more time to grow. We haven't even finished painting the nursery yet.'

'Try to stay calm. I know, ideally, Quinn would stay in there for forty weeks but thirty-five is still OK. My daughter was fine and she was born at thirty,' Meadow said.

'She was?' Emma said.

'She was perfect. She'll be eight in a few months and you'd never know she was premature, she's so clever and brilliant. Early babies are fairly common. Now are you comfortable, would you prefer to be in a different position?'

Emma nodded. 'I think I'd like to walk around a bit, it seems to help with the pain.'

'OK, let's do that,' Meadow said. She moved round to the side of the bed and helped Jason to heave her to her feet. Jason held her hand as she walked around the room.

'This would be a beautiful place to give birth to our son,' Emma said.

Her husband paled at this. 'No way, we're having this baby in a hospital surrounded by doctors and nurses.'

Emma suddenly gripped her stomach again, groaning with the pain of another contraction.

'You might not have much choice,' Meadow said. 'Quinn is on his way.'

'Meadow!' Bear called from downstairs. 'The paramedics are here.'

'Thank God,' Jason said.

'Bring them up,' Meadow called.

She heard footsteps on the stairs and a man and woman

dressed in green entered the room. Bear stood at the doorway, looking on anxiously.

'All right love, how you feeling? How far apart are your contractions?' the female paramedic said.

'I'm not sure,' Emma said.

'About five minutes,' Meadow said.

'OK, let's get you on the bed for a moment just so we can have a look.'

Meadow moved to the door, Emma didn't need a huge bunch of strangers gawping at her undercarriage. 'We'll be downstairs if you need anything.'

She and Bear went back downstairs.

Bear put his hands on her shoulders. 'Are you OK?'

'Yeah.'

'Is it bringing it all back?'

'Yes, the panic and uncertainty, I remember it like it was yesterday. They must be so scared.'

Bear enveloped her in a huge hug, holding her close, and she realised she was trembling slightly as she leaned her head against his chest and slid her arms round his back. When Jason had said the baby was premature, that fear she had felt eight years before had slammed into her again. All the appointments, all the books, all the prenatal classes, none of it could prepare you for giving birth to your baby ten weeks early. She had never felt fear like it. Bear held her there for the longest time, not relinquishing his hold, and she knew she loved this man with everything she had. And tonight, when they were alone, she would tell him.

She eventually stepped back. 'Thank you.'

'Always.'

'Listen, I should stay here, just in case they need anything, but you get off and take Star camping. She's been so excited about it all day, I'd hate for her to miss it and there's no point in both of us being here.'

'I'm not leaving you.'

She smiled. 'Bear, I'm not the one having this baby. I'll be fine.'

Bear sighed and looked at his watch. 'Are you sure? I can wait a bit longer.'

'No, go, I promise I'm all good. The paramedics are here, I'll just be on warm water and clean towel duty if they need me.'

'OK, well if you need me, for anything, even if it's just another hug, call me,' Bear waved his mobile at her and she nodded.

He bent his head and kissed her on the cheek and then with a wave he left. She listened to the voices up above to try to ascertain what was going on but everyone seemed fairly calm. They weren't telling Emma to push just yet but it didn't seem like they were making any move to get her to the hospital either so it looked like they were going to have their first treehouse birth. Meadow looked at her watch. It was going to be a long night.

CHAPTER FORTY-FIVE

'So what do we do if we see the dog?' Star asked, clutching her camera, her notebook lying open in her lap.

They were sitting in the mouth of the tent, their sleeping bags, pillows, duvets and blankets already laid out behind them. Alex, the chef, had provided them with enough snacks and food to last them a few days, rather than just one night. They also had plenty of food for Snuggles, as Star had taken to calling him. Or any other animal that might come along – though the others would smell human and probably stay away. Or Snuggles would scare them off.

'Well, I don't think we should try to catch him tonight. We've got the food here in two places. One around ten metres from the tent and this one right here. If he's nervous he might not come at all or he might only take the food from over there and not come near us. And then tomorrow night or maybe the night after we might persuade him to come closer. If he comes up to us tonight then he might be a lot more used to humans than we think he is, which will make him a lot easier to catch, but we still need him to trust us before we wrap a collar round his neck and put a lead on him. So tonight if he comes close we'll try to feed him by hand too and we might even get to stroke him but then we let him go and try again tomorrow. But let's play it by ear.'

Star nodded. 'Mummy says we have to be really quiet.'

'I think if we stand any chance of seeing any animals tonight, then yes we do, but a lot of the animals will smell us so might not come anywhere near us anyway.'

'I had a shower today,' Star said. 'I don't smell.'

Bear nearly laughed. 'Animals' sense of smell is really good, far far better than ours. It has to be to sniff out food. Where we just go to the cupboard or fridge to get food they have to hunt it out in trees and bushes. And they don't just sniff out bad smells, they sniff out good ones too. We give out scents that we're not even really aware of. But they will absolutely know we are here.'

'Will Snuggles know we are here?'

'Yes, dogs have a brilliant sense of smell. He will know we are here but there are lots of other humans who are walking around and staying in this wood so our scents will mix with those. The cat food will also smell really good so he might come regardless of smelling us if he's that hungry.'

'What do we smell like?'

'I don't know. But they will know that the scent is human and foxes and badgers will be able to smell Snuggles too and will stay away if they think it's a threat.' Bear took a swig of water. 'You know tonight, me and your mum went to a place to meet some new friends and the lady who was running it told us that scent is a really important factor when it comes to choosing a new friend. You know how wolves mate for life and some humans do too? Well, apparently we choose the person whose smell appeals to us the most. I bet wolves are the same. So we had to do a lot of sniffing tonight to choose which friends we wanted to get to know more. Some people were sniffing each other's neck, other people were sniffing a t-shirt other people had worn to see if they liked the smell or not.'

Star wrinkled her nose. 'That sounds gross.'

'I know, I thought that too.'

'Did you and Mummy sniff each other?'

'Yes we did.'

Star smiled. 'Mummy smells nice.'

'Yes she does, I thought she had the best scent out of all the other people there tonight. And she seemed to enjoy sniffing me too.'

'Does that mean you two will mate for life?'

'I don't know. Maybe. But I think we have to figure that out for ourselves, without any interfering from you, missy,' he poked her gently in the ribs and she giggled.

Just then there was a noise in the bushes and Bear put his finger to his mouth to indicate to Star she should be quiet. Although if the animal had come that close to them while they were talking, it clearly wasn't put off by them.

They watched the bushes as they moved and suddenly Snuggles was standing in front of them. Star let out a little gasp of delight and then clamped her hand over her mouth. Snuggles was huge and he looked so wolf-like it was a little unnerving. But when he wagged his tail at seeing them, Bear relaxed a little.

They watched him eat the food that was on the far side of the clearing from them, and Bear noticed how gentle his face was and how completely unbothered he was by their presence. This was definitely a pet dog, or at least a dog that was used to humans.

Snuggles finished the food and eyed the other bowl right in front of them.

'Hey boy, come on, it's OK, we won't hurt you,' Bear said.

'Come on Snuggles, plenty of food over here,' Star said.

Snuggles hesitated for a moment and then picked his way carefully and slowly across the clearing towards them.

'OK Star, don't make any sudden movements. Just move really slowly.'

The way Snuggles moved towards them was really submissive, his head down low, his tail wagging. The dog was clearly as wary of them as they were of him.

Snuggles got closer and started eating the bowl of food that was right in front of them, watching them carefully.

Bear picked up one of the sausages that Alex had given them for Snuggles and offered it out. Snuggles stepped closer and took it gently from Bear's hand. The dog had definitely been fed like this before.

'Can I feed him?' Star said, quietly.

'Yes, go for it, just move slowly.'

Star picked up the sausage and held it out and Snuggles moved over towards her, eagerly. He very gently took the sausage from her hand and ate it and then, because her hand was still outstretched, he licked her hand too. This made Star giggle and Snuggles wagged his tail at the noise.

'Can I stroke him?' Star asked.

'Yes, but not on top of the head, try his chest or his shoulder,' Bear said. 'Move slowly and be really gentle.'

Star reached out a hand to stroke the dog's chest and Snuggles was obviously quite happy to let her do it, wagging his tail as she gently touched his fur.

To Bear's surprise, Snuggles even sat down next to Star so she could continue the stroking.

'He's beautiful,' Star said, reverentially.

'He is. Here, give him another sausage.'

Star reached down and grabbed the sausage and as she continued to stroke him with one hand she fed him with the other. Snuggles was very calm and clearly enjoying the attention.

Bear had a good look at him: his claws were slightly long and his coat was a bit muddy in patches, but he looked in fairly good condition, which meant he probably hadn't been out here too long, maybe a few weeks, and he'd managed to keep himself fed. It was hard to tell underneath the mass of fur but he didn't look too skinny.

Snuggles suddenly leaned forward to sniff the side of Star's neck and Star giggled at the feel of his whiskers on her skin. Then Snuggles lay down with his head in Star's lap, looking up at her with such adoration.

'Wow, Star, he really likes you,' Bear said.

'I like him too. Do you think Mummy and Daddy will let me keep him?'

'We have to try and find his previous owner first. Snuggles may have slipped out of his home and his owners have been worried about him ever since. If we can't find his owners then we can have a chat about looking after him here, but that's something we'll have to ask your mum and dad. He's a big dog and he might not be too happy in a treehouse.'

Suddenly there was the noise of loud laughter nearby as no doubt people returned to their treehouses possibly after being down the pub.

Snuggles was up on his feet like a shot and disappeared into the trees.

'Oh, he's gone,' Star said sadly.

'But that was excellent progress tonight. We fed him by hand, stroked him and he was happy to lie down next to you. I didn't think we'd be able to do any of those things tonight. This will probably make him a lot easier to catch. We can camp out again tomorrow or put food out by the front of your house or mine to see if we can get him closer to a house and other people. If we can get him to go up the steps to your treehouse that would be great. And your treehouse smells of you so Snuggles will know you live there. He trusts you so, you never know, we might get lucky.'

'Then he can sleep in my room.'

'I think he'll probably need a bath first before we let him do that. Also, if we do end up keeping him, the poor dog will probably need a better name than Snuggles.'

Star laughed. 'I'll think of something.'

CHAPTER FORTY-SIX

Meadow approached the tent expecting to see a flurry of activity, or at least Bear and Star lying in the entrance to the tent looking out for wildlife, but there was silence and no sign of movement at all.

Maybe they'd gone to bed.

Meadow quietly unzipped the tent and peered inside, a huge smile spreading across her face. Bear was on his back fast asleep and Star was lying cuddled into his side snoring softly. Bear had his arm wrapped around her tightly.

Meadow's heart felt like it was going to burst with complete and utter love for him. This man was the most incredible, kindest most wonderful man she had ever met and she loved him with everything she had.

Suddenly sensing she was there, Bear's arm tightened protectively around Star as his eyes opened. Realising it was her, a big smile appeared on his face.

'Hey!' he said softly.

'Hi, I thought you guys might want a hot chocolate,'

Meadow whispered, waving the flask. 'Didn't expect to find you sleeping on the job.'

Bear grinned. 'Star was getting tired. I suggested we have a little nap and that we could always get up later to do some more nature watching.'

'She'll probably be out for the rest of the night now.'

'Yeah, I guessed as much,' he said and then after a moment he patted the bed area next to him.

She crawled inside the tent, zipped it up, kicked off her shoes and then, as Bear held up a blanket, she cuddled up next to him.

'Was the baby OK?'

'Yes, in the end. It all happened so quickly after you'd left, her contractions getting closer together, but then they suddenly seemed to stop. Every time they tried to move her, the contractions started again and they'd get her back on the bed and then they'd stop. They could have got to the hospital five times over but the paramedics weren't really keen to move her and in the end Emma didn't want to move either. She said it was so peaceful there in the treehouse and she wanted it to be beautiful for the baby. Anyway, a little girl was born about an hour ago.'

'A girl, I thought they were having a boy?'

'They did too but nope. They're still using the name Quinn though. She was screaming loudly when she arrived and the paramedics were really pleased with how she was doing but they've taken them all off to hospital now to check her over just to be sure.'

'And you were OK?'

She smiled. 'I am and thank you for asking. You get me like no one else does.'

'Meadow, you mean the world to me.'

They lay there, staring at each other for the longest time, not saying a word but not needing to either.

She reached up and stroked his face. 'I love you.'

His eyes widened. 'Carousel or rollercoaster?'

She smiled. That felt like the easiest and the hardest question to answer.

'Mummy,' Star said, sleepily. She peered at her mum blearily. 'Did the lady have her baby?'

'Yes, a little girl. Sorry I wasn't here sooner.'

'That's OK, me and Bear saw Snuggles,' Star said.

'The dog?'

'Yes and I fed him and stroked him and he lay down with his head in my lap.'

'Sounds like you've made a friend.'

'He was smitten with her,' Bear said.

Star climbed over Bear, shoehorning herself into the tiny gap between him and Meadow, forcing them to shuffle apart to accommodate her.

'I saw a hedgehog, Mummy,' Star said, sleepily. 'And a baby rabbit. But no foxes or badgers.'

'Maybe the webcams might pick something up again,' Meadow said, sliding an arm around her daughter.

Bear shifted onto his side and wrapped an arm around them both. There would be no more conversations tonight, at least not while Star was awake and between them. But that was OK, there was time. She closed her eyes and went to sleep with a huge smile on her face.

CHAPTER FORTY-SEVEN

Meadow woke the next morning when Star climbed over them, unzipped the tent and crawled out.

'Don't go too far,' Meadow said.

'I'm just here,' Star said and Meadow could see through the fabric of the tent that she was sitting right outside the door. The tent flap was fluttering in a gentle breeze, letting in the warm summer air, but largely shutting out the world.

Meadow turned her attention to Bear, who shuffled a bit closer to her now that Star had gone.

'Hi,' Meadow said, softly.

They were so close now, she only needed to stretch forward a few inches and she could kiss him.

'I love you too,' he whispered so that Star couldn't hear him.

Her heart leapt at hearing those words. She swallowed down the excitement that was building in her chest. 'Carousel or rollercoaster?'

He studied her face and then cupped her cheek, trailing

his thumb gently across her lips. He leaned forward slightly as if he was going to kiss her but, before he could, his mobile phone rang loudly and insistently.

He sighed and sat up to grab it.

'Hello? Oh hi Heather.'

Meadow sat up, looking away from him so he couldn't see the disappointment on her face. He'd given Heather his number. That thought didn't fill her with joy.

She pushed back the duvet and climbed out the tent, leaving him to talk to her alone.

'Shall we go home and get changed and then go and have some breakfast?' Meadow said.

Star nodded, getting to her feet. 'Last night was fun but camping makes me tired.'

Meadow nodded. 'I know what you mean. Come on, you'll probably feel more awake after a shower.'

Star took her hand and then stopped. 'Is Bear coming?'

'He'll probably see us at breakfast,' Meadow said and as they walked off through the trees she couldn't help but feel thoroughly confused.

CHAPTER FORTY-EIGHT

While Star was in the shower, Meadow decided to drop AstralSurfer a message. She had done what he suggested the night before and it had worked out wonderfully. She opened Connected Hearts and clicked on their conversation.

Thought I'd give you an update on last night's dating event. It was weird to sniff so many people's t-shirts, some were nice, most were not. And I did what you suggested and asked my friend to sniff me directly to see if he liked my scent. And he did, very much. Then when we were sniffing t-shirts we both made sure to only scan each other's t-shirt so we matched. It was lovely and I thought maybe this was it, we had finally admitted we wanted each other. We camped out last night with my daughter which is obviously not the right time for huge declarations of love, but this morning, when she got up and left us alone in the tent, I thought he was going to kiss me, but then his phone rang and it was the woman he matched with at the speed dating. I left him in the

tent to talk to her and I have no idea where I stand. If he gave her his number then he must be interested in her.

He started replying almost straightaway. **Is your friend the kind of man to sleep with or date multiple women at once?**

Meadow smiled. **Not at all, he is the loveliest man I've ever known.**

He replied. **Well I wouldn't worry about this other woman. If he matched with her at speed dating, then his details would have been automatically shared by the event. I've done these things before and that's how they work. I would listen to the lady who organised the event and trust that he matched with her because of your date not hers.**

Meadow groaned. Of course that was why Heather had Bear's number. She had also received an automated email with his telephone number after they had matched too. Her heart soared with hope again. He had been going to kiss her right after he had told her he loved her. Maybe they did have some kind of future after all.

Thank you for that. Of course you're right. I'm so rubbish at all of this and I would have been lost without you. I'm sorry that our conversation seems to have shifted from us dating to you giving me advice on how to date someone else.

I just want you to be happy, Twilight. Do you have another event tonight?

Yes, kiss speed dating followed by dinner in the dark.

So you'll finally get to kiss him again after all these years. I think you'll soon be able to tell if he loves you or not from the kiss.

Her heart leapt at the thought. **It is in the dark though, we might not be able to tell who we are kissing.**

I have no doubt at all that you will know and so will he.

She smiled at that. **I'll keep you posted.**

CHAPTER FORTY-NINE

Bear hadn't come to breakfast so it kind of felt a little awkward when he turned up in the office after. Meadow had no idea what to say to him. They had nearly kissed. But then he'd spent the last hour or so chatting to Heather so, despite what AstralSurfer had told her, she still felt a bit confused.

He seemed really happy though, walking into the office whistling to himself and sitting at the desk with a big grin on his face.

After he had done his daily checks on the website, he turned to Meadow. 'So, last event tonight.'

Meadow forced a smile on her face. 'Yes. Umm, two events actually. Kiss speed dating and dinner in the dark. I'm not really looking forward to the kissing one, but the dinner in the dark should be fun.'

'Kiss speed dating?' Indigo said.

'We have twenty seconds to kiss someone in the dark to see if there is an intimate connection before we move on to the next person.'

Indigo wrinkled her nose. 'Is it me or is that a bit gross?'

'It's not just you,' Meadow said.

'I'm quite looking forward to it,' Bear said.

Meadow stared at him, feeling a little bit hurt by that after what they nearly shared this morning. He was looking forward to kissing thirty different women?

'And how do you think Heather will feel about you kissing so many people?' Meadow said.

'I don't think she'll care, I told her this morning that it wasn't going to work between us.'

Meadow's eyes widened. 'You did?'

'Yes, it was not a great conversation to have, but we ended up having a chat about dating and relationships. She's been in love with her neighbour for three years so her heart wasn't really in it anyway. I talked to her about being brave and telling him how she feels. We actually left on good terms.'

'What excellent advice,' Indigo said.

Bear nodded. 'Love is a risk, but the positives far outweigh the negatives.'

'So how many people will you be kissing?' Indigo said.

'Around thirty,' Meadow said.

Indigo's look of disgust deepened. 'You're going to kiss thirty different people in one night?'

'I know, I'm not looking forward to it at all. I was actually thinking of skipping that one and just turning up for the dinner.'

'You have to go,' Bear said, insistently. 'How will you meet your soul mate if you don't attend all the events?'

'I'm not going to meet my soul mate by sharing my saliva with thirty different men.'

'Look, you made me go to the pheromone event when the thought of sniffing all those t-shirts repulsed me, you have to do this one in return,' Bear said.

He had a point but she couldn't help being really hurt that he was so looking forward to kissing all these women.

'The way I see it, if you find someone you really enjoy kissing, why not stick with them. Remove yourself from the dating event and just kiss the person you really want to be with,' Bear said, his eyes locked on hers.

Her heart leapt. Was that why he was so looking forward to it because he would get the chance to kiss her?

'I suppose the silver lining in this event is that at some point in the evening you two will get to kiss each other,' Indigo said, voicing Meadow's thoughts.

Meadow looked at Bear to see his reaction to that. He looked like he was trying to keep the smile off his face.

'Oh yes, we will. I hadn't really thought of that,' Bear said, innocently, and looked back at his computer as if he was completely blasé about the idea. Although the tone of his voice belied that.

Meadow couldn't help the smile from spreading across her face. She glanced across at Indigo, who had obviously picked up on Bear's tone of voice, too, and was grinning at her.

Suddenly the kissing event was looking up.

CHAPTER FIFTY

Cars and vans had been leaving all morning as Dwelling packed up for another year. It had been a huge success and all the guests had enjoyed the different workshops and the music. As always there was much talk about how to make it bigger and better for the following year. Meadow was hopeful that it wouldn't get much bigger because, in her eyes, the attraction of the event was that it was small, intimate, somewhere everyone knew everyone else. If it was bigger, she felt it would lose that.

There were a few honks of horns outside as people shouted goodbye and Meadow moved to the door to wave a few visitors off. She was hoping to see Leah before she left, although Leah had promised to come and say goodbye.

Leah's car was still there and as Meadow stepped outside she could see her giving someone a hug goodbye. Meadow waited for her to finish and waved at the man who was walking out with Cucumber the iguana on his shoulder.

Leah spotted her and came over, linking her arm with

Meadow and casually walking her away from the reception area.

'Well, I think this year's festival went well,' Meadow said.

'It did, another big success,' Leah said.

'It was lovely seeing you again.'

'You too.'

'You're welcome to stay here anytime. It doesn't just have to be once a year.'

'Oh, we'll be back for the wedding,' Leah said.

'River's?'

'Yours.'

Meadow smiled and rolled her eyes. Leah turned to face her. 'Just tell him you love him. You will always regret not telling him if you don't. Life is too short for regrets and something that big and powerful should be celebrated, not buried away.'

Meadow sighed. 'I will try.'

Leah smiled and hugged her. 'I'll see you in a few months. I feel an autumn wedding is on the cards.'

Meadow smiled and hugged her back.

'Good luck with the baby.'

Leah walked over to Charlie and took his hand, giving Meadow another wave.

Meadow watched her go. It really was time to tell Bear how she felt. She didn't want to hide it any more.

CHAPTER FIFTY-ONE

Meadow stood nervously in the holding room waiting to be taken off into the kissing corridor.

Imogen had already done her big speech about how things like kissing, cuddles and sex release completely different chemicals in the brain than talking to someone. She'd explained the rules, twenty seconds of kissing, no talking, and then move on when the bell rang. If people enjoyed the kiss they were to push a button on their wristband to say they wished to be matched with the other person and if the other person did the same then they would be matched after. There was a strict no touching rule. Faces and heads were allowed to be touched but nowhere else.

All the men had been taken off to line one wall of a dark corridor and the women were just about to be called in to join them.

Imogen tapped the microphone to get everyone's attention. 'Ladies, if I can ask you all to make a line over here at the entrance to the corridor, but can you stand in numerical order.'

Meadow frowned. That was a bit odd. If they were going to kiss all the men, why did it matter what order they were in? Perhaps it was to do with the computer program that would match them. But as she was number one, she joined the front of the queue.

There were murmurs of excitement around the room as women moved to take their place in line. Imogen carried on talking as the last women joined the queue behind Meadow. 'We're going to walk you into the dark corridor in a moment, you'll be next to a wall and I want you to find the right-hand wall where you should find a rope, follow that rope as far as you can. Me and my assistants will make sure you are standing in front of a man. When the bell rings you will have twenty seconds to step forward and kiss that man. No touching, no talking. Tonight is purely about the kiss. When the bell rings again you should stop, find the rope to the man's right and follow it until you meet another man. If you enjoyed that kiss, don't forget to press the button on your watch to signify you'd like to be matched with that person. Me and my assistants will be in there making sure you're all OK. So if you want out just move back against the back wall and wave your hands and one of us will remove you.'

Imogen pulled on her night-vision goggles and Meadow saw her assistants doing the same and, the next thing, she was marching off into the darkened corridor and Meadow and the other women followed her.

They were plunged into darkness almost immediately and Meadow quickly found the wall to her right and slowly followed it along without any idea where she was going. She heard shuffling behind her but couldn't see any men.

Suddenly a hand reached out to her arm to stop her.

'Here you go, if you turn to your left you'll be facing your first kiss,' Imogen said.

Meadow turned tentatively to the left, her eyes scanning the impenetrable darkness but she couldn't even see her hand in front of her face.

'Don't start kissing until you hear the bell ring.'

Meadow heard her move away and she thought she heard the sound of a curtain being pulled across a rail but she wasn't sure why.

She wondered what the first man would be like to kiss and when she would get to kiss Bear. Would he recognise her? Would their kiss bring back memories for him? Would she recognise him? It had been several years since they had kissed.

Suddenly the bell rang and Meadow immediately moved forward.

She reached out tentatively and made contact with what felt like the man's chest, she moved carefully forward, reaching out for his face and found his lips. She leaned up and kissed him. He let out a little moan of need against her lips and cupped her face and really started kissing her back.

Suddenly she knew without a doubt that she was kissing Bear. His kiss was so familiar, his scent surrounding her, it was him.

Had he recognised her? Did he know who he was kissing? This kiss was everything. Her heart soared. There was so much passion, need and desire in this kiss, like it could very easily lead to something much more if they weren't in a room with fifty-eight other people. He moved his arms around her, pulling her close which was completely against the rules but she didn't care. She slid her arms around his neck, pressing herself tight against him.

The bell rang to say their twenty seconds were up and Bear let out a moan of protest against her lips. She wasn't done either, far from it. She clung onto him, continuing the kiss, and he shuffled her against the rear wall and into the furthest corner, removing them both from the kissing fest.

Her dress was low at the back and when he slid his hands up and stroked her skin she nearly exploded from a sheer desperation to be with him. She let out a groan that sounded like a roar, thankfully stifled by his lips. He cradled the back of her head in the sweetest way, tilting her head back, and he took advantage of that by pressing his mouth to her throat.

She was panting. There was no other way to describe the heavy breathing, the increased heart rate like she'd run a hundred miles. Her legs felt like jelly and the only thing holding her up was Bear's weight pinning her to the wall. She heard the bell ring again to indicate the next kiss was over. They were getting through them way too quickly. He moved his mouth to her shoulder, running his hand down her arm as she stroked the hair at the back of his neck. This kiss was the most magnificent kiss of her entire life.

It was so much easier, kissing in the dark, hiding their identities, no talking or explanations, just kissing. What would he do if she stopped him now and told him who she was? Would he carry on kissing her regardless? Would he be appalled? He must know, there was no way he would kiss a stranger like this, he would be too respectful for that. This kiss was the kind you shared with someone you knew.

He returned his mouth to hers, pressing himself impossibly tighter against her. She hooked a leg around his hip. His greedy hands were devouring her, wanting her.

She had to put a stop to this because if she didn't he'd soon be making love to her against the wall and she didn't think she would have the willpower to stop him.

She pushed him back ever so slightly and he responded instantly, his breath heavy against her lips as he pulled away.

'Sorry,' his voice was croaky and no more than a whisper.

She leaned up to kiss him again, only this time she took it really slow and gentle and he understood, kissing her back with equal tenderness, his hands now were caressing, stroking, loving her.

She lost track of how many bells she heard, but she could have stood there kissing him all night and never have tired of it.

Suddenly a different kind of alarm went off.

'Ladies and gentlemen, your kissing time is over. Ladies, if you can step away from your men and find the wall behind you and start following it out to your left. My assistants will be there to help you if you are having trouble. Men, if you could stay where you are for a moment until all the women are out and then we'll help you out too.'

Bear pulled away slightly, both of them were breathing heavily. He kissed her on the forehead and then stepped back to let her go.

She took a moment or two to catch her breath, to make sure she could stand without her legs giving way beneath her, and then she moved towards the entrance along the wall. She paused as she heard other people shuffling around her to make sure she pressed the button on her wristband so she would match with him. After a kiss like that how could she not? It might be awkward if he had no idea he'd been kissing his best friend like his life depended on it but it was time things came to a head. Maybe it was time, once and for all, to find out whether he had feelings for her too. And if he didn't maybe she could finally move on with her life. She pressed the button a few more times for good measure. She followed the wall back out into the waiting area, blinking at the bright lights as her eyes became accustomed to them.

Imogen was waiting at the front of the room and gave Meadow a knowing smirk. Christ, Meadow hoped she hadn't seen too much of their kiss. Things had got a bit too heated for them to have an audience.

Meadow watched as Bear finally came out and he looked around the room, his eyes finding hers. He immediately walked over to her.

'I have just had the best kiss of my entire life,' Bear said.

She smiled. 'Really?'

'Oh god, it was insanely good,' his eyes locked with hers and in that instant she knew he knew who he'd been kissing. 'If she hadn't slowed things down I would have made love to her right there and then in the corridor, the kiss was that good.'

She gasped at hearing him say that and tears filled her eyes, a huge smile spreading across her face.

He stepped closer and wiped the tears gently from her cheeks. 'It's OK,' he whispered. 'I think we both knew we would end up here eventually. It just took us a little time.'

More tears joined the others. 'Just to be clear, I wanted you to make love to me too. I just didn't want fifty-eight other people to hear us.'

He stared at her. 'Christ, we need to get out of here.'

He stepped back and looked around, just as Imogen switched on her microphone.

'Ladies and gentlemen,' Imogen started. 'Thank you for taking part in our kissing speed-dating event this evening. I hope you had fun. Now we're running a little behind tonight, so we're going to go straight ahead with our dinner-in-the dark event. After that has finished you will be matched with your kissing partners.'

Meadow smiled at Bear, knowing she had already found her match.

'Now, as you know, this event is about matching you genetically and we've done that by using the saliva swabs you gave us at the beginning of these events,' Imogen went on. 'We use information found in your DNA to find someone who is genetically different, specifically in chromosome six. Not only that but many aspects of your personality are also part of your genes and, based on some of the questions you answered when you registered, we can help match you to the correct personality types found in your DNA. Now this isn't an exact science, there are many studies to prove this works and just as many that prove it doesn't. Our personalities, our likes and dislikes are also shaped by our life experiences and that cannot be taken into account when looking at DNA. But it's certainly something that's worth a look.'

Meadow wondered if being matched genetically actually worked. She could understand the previous ways they had matched people but being matched because it was written in your DNA seemed a step too far.

'In a moment we will move into the restaurant, which is all in darkness. Ladies, we will seat you first and then we will bring in the men. If you are happy with your match at the end of dinner, please press the button on your wristband. Meadow, as you are number one, can I ask you to come forward first. I'll call the rest of you in numerically.'

Meadow looked at Bear. 'I'll explain that we're leaving.'

Bear nodded and Meadow walked over to Imogen.

'Me and Bear are leaving so—'

'No you can't. We've matched everyone here tonight, if you two leave, your matches will have no one to have dinner with.'

'Well, they can have dinner with each other.'

'No, they won't be genetically matched with that person, that's not fair. Look, I know you and Bear have something going on, that much was obvious by the kiss, but this is an hour out of your time. Just go in there, have dinner and conversation with someone nice, enjoy the dinner-in-the-dark experience and then you can leave. It's not a big deal. Come on. Jacob,' she called one of her assistants. 'Can you take Meadow to table one.'

Jacob appeared at her side. 'My pleasure. Meadow, you're looking fabulous this evening. Who designed this magnificent dress?'

'Umm, I did, but I…' she looked round for Bear who

was watching her with confusion.

'You made this? It's stunning. Right, put your hand on my shoulder and I'll guide you to your seat,' Jacob said, flipping his night-vision goggles over his eyes.

She glanced around at Bear again and shrugged helplessly, putting her hand on Jacob's shoulder as he guided her into the darkness. The door closed behind her and the darkness was completely consuming and very claustrophobic.

'OK, my darling, here is your seat to the left,' Jacob said and she reached her hand around until she found a sofa and sat down on it. 'I'm going to get your date now and you'll have a chance to chat for a little while before we start bringing out the food. If you need me, just shout my name and I'll come running.'

'Thanks Jacob.'

She sat there for the longest time, straining her ears to listen as other people also came into the restaurant. She listened for Jacob's return, but all she could really think about was Bear, kissing him and being with him. She didn't care who her genetic match was. Bear was the only one she was interested in. Why had she let herself be cajoled into coming in here when she and Bear had just finally got together after all this time?

She stood up. But there was no way she could find her way out without causing herself an injury.

'Jacob.'

'I'm here, my darling, and I've brought you a lovely young man. Meadow, this is Bear.'

She let out a little gasp. He was her match. She wanted to cry with relief.

'Here's your seat, just here on your right. Careful not to sit on her,' Jacob said.

She quickly sat down and she felt a hand on her head as Bear tried to find his seat safely.

'Sorry,' Bear said.

She felt him sit down next to her. Her heart was racing so fast she felt like she'd run a marathon.

'I'll leave you two lovebirds to get acquainted and I'll be back soon with your food,' Jacob said.

'Hi,' Bear said, softly.

She reached out for him, finding his shoulder and tracing up it so she could cup his face. She stroked her hand through his stubble. 'Hello.'

She found his lips with her thumb and then leaned forward and replaced her thumb with her lips, kissing him hard.

He kissed her back, caressing her face, then letting his hands wander down her arms. He sank back into the sofa, bringing her with him as the kiss continued. He was so gentle, his kisses filled with absolute adoration and tenderness. He moved back slightly, leaning his forehead against hers, his breath ragged.

She stroked his face. 'Bear, it's always been you. Always.'

He groaned. 'All those wasted years.'

'I know, but maybe we would never have made it back then, maybe we had to grow by ourselves to be ready to be together,' Meadow said. There was no point in dwelling on the past, they were here now.

He kissed her again and she ran her hand down his chest, touching the bare skin at his open collar which caused him to moan softly against her lips.

She pulled back. 'We need to get out of here.'

'Yes we do.'

Meadow sat up. 'Jacob!'

After a few moments Jacob arrived. 'I'm here, my darlings.'

'We need to leave,' Bear said.

'Oh, fallen in love already, have we?' Jacob said.

'Something like that,' Meadow said.

'OK, no problem,' Jacob said. 'Meadow, I'm standing next to you, if you can stand up and then reach out your hand, I'll place it on my shoulder, and Bear, if you can place your hand on Meadow so you can follow her, I'll guide you both out.'

Meadow did as he asked and Bear stood up behind her and slipped his hand into hers, which made her smile at how right it felt. They shuffled out through the darkness, following Jacob until suddenly they were blinking under the light of the bar area.

Imogen was still guiding people inside so Meadow and Bear said thanks to Jacob and quickly slipped past her to go outside. As soon as they were outside in the warm night air, Bear pulled her into his arms and kissed her again. The kiss went on for some time as people walked past them on the street but she couldn't have cared less what people thought.

Eventually he moved back slightly. 'I could do this all night.'

She grinned. 'Then let's do that.'

'Let's go back to mine,' Bear said.

She nodded, excitement building for what might happen when they got there. After her first disastrous experience of sex she'd never really been bothered about having it again. She wasn't scared off by it, she just hadn't been fussed about going on dates and finding someone to do it with. She'd wanted someone special and amazing to share that with, not just have sex for the sake of having sex, but now she wanted that with Bear more than ever. He ticked those boxes for her in every way.

They hurried down the street towards Bear's car and he quickly opened the door for her before running round to the driver's side. Was he having the same thoughts as she was?

They drove a short while through the town and she couldn't take her eyes off him the whole time. She couldn't wait to get her hands on him. She reached over and put a hand on his thigh and laughed when he nearly swerved off the road.

He gave her hand a squeeze and then gently removed it. 'There's no way I'm getting us home safely with your hand there.'

She smiled and looked out the window to see they were pulling into the driveway of Wishing Wood and her heart danced in her chest with nerves and excitement.

He parked next to his lodge, which was at the other end of the car park to the reception area. They both scrambled out of the car and Bear came round to her side, kissing her briefly before taking her hand and running to his lodge.

As soon as they were inside they kissed again, Bear cupping her face gently, her arms round his strong back. The kiss was everything, tender, loving, with an edge of desire and need for each other.

She barely noticed that he'd unzipped her dress and

pushed it gently off her shoulders so it fell at her feet, she was too busy enjoying the kiss to notice anything else, until he caressed his hands across her skin, lighting a fire inside her for more.

She was desperate to feel his body against hers, so she started unbuttoning his shirt, stroking his chest as she pushed it off him. The rest of their clothes came off very quickly until they were both standing there naked in his lounge, kissing and stroking and touching as if they couldn't get enough of each other.

Bear started shuffling her backwards across the lounge and into his bedroom, still kissing her. He pulled away to switch on the bedroom light and then stepped back so he could look at her, his gaze warmed her from the inside.

'Meadow, you are so beautiful.' He took her hand and led her to the bed.

She lay down and he moved to lie next to her, taking her in his arms and kissing her again, his hands wandering over her body with such love and affection. She gasped against his lips as he slipped his hand between her legs.

His touch was so gentle but confident. He knew exactly how to make her go weak and within moments she was shouting out his name, feelings crashing through her that she'd never experienced before. As the feeling subsided he kissed her hard. He pulled away slightly to grab a condom from the bedside drawers and put it on and then rolled on top of her. Her body trembled at the thought of what was coming next, she felt like she'd been waiting for this moment for years. But it was enough to make Bear pause.

'Meadow, we don't have to do this if you don't want to.

I will be blissfully happy spending the rest of the night just kissing and cuddling you.'

Meadow smiled. 'While that sounds lovely, I want to do this with you. I trust you completely and there is not a single doubt in my mind that we should be doing this, right here and now.'

He smiled and kissed her, moving deep inside her so carefully like he thought he might break her. Her heart filled with love for him at his gentleness. Every move from him was slow and considered, tender and loving, until every nerve and cell in her body was humming with complete and utter bliss.

He paused to look at her and she stroked his face.

'You OK?' he asked.

'I'm in heaven.'

He grinned and kissed her again, sliding his hand under her bum, holding her impossibly tighter against him, and that tiny movement sent her flying high, grasping at his shoulders, her breath ragged as the most incredible feeling built in her and then exploded through her like a million fireworks going off at once. He pulled back to stare at her as he fell apart too, his body trembling as he collapsed on top of her. They lay there for a while, both panting as if they'd run a marathon. He rolled off her, taking her with him so she was lying on his chest and then he scooped up one of the blankets and wrapped it round her as they tried to catch their breath. He kissed her on the head. They didn't speak because they didn't need to, but for Meadow she'd just experienced the most incredible moment of her entire life.

CHAPTER FIFTY-TWO

Meadow lay on Bear's chest looking at the stars through the huge skylight above his bed. Her body was still buzzing from the incredible sex and it had been quite a while since they'd finished. She was still stunned that her evening had ended like this, not just that she was here in Bear's arms after all this time, but the fact that she'd had earth-shattering sex.

A laugh bubbled up in her throat and she giggled into his chest.

He stroked her head. 'Just what any man wants to hear after they've had sex.'

She propped herself up to look at him. 'I just never realised sex would be like that. I knew that it would be good or nice, with the right person. I just didn't expect it to be so... magnificent.'

She realised that, as far as Bear was concerned, her limited sexual experience was with Heath and what she'd just said made it sound like he was awful in bed. She didn't want Bear to think that but for some reason he didn't even question it.

'It was magnificent because it was us, because we're meant to be together,' Bear said. 'Hands down, it was the best sex of my entire life, but I think that's because it's you and I've been waiting for this moment for the last eight years of my life.'

'I'm so sorry I messed everything up when we were younger, I wonder if I hadn't we'd be married with children of our own by now.'

'We were kids. Maybe we would have only lasted a few weeks, but now we're older we know what we want and I want you.'

She leaned up and kissed him. 'I want you too.'

She pulled back to gaze at him and he stroked her hair, the look he was giving her was one of complete and utter love.

'I can't believe we're here,' she said. 'I never thought I would ever find someone who loved me as much as I loved them. And it's you, the man I've been in love with almost my entire life. It feels like it's too good to be true.'

He frowned. 'It is true. I love you with everything I have. Don't ever doubt that.'

He kissed her again and it was quite obvious, as the kiss went on, that he wanted more.

She put a hand on his chest to stop him. 'Hang on a moment. I should text Heath and tell him I'm not coming home tonight. He might worry when he realises I'm not there later or in the morning.'

Bear nodded. 'Go for it, but be quick.'

She grinned and climbed out of bed and walked into the lounge to grab her phone from her bag. She sent a quick text.

Hey, I'm not coming home tonight, I'm staying with a wonderful man.

He was quick to reply. **Wow, how exciting. Good for you, hope you enjoy your night.**

She thought about what to reply.

'There is no finer sight in the world than you standing naked in the middle of my lounge... texting another man,' Bear said.

She looked up to see him leaning against the doorway, holding his phone in his hand.

She laughed. 'Oh shush, you know he would worry if I'm not there, just like you would.'

He grinned. 'It's fine. He's just texted me too. He knows how I feel for you. He wants to know if I'm OK as he clearly thinks you've gone home with a complete stranger and abandoned me. Shall I tell him?'

'Let's tell them tomorrow at breakfast, knowing Heath he'd be round here with a bottle of champagne to celebrate if we tell him now. Reply vaguely but positively. We don't want him to come round with a bottle of beer to commiserate you.'

Bear started typing away on his phone and Meadow did the same.

I've had the best night. I'll bring him to breakfast tomorrow so you can meet him.

Heath was quick to reply. **Isn't that a bit soon? What about Star, we should make introductions slowly.**

Meadow smiled. **Star will love him and you will too. Trust me.**

She tossed her phone back into her bag and turned back to Bear who was watching her with a smile.

'What did you tell him?' Meadow said.

'That I was having a great night.'

Meadow laughed, walking back over to him and slipping her arms around him. 'Oh he'll probably guess, I told him I was bringing my wonderful man to breakfast tomorrow to meet him. Let's hope he has the decency to stay away. Now, why don't you take me back to bed?'

'Why don't I take you right here?' Bear said, kissing her.

'Oh I'd like that very much.'

He shuffled her back against the wall and pressed a condom into her hand before his hands started exploring and caressing her.

'You wanted me to make love to you in that corridor, let's go back there,' Bear said, switching the bedroom light off, although light was still coming in from the lounge. 'I started kissing you like this,' he kissed her neck, trailing his mouth ever so slowly down to her bare shoulder. She cupped the back of his head, tilting her own head back to give him access.

'Bear!' she said, softly.

'And then you put your leg around my hip,' Bear said, hooking her knee and wrapping it around him, then kissing her again on the mouth. 'And then you slowed things down.'

'What would you have done if I hadn't?'

'Well I wouldn't have undressed you, not there in front

of everyone, but certain items would have needed to be removed, so I might have pushed your dress down slightly so I could do this.'

He bent his head and kissed her breast with the slightest of touches but it made her desperate for more. He moved his mouth across her breast, slipping her nipple into his mouth which made her cry out.

'Then I would probably have removed your knickers, so I could do this,' Bear said, slipping his hand between her legs, making that sensation build in her stomach, making every nerve in her body come alive as the feeling grew and then suddenly exploded through her, causing her to shout out noises she had never made before.

She clung to him, trying to catch her breath.

'And I would have kissed you to drown out those noises, but here, well, I love to hear it.'

'And then what would you have done?'

Bear took the condom from her and put it on. 'Well I didn't have one of these in the corridor, another reason why sex would probably have been a bad idea, but if I had, then I might have picked you up like this.'

He lifted her and she wrapped her arms and legs around him and he moved inside her, making her gasp against his lips as he pinned her against the wall.

There were no more words after that, there was no need as he held her tight, moving against her slowly, kissing her leisurely as if he had all the time in the world. He dropped his mouth to her throat, giving her gentle kisses there too. He started getting faster and that feeling built in her quickly, fizzing through her body and then bubbling over like a bottle of champagne, her body trembling as their groans mingled on their lips.

She pulled back slightly to look at him, her breath heavy against his lips. 'As second kisses go, that would have been amazing.'

CHAPTER FIFTY-THREE

Meadow walked towards the restaurant holding Bear's hand. She was feeling happier than she'd ever been in her life but, as he pushed his way through the entrance, letting go of her hand as he grappled with the door, she was surprised to see Heath waiting for her just inside.

'Is everything OK? Where's Star?' Meadow said.

'She's inside with River and Indigo. I thought I better meet the man first before we introduce him to Star,' Heath said, looking over Meadow's shoulder. 'I have to say this all feels a bit quick. I'm happy you're out meeting people and having fun, but we did say that we wouldn't tell her until things got serious. Just because you slept with him doesn't mean it's going to last.'

Meadow smiled; he clearly hadn't cottoned on. 'I have every confidence this man is going to be my forever.'

'I know the guy really well,' Bear said. 'I think he's a good bloke.'

Meadow stifled a giggle.

Heath frowned. 'Where is he then?'

Meadow took Bear's hand again and lifted it up. 'Right here.'

Heath took a few seconds to take in the situation before a huge smile spread across his face. He reached forward and grabbed his brother into a huge hug. 'I'm so happy for you, for you both.' He let go of Bear and hugged Meadow too. 'This is wonderful news. You two have always been so close. And I know Bear has always had feelings for you, I just had no idea if you felt the same way. This is brilliant news.'

'It is really,' Bear said. 'She's made me the happiest man in the world.'

Meadow smiled as Bear kissed her on the forehead.

Heath frowned slightly. 'How do you want to play this with Star? I know she absolutely adores Bear but this will be a new dynamic she will need to get her head around.'

'Your daughter has been trying to matchmake us all week,' Bear said.

Meadow nodded. 'She has. I've got the feeling she will be OK with this. Let's just go in there holding hands and see what she says, we don't need to announce it to her formally, she'll just get used to Bear being in our house a bit more and us kissing and cuddling together.'

'OK, let's do that, but genuinely, this is wonderful news,' Heath said.

They went into the restaurant, Meadow and Bear holding hands, and as soon as Star saw them she came running over. 'Bear, I saw Snuggles again last night at our treehouse. He came for the food at the bottom of the steps and then climbed up them to eat the food at the top and I came out to see him and he let me stroke him again and he was wagging his tail but when I went to get Daddy he ran away again. Come on, we need to come up with a plan to capture him.' Star grabbed Bear's hand and dragged him off back to the table.

Meadow looked at Heath with a smile. 'Well, that was a lot smoother than I expected.'

Heath rolled his eyes. 'She either didn't notice or Snuggles news trumps you and Bear being together.'

'It's OK, I actually prefer it this way, we'll just continue being together and if she has any questions about it, we'll answer them as they come up.'

'Good plan.'

Meadow sat down at the table next to Indigo. She smiled at River who was helping Tierra with a puzzle book she had open.

'How did it go last night?' Indigo asked. 'With the, erm…' She made quick kissing sounds with her mouth so that Star and Tierra wouldn't pick up on what they were discussing. Although neither of them would have heard anyway, Tierra's puzzle book was holding all of her attention, a little frown on her head as she tried to find the right curly line that joined the rabbit to the carrot. Star was talking very animatedly with Bear about a very convoluted plan to capture Snuggles. 'Heath said you'd found a nice friend who you had a sleepover with last night?'

'I did,' Meadow confirmed, inclining her head towards Bear. 'And it was utterly wonderful.'

Indigo looked between Meadow and Bear, her eyes widening. 'You two?' she said, her voice a near squeak with excitement.

'Yes.'

'Oh my god, that is amazing,' Indigo hugged her.

River looked up from the puzzle book in confusion. 'What's going on?'

Indigo did some elaborate gestures with her head, pointing to Meadow and Bear and then waggling her eyebrows.

'Oh,' River smiled. 'That is good news.'

'What's good news?' Star asked.

Meadow glanced at Heath and he nodded.

'Me and Bear, we're—'

'Mated for life?' Star asked.

'Yes,' Meadow said.

Star looked at Bear, who nodded.

Star grinned. 'Finally!'

Then she turned her attention back to the plan she was drawing out on a piece of paper. That was it, as far as Star was concerned. No big deal.

'Right, we have something far more important to discuss,' Bear said, giving Meadow a wink. 'Operation Catch Snuggles. It seems our little canine friend has a sore paw and I think we need to catch him sooner or later so we can have a look at it and make sure it doesn't get infected. We're going to get some sausages and meat from Alex, if everyone can carry some around with them that will be a start.'

'What about my trap idea?' Star said, pointing to her elaborate design that looked like it had come straight from an episode of *The Road Runner Show* or *Tom and Jerry*.

'We'll call that plan B,' Bear said.

CHAPTER FIFTY-FOUR

'I want to know everything,' Indigo said, sitting down next to Meadow in the office. Bear hadn't come in yet, he and Star were going out to look for Snuggles with various food treats to tempt the dog.

'I'm not telling you everything,' Meadow laughed.

'I don't want the sordid blow-by-blow,' Indigo said. 'Just how it happened.'

'Somehow we were each other's first kiss when we were doing the kiss speed dating last night, I knew straightaway it was him and I think he did too. We didn't move on for our second kiss, we just stayed in the darkness kissing each other for twenty minutes and it was wonderful and lovely and hot as hell. Then, wonderfully, he ended up being my match on the dinner-in-the-dark event too but it wouldn't have mattered if he wasn't, we'd already told each other how we felt. We skipped dinner, came back here and...' Meadow gave a contented sigh. 'It was utterly magnificent.'

'Awww, you two were meant to be together, I could see

that almost from the first moment I arrived here. I'm so glad you've finally told each other how you feel.'

'I am too.'

The phone rang and Indigo picked it up.

There was someone else she needed to tell too. She logged in to her Connected Hearts profile and wrote a message to AstralSurfer.

So last night, me and my best friend finally declared our feelings for each other and I have never felt happier in my entire life. We just fit together in a way that I share with no one else. He is my soul mate, I have no doubt about that. Thank you for all your help.

His reply took a few moments to drop through.

I'm so happy for you, honestly. This is wonderful news.

Meadow smiled. **Thank you.**

I guess this is goodbye then.

She frowned. She hadn't thought of it like that.

I'd like to stay in touch, it's been great chatting to you over the last few days. We can still be friends, if that's what you want. You have given me such wonderful advice and I'd love to return the favour when you meet the woman of your dreams, give you the female perspective. I promise not to bombard you with how loved-up I am.

He took a while to respond this time.

OK, that sounds good. I better go.

She watched his online light go out and frowned. Was it weird to offer that to a man she had been flirting with earlier in the week, someone she was potentially going to date? Was he hurt that she had found someone else? She hoped he would be OK about all of this but maybe he just needed a few days to get his head around the idea.

CHAPTER FIFTY-FIVE

Indigo had left to do some baby shopping with River, leaving Meadow and Bear alone. He was on her computer fixing a glitch with the booking system that wasn't loading properly on her screen and she was working on his.

Suddenly an email popped through from Imogen on her phone.

Dear Meadow,

I am so happy that you and Bear have finally got together, I have never known two people who were meant to be together as much as you. However, I feel I should explain a little about what happened last night.

Bear contacted me about the kissing event and asked if it could be arranged to kiss you first. As I was desperate to see you two together I was more than happy to oblige. I told him that if you two connected during that kiss to feel free to continue kissing each other and that the other women would be diverted to simply bypass him so you two would be left in peace. As that event was about connecting with someone on that intimate level I have no concerns that you matched with each other fairly. You two did connect on that level.

However, as you did sign up to be matched genetically as well as in the other ways, I feel it is my duty to tell you, you did not genetically match to Bear last night. While I was distracted taking couples to their tables, it seems Bear paid Jacob fifty pounds for him to seat Bear at your table. I'm sure this won't make any difference to your relationship with him, however if your decision to be with him was based on your belief that you were genetically matched then I'm afraid that isn't the case and I felt like you should know that.

Kind regards,
  Imogen

Meadow read the email a few times as she thought about what this meant. Bear had arranged that kiss but there was something really sexy about that, he wanted to kiss her and only her and there'd been nothing fake about his reaction to her. The genetic match thing was a bit weird but, in reality, it didn't change anything. Even before he'd come to join her inside the restaurant, she had decided she didn't care who her genetic match was, that she just wanted to be with him. They'd planned on leaving after the kissing event so she would have never found out who her genetic match was but it felt a little dishonest because she had believed that Bear was her genetic match last night and he must have known that.

She shook her head. It didn't matter. She would have probably done the same thing if the situations were reversed just so she could be with Bear again after that incredible kiss. But she would have told him what she'd done.

Just then the computer pinged with a notification from Connected Hearts and she absently clicked into it. A message from *RebeccaSexKitten*.

Hello sexy, want to get together for a good time. Love Becca

She frowned in confusion. Dick pics from men were one thing, now she was getting messages from women offering her a good time. She smiled as she realised that of course this wasn't her profile, this was Bear's as she was on his computer. Her eyes scanned the profile name at the top of the webpage to confirm it and her heart fell into her stomach. *AstralSurfer*.

No, no, no, this couldn't be right. Bear couldn't be AstralSurfer. She stared in horror at his profile name and felt sick, tears pricking her eyes.

'You OK over there?' Bear said.

She looked at him and his face fell in concern. 'What's wrong?'

'You're AstralSurfer?'

He paled. 'Shit!'

'Oh my god, you are.' Meadow got up from the computer, her hands on her face in horror.

'I wanted to tell you, I did, I hated lying to you but—'

'Oh god, you knew you were talking to me, all this time.'

'Not right away.' Bear stood up and moved towards her but she stepped back away from him and he halted. 'You told me your name was Iris Starfish, I had no idea when I started talking to you.'

'But you soon figured it out,' Meadow snapped. 'Christ, I was so stupid, how did I not see it? Oh wait, because you lied to me and said you were away with work, you were in a breakfast meeting, you were stressed out with work, and I bought it hook, line and sinker.'

'No, you don't understand, when I told you I was away with work, I didn't know then who you were. I was excited about what was happening between us after that wonderful first date and I didn't want to encourage Twilight if something was going to develop between me and you.'

'So you just kept Twilight on the back-burner just in case we didn't work out.'

'You were still messaging AstralSurfer after our wonderful date, so you were obviously keeping your options open too.'

'I didn't know how you felt,' Meadow said.

'I didn't know how you felt either. That's why I didn't want to meet Twilight, I didn't want to start something with her and then have to end it because no one mattered more to me than you. I was trying to do the right thing for both of you.'

'And the right thing by me was lying about who you are?'

He pushed his hand through his hair. 'I didn't know then.'

'When did you figure it out?' Meadow said.

'It doesn't matter.'

'It does, because I need to know how long you've been lying to me.'

He shook his head.

'How long?' Meadow said, she could hear the coldness in her words.

'I guessed when you said you needed to distract your daughter away from the iguana and then met Star shortly after and she told me how cool the iguana was. But I convinced myself I was wrong because I found Iris Starfish online. I even messaged her and when she replied I presumed that was you because, let's not forget, you lied about that too.'

'But at some point after that you knew for definite,' Meadow bypassed her tiny lie.

He swallowed. 'Yes.'

'Why didn't you tell me?'

'I couldn't.'

'What does that even mean?'

'I wanted to. God I was desperate to.'

A new thought occurred to her. 'I told you about my feelings for my best friend. You told me to let him sniff me to see if he was attracted to me. You knew then and you were playing with me.'

'No, it wasn't like that. I wanted to tell you I was in love with you, I really did. That night you were drunk I tried to tell you then, but you weren't exactly coherent, and after it was so hard to find the words. You know how hard it was, you never told me you loved me either. Eight years on after we should have said the words back then and we still couldn't be honest with each other about our feelings. I didn't know for sure how you felt before the pheromone event, other than that you thought I smelt amazing. I thought this could be a way we could share our feelings for each other without saying a word.'

'You used it to your advantage.'

'No, it wasn't like that.'

'I'm so embarrassed. I told you some really personal stuff,' Meadow said.

He had the good grace to look uncomfortable. 'I know,' he said, softly. 'I wanted to be here for you as a friend.'

'And you treated the whole thing like a game.'

'No, Meadow, this wasn't a game to me.'

'Imogen emailed me this morning to say you'd set up the kissing event and then I find out you paid Jacob so you could be my genetic match too.'

'What does that matter? We had just shared the best kiss of my entire life, there was no way I could sit politely talking to some other woman for the next two hours, when all I wanted was to be with you. That's what happened with Heather after the speed dating and I was left with her instead of being able to tell you how I felt. I didn't want a repeat of that. You said you wanted to leave before the dinner-in-the-dark event so we could be together and I could see you were getting coerced to go in there anyway, so I came in to get you out.'

Meadow shook her head. 'Was this whole thing a big game? From the beginning? You were so intent on me doing online dating and then we matched at ninety-six percent, you said that never happened. Then we conveniently matched at every event too. Was this just some big ploy to get me into bed?'

As soon as the words were out she wanted to snatch them back, because she knew she had hurt him with them. But she had already gone to bed with one man because of a lie and now she felt like it was happening all over again.

His face was like thunder when he spoke. 'Jesus Christ, Meadow, if you think that little of me, then what the hell are we even doing here? I should have told you who I was and I'm sorry I didn't. But what you've just accused me of is sickening. I have no control over us matching at ninety-six percent. We matched at the first two events, the speed dating and the group dating, because we love each other, it's as simple as that. Yes, I made damned sure I only scanned your t-shirt at the pheromone event because after sniffing you I didn't want anyone else. But you did the same too. And yes, I arranged to kiss you first at the kissing event but I certainly didn't hear any complaints from you when you were wrapped around me, panting in my ear because you were enjoying the kiss so much, so don't you dare make this into that I tricked you somehow. I know you were lied to in the past but I am not that man and if you really loved me you would know that. But then I've never been good enough for you, have I? Eight years ago you chose my brother over me because I wasn't good enough—'

'No, Bear, I didn't—'

'Yes you did. I held your hand while you gave birth because I love you, I sat with you for the next few weeks while your daughter was in an incubator because I love you. I took Star into my life because she was your daughter and so I loved her too. I have been in love with you my whole life, but it's not enough, is it. You're so scared that you're unlovable you'll latch onto any reason to prove you're right, to prove that what we have isn't real when you know in your heart that it is. I could never do anything to hurt you but if you truly believe that I have just been playing some sick game with you from the beginning then I think we better call a stop to this now.'

He turned and stormed out. She watched him go. What the hell had she done? Why had he lied about who he was? They'd been talking online for a week, why wouldn't he tell her the truth? She knew she had no right to accuse Bear of playing a game with her, he wouldn't do that, but right then she felt so confused.

CHAPTER FIFTY-SIX

Bear marched off through the trees with no idea where he was going until he arrived at the wedding chapel. He heard Heath working away inside and climbed the stairs to talk to him. His brother looked up as he walked inside.

'Hey, you come to give me a hand as River is off swanning around somewhere?'

Bear was so hurt and angry right now that handling a hammer or drill was not in his best interests.

Heath sat back on his heels as he looked at Bear. 'You OK?'

'Meadow has just found out that I'm AstralSurfer.'

'Oh shit.'

'My words exactly. I was going to tell her, I just wanted to wait a few days as you suggested so she'd forget that she might have blurted out the truth about Star in her drunken state. And the more she was talking to me about all her worries and pain from the past, it was harder to say, oh hello, it's me. And I was kind of hoping that once me and her got together, then she wouldn't want to message

AstralSurfer any more, but she told him this morning that she still wanted to be friends, help him with his dates as I had helped her. It was just getting more and more complicated.'

Bear paced across the wedding chapel. He should have come clean about all of this before, maybe not as Meadow was pouring her heart out in a drunken emotional state but certainly the next morning. He had lied to her and many times. And he supposed she was right that he had used it a little bit to his advantage when she was talking about the dating events she was going on with her friend. But it had never been malicious or with any intent to play any kind of game with her. He could understand she was pissed about him hiding behind AstralSurfer but to suggest that it had all been part of some convoluted plan to get her into bed was horrible.

'I take it she didn't react well to it?' Heath said, getting up.

'That's the understatement of the year,' Bear said and briefly told him what was said.

Heath shook his head. 'Christ, that lie that caused her to get drunk and let that dick get his hands on her messed her up a lot more than I thought.'

'Plus her parents just generally being crap and making her think she isn't worth anything. We've both been there with our own upbringing so I know how she feels, but she told me her parents hated her, that's a heavy burden to carry,' Bear said. He looked out the window at the sea beyond. He should have been more sympathetic to her past instead of getting hurt by her lashing out to protect herself. He needed to prove to her that he would always be there, that she might get scared but his love for her was constant. He sighed. But she had to play a part in that too, she had to trust him enough to let him in.

'I need to talk to her,' Bear said.

'At the risk of giving you more crappy advice, as it's my fault you didn't come clean initially, I think you might need to give her a few hours to calm down.'

Bear let out a heavy sigh as he looked out the window again. He could see Wisteria Cottage peeking through the trees, he could see the purple front door and the purple window frames. He had hoped he might move in there with Meadow one day, but she had to want that too and maybe he needed to give her some time to realise that.

CHAPTER FIFTY-SEVEN

Amelia walked into the office a short while later, but stood in the doorway, glancing over her shoulder.

'Where's Star?' Meadow said.

'Out here, putting sausages down everywhere, she is determined to catch this dog,' Amelia said.

Meadow smiled weakly.

'River and Indigo not back from their baby shopping spree yet?' Amelia asked.

'Not yet.'

'And where's your young Bear?'

Meadow looked away, biting her lip so she didn't cry again.

'Oh no, what's happened?' Amelia said as Meadow moved to her side to keep an eye on Star.

Meadow explained what had happened.

'But the worst thing is that he thinks I slept with Heath to get back at him. He thinks I chose to sleep with Heath instead of him and I'm not sure he will ever get over that.'

'I'm pretty sure the thing that has Bear most upset is

that you chose Heath to raise Star with and not him. In his eyes, you didn't think Bear was good father material.'

Meadow stared at her in horror.

'Bear grew up thinking he wasn't good enough, just like you did. It's got to hurt him that you didn't think he was enough either.'

Meadow swallowed, tears pricking her eyes again. 'You know?'

'Of course I knew. You and Heath had never ever looked at each other romantically. It just didn't make sense that you would end up in bed together. I don't blame you for doing what you did, not for one second. As you know, I was fourteen when I got pregnant with Bear's dad and his twin brother and was forced to give them up for adoption. I have never ever forgiven myself for it. If a knight in shining armour had come along and offered to marry me and help me raise my boys, I would have leapt at the chance if it meant I didn't have to give them up. And I know, for you, giving up Star for adoption would never have even entered your head, but I know you would have struggled without a home or a job. You absolutely did the right thing. But I did wonder why you didn't choose Bear instead of Heath and I think he must wonder that too. Was it his age? I know he was only sixteen but he would have moved heaven and earth to give Star the best upbringing he possibly could.'

'Bear knows too?' Meadow asked quietly.

'I would imagine so. I don't know for sure, it's not something we've spoken about. But I can't see that he would get that upset about you and Heath sleeping together eight years ago, he's slept with his fair share of women over the years and you two weren't together at the time. When Bear said you chose Heath over him because he wasn't good enough, I'm guessing he means that you chose Heath to be Star's father.'

Meadow glanced around to see that Star was on the other side of the grassy field, placing sausages in the trees. There's no way she could have heard.

Meadow shook her head. Christ, she'd had no idea that anyone outside her and Heath knew the truth. All this time, she'd been so fearful that people would judge her for her deceit or not accept her or Star into the family when the Brookfield brothers had always been there for her, giving her the family that she had missed out on for so long. To think that Bear knew and was hurting over her *choice* eight years before, that made her heart break for him.

She was still angry over his lie about AstralSurfer but she had lied to Bear for the last eight years.

She really needed to talk to him.

CHAPTER FIFTY-EIGHT

Meadow was lying in bed staring at the ceiling. It was gone two in the morning and she couldn't sleep. She had gone to Bear's house as soon as Indigo had got back but there was no sign of him and she still had no idea what she was going to say to him. Then she'd got caught up in the normal night-time activities of cooking Star some dinner and watching a movie together. Heath had gone out to his weekly pool night so she hadn't even had a chance to talk to him about the whole thing, not that they could have any kind of real conversation with Star around. She had hoped Bear would come to see her but she guessed he was still hurting over the whole thing and she hated that.

She picked up her phone and was just about to send him a text when a scream from Star made her leap out of the bed. She ran to Star's bedroom. Her daughter was sitting up in bed, her breathing heavy, visibly upset.

Meadow switched on the light, quickly moved over to the bed and picked her up. 'Hey, what's the matter?'

'There was an alien,' Star snuffled, wrapping her arms

tight around Meadow. 'It had lots of arms and legs and big teeth.'

'It was just a dream, baby,' Meadow said, stroking her head.

'It ate Bear.'

'Bear is fine, I promise you. It was just a dream.'

Star's breath shuddered as she buried her face in Meadow's shoulder. 'Can we go and see Daddy?'

'Of course we can,' Meadow said. She grabbed the blanket from Star's bed, wrapped it around her and carried her downstairs. Whenever she had a nightmare, which thankfully wasn't that often, it was always Heath she wanted to cuddle. Although when Star stayed with Heath, she always wanted Meadow if she woke with a nightmare.

Meadow slipped outside onto the rope bridge and walked across to Heath's treehouse, letting herself in. She'd got halfway up the stairs when Heath came running down them – obviously she'd just woken him up, judging by his dishevelled sleepy state.

'Hey, is she OK?'

'Just a dream about aliens,' Meadow said, passing her daughter into her dad's arms.

'Hey,' Heath murmured into Star's ear. 'You OK?'

Star nodded against him as he carried her back up the stairs. Meadow followed them up. She watched as Heath settled Star in the bed next to him and then held up the duvet for Meadow to come and join them.

Meadow climbed into bed behind Star, curling her body around her as Heath held Star against his chest.

Star let out a sigh of contentment and within minutes seemed to drift straight back off to sleep. It occurred to

Meadow that it wasn't Heath Star wanted when she had a nightmare, it was both of them cocooned around her protectively like this.

'How you doing?' Heath whispered, when Star started snoring softly.

Meadow sighed. 'I don't know.'

'Bear loves you, you know that.'

'He lied to me.'

Heath shook his head. 'Yeah and that was my fault.'

Meadow frowned in confusion. 'What do you mean?'

'Do you remember that night you came home drunk after that group dating event a few days ago?'

'Yes of course.'

'Well you started texting Bear, well AstralSurfer. You told him all about your first and only experience with Henry.'

Meadow gasped. 'No! No I did not. I have never told anyone that.'

But even as she said it she knew that wasn't true. She'd woke up the next day with the absolute certainty that she'd told someone.

'Well alcohol loosens those lips, you told Bear everything. He came to me ready to punch my lights out because he thought I was the scum who lied to you to get you into bed. I had to tell him the truth.'

Meadow felt tears prick her eyes. 'Heath, I'm so sorry.'

'It's OK, really.'

'No it isn't. We promised each other we'd never tell anyone.'

'I promise you I wasn't angry. I was more concerned about you.'

'I can't believe Bear knows, Amelia knows too and she said she suspected he knew, but he never said anything.'

Meadow swallowed the lump of emotion in her throat. All her worries that Bear would treat her and Star differently if he knew were completely unfounded. He'd gone camping with Star, played with her, his love as strong as it had always been. And his relationship with Meadow had obviously deepened in the last few days too, despite knowing her deepest secrets.

'He never said anything because I made him promise not to. You were always so worried about my brothers finding out, unnecessarily it seems. In the beginning you were scared they wouldn't accept you into the family if they knew the truth and later you were scared about them finding out the lie. I always knew they would have taken you in, just like I did. They love you. Well, Bear more than River obviously. But I knew you'd be upset that you'd told anyone and that Bear of all people knew, so I convinced him to hide it from you. Bear logged in to your Connected Hearts account and deleted that whole conversation and then I persuaded him not to tell you that he was AstralSurfer just in case you did remember telling him. He only found out that night that you were Twilight Rose and he wanted to tell you who he was but what you told him made it really awkward for him to come clean. I suggested that he just stop messaging you as AstralSurfer and he would slowly fade away and then you'd never need to know. But that didn't happen.'

'He said he wanted to be there for me as a friend,' Meadow said, her voice choked. 'But he kept quiet about who he was just so I wouldn't be upset by my own stupid blabbermouth?'

Heath nodded.

Meadow groaned softly. 'Even when we had that stupid row about him lying to me, he never told me why. Even then, he was trying to protect me.'

'Yeah.'

'Christ, I need to talk to him.'

Star stirred and Meadow curled herself tighter around her.

'Go and see him before breakfast,' Heath whispered.

Meadow nodded. 'I think we need to tell River and Indigo too, I don't want them to have to worry about a premature birth with their baby. I mean, premature births can happen for many reasons but genetics is one of them and they shouldn't carry that extra burden of worry unnecessarily. And as Bear and Amelia know, it's only right that they do, too.'

'I agree.'

'I am sorry that this has all come out.'

'Please don't be, it doesn't change anything.'

'You're a good man, Heath Brookfield.'

He smiled. 'I'm the best.'

Meadow laughed and then stifled it in her pillow.

She closed her eyes and crossed everything she had that Bear would forgive her.

CHAPTER FIFTY-NINE

Meadow woke while it was still dark. She opened her eyes and immediately realised Star wasn't there. She sat up and put a hand out to where her daughter had been. The sheets were cold.

She got out of bed and wandered to the toilet to check if Star was in there but there was no sign of her and the treehouse was unnaturally quiet.

'Star!' Meadow called out, her heart starting to race. There was no answer.

Heath was already up out of bed, hearing the alarm in her voice.

'Shit, did she go to her room?' he said, running up the stairs to the second floor.

Meadow knew from the silence she wasn't there. She raced down the stairs, out the door and across the rope bridge, bursting into her own treehouse. 'Star!'

There was no answer but Meadow checked all the rooms just to be sure but there was no sign of her. She grabbed her shoes, her phone, her walkie-talkie and a hoodie she threw on over her pyjamas, then grabbed Star's spare inhaler and flew back across the bridge.

She shook her head at Heath's hopeful face. 'Fuck, Heath, where the hell is she?'

'She got up to go to the toilet maybe half hour or so ago, I thought she would come back when she was done but I must have fallen back to sleep again so I didn't notice. Jesus Christ, why would she leave? Where would she go?'

Heath snatched up his phone and called River, explaining the problem, and Meadow quickly phoned Bear.

He answered on the second ring. 'Hey, you OK?'

'Star's gone missing. She's not at Heath's or mine.'

'Bloody hell. I'll check the east side down towards the river. That's where we camped, maybe she headed down there. I'll take my walkie-talkie and let you know if I find anything.'

'I'll head up to the reception and the restaurant,' Meadow said.

'I'll take the area where the new treehouses are. River is going to take the north side and Indigo is going to the west,' Heath said.

Meadow nodded and ran out the house.

CHAPTER SIXTY

Bear tore through the trees, his torch beam flying over every surface, shouting out Star's name. Though maybe he needed to go slower, if she called out he wouldn't hear her with the speed he was going through the woods. He stopped for a second, his torch scanning the trees, the ground, the bushes.

'Star!'

There was no answer so he carried on running. She had to be in the woods somewhere.

Suddenly he heard a dog bark. He stopped still, his breath heavy, his chest panting. Could it be Snuggles?

'Star!'

The dog barked again. With nothing else to go on, Bear ran off in the direction of the bark.

'Star!'

'Bear!' Star called out.

He nearly sank to the ground in relief. She was here and she was alive, he could cope with anything else.

He burst through the trees into a small clearing and

stopped when he saw Snuggles lying on the ground next to Star, as she propped herself up against the dog.

He grabbed his walkie-talkie. 'I've got her, she's OK, I'll bring her back to Wisteria Cottage.'

Meadow's voice came over the airwaves immediately. 'Oh my god, is she OK? Where are you, I'll come down. Does she need her inhaler?'

Star shook her head.

Bear looked around. They weren't near any treehouses for him to be able to direct her. In fact he had run through the trees in such a rush he couldn't exactly pinpoint where he was.

'She's fine, I promise, I'll be back at your house soon,' Bear said. They didn't need Meadow wandering aimlessly through the dark woods too. He put the walkie-talkie back in his pocket.

'Star, thank god you're OK. We've all been so worried. What are you doing out here?' Bear moved very slowly towards them just in case any sudden moves upset Snuggles.

'I heard barking and when I looked out the window I saw Snuggles. You said we need to catch him sooner rather than later because of his poorly leg and you said that maybe some dog toys or a ball might be the way to do it, so I took one of my balls and came outside. He loved it. I thought if I played with him for a bit he might let me catch him. We were running and playing together and I didn't realise how far I'd gone and when I tried to go back home I got lost and scared, then I fell over and hurt my ankle and couldn't get back up. But Snuggles lay down with me and he's kept me warm.'

'Oh Star.' Bear moved closer, kneeling down. Snuggles eyed Bear but he clearly could tell he didn't mean either of them any harm. 'You shouldn't have come out here alone in the dark. And how would you have caught him, you don't have a lead or anything like that?'

'I didn't think of that, I just wanted to help Snuggles.'

Bear smiled. 'Let me look at your ankle.'

Star indicated which one it was and Bear gently felt around. Nothing seemed out of place so it was more likely to be a sprain than anything else.

'You better tell your mum you're OK, she'll want to hear your voice,' Bear said, offering out his walkie-talkie.

Star pressed the button. 'Mummy, I'm OK, Bear is here and Snuggles is here too.'

'OK, honey, I love you,' Meadow said, her voice clearly tearful.

'Right, let's get you home.' Bear stood up and then lifted Star so she was sat on his hip.

'What about Snuggles?' Star said.

'I haven't got a lead either, but maybe he might follow us. He seems attached to you.'

'He looked after me, Bear, we need to look after him as well.'

'We will. I think we need a new cooler name for him though. How about Hero?'

Star smiled. 'I like it. Snuggles didn't really suit him anyway. Come on, Hero.'

And whether it was the new name or whether the dog would have come anyway, Hero was quick to follow as Bear started walking through the trees.

After a short while, Bear spotted a few treehouses and

joined the main path that led through the trees, starting to recognise where he was.

'Was Mummy angry?' Star said.

'I think probably more scared than anything,' Bear said, taking another path that would lead them to Wisteria Cottage.

'I didn't want to wake them, I thought I'd only be outside for a few minutes,' Star said.

'I'm sure your mummy and daddy would prefer that you wake them than for you to go outside alone in the middle of the night and they could have helped you catch him.'

Wisteria Cottage came into view and Bear could see Meadow pacing around at the bottom of the steps. God, his heart hurt just looking at her. They had to sort this out between them, he refused to believe this was over. But she had called him when she needed him so maybe all hope wasn't lost.

Meadow spotted them and ran flat out across the wood to meet them.

'Oh my god, Star, I was so worried, what were you thinking?' Meadow said, as Bear passed Star into her arms. Meadow hugged her tight.

'I wanted to help Snuggles,' Star said, her voice muffled against her mum's chest. 'I mean Hero. Me and Bear renamed him. When I fell over, Hero stayed with me and kept me warm until Bear found me.'

'Well, it sounds like they are both heroes,' Meadow said. She looked at him. 'Thank you.'

'I'm always here for you,' Bear said.

'I know,' Meadow said, softly. 'I—'

Just then Heath burst through the trees and swallowed Meadow and Star up in a big hug.

'Star, don't you ever do that again, I have never been so worried in my entire life as I have been tonight,' he said, kissing the top of his daughter's head.

'I'm sorry Daddy, I just wanted to help the dog. He was outside and I wanted to try and catch him.'

Heath sighed as he held them both tight.

'He looked after me when I fell over, we need to look after him,' Star said.

'We will, I promise,' Heath said.

Bear glanced around for the dog but, true to form, he'd run off again.

'Let's get you back inside and warmed up and get you checked over,' Heath said.

'She said she's hurt her ankle, her left one,' Bear said. 'I did look at it and I don't think it's broken.'

'Thank you,' Heath said, with such gratitude that Bear knew it wasn't just for the information. Heath turned back to Meadow. 'River and Indigo have taken Tierra back to their house but they've said to call them if we need them.'

'I should go too,' Bear said.

'Absolutely not,' Heath said. 'I think I owe you a can of beer.'

'No, it's fine, don't worry,' Bear said. He didn't want the awkwardness of being somewhere he wasn't wanted.

Heath shifted Star onto one hip. 'Why don't I leave Meadow to persuade you to stay?'

Meadow smiled as Heath moved off. 'I think I owe you an explanation and an apology. Will you stay for that?'

He stared at her, his heart leaping in his chest. 'You don't owe me anything. It's me who should be sorry.'

She shook her head and glanced over at Wisteria Cottage where Heath was climbing up the stairs. 'I need to go and make sure Star is OK, and then we can talk. Please stay.'

Bear nodded.

Meadow quickly ran to catch up with Heath. Bear had a last look around for Hero but, with no sign of the dog, he climbed up the stairs and waited in Meadow's lounge. He could see through the window that over in Heath's treehouse they were both making a big fuss of their daughter.

Bear went to the fridge and grabbed some food and then went back downstairs to the wood and put it on the ground for Hero. He then returned upstairs and left some more near the door in the hope Hero might come upstairs again and they could catch him. He went back into the lounge and paced and sat then paced some more.

He heard the door open and looked up to see Meadow had come back. Before he could say a word, she moved quickly across the room towards him, tugged his t-shirt down towards her and kissed him. He immediately wrapped his arms around her and kissed her back, sighing with relief against her lips.

She looked at him. 'I love you with everything I have. And yes, I might get scared sometimes but I promise I won't ever push you away again.'

'I promise never to let you.'

She smiled. 'I'm so sorry for what I said yesterday about you manipulating the dating and us matching. That was stupid and thoughtless. I never really believed that, I was just scared because you'd lied to me and I was hurt so I lashed out. I should never have doubted you. You have always been there for me, when Star was born and ever since then, for every tiny and huge thing. You have been my rock and I love you so much.'

'I will always be there for you,' Bear said. 'Because I love you too. But I need to explain about why I never told you the truth...' he stopped talking when she put a finger over his lips.

'Heath told me you did it to protect me and I think I've impossibly fallen in love with you a little bit more. I told you my secret.'

Bear nodded. 'Yes and I didn't want you to get hurt because of it.'

'You are a beautiful, wonderful person, Bear Brookfield, and you will never know how completely grateful I am to have you in my life. But there's something I need to clear up. I never chose Heath to be Star's dad over you. I came here after my parents chucked me out because this place and you three have always been my home. I came here because I needed a shoulder to cry on, because I had nowhere else to go. Heath was the first to find me and brought me back to his lodge where I sobbed my heart out. I never came here looking for marriage or a dad for my baby, that thought never even entered my head. When Heath offered to marry me and help me raise my baby, I was so scared about my future that I said yes. And when we got married in Scotland with two strangers we'd grabbed from the street to witness it, my heart broke a little because in my dreams I would always be marrying you. And in some ways, I wish I had never trapped Heath in a loveless marriage, that I had raised my baby alone. But I can never regret the decision I made because Star has the most incredible dad in the world with Heath. But I never chose him over you. He chose us.'

Bear swallowed the lump in his throat. 'I get it now. I understand.'

'I have always loved you,' Meadow said. 'And I always will.'

'I love you too, you have always been my world.'

Bear kissed her.

The kiss turned to something more and she dragged his t-shirt off. He pushed the hoodie off her shoulders and slipped his hands underneath her pyjama top, running his thumbs over her breasts, and she made a noise against his lips that was pure need.

Suddenly a movement caught his eye and standing at the still open door was Hero, cocking his head as he watched them.

Bear pulled back slightly from Meadow. 'We have a visitor.'

Meadow looked around and smiled when she saw Hero. 'We need to catch him, if nothing else to stop Star wandering round the woods in the middle of the night trying to find him.'

'I agree.'

'Let me grab some more food,' she said, running to the kitchen.

Bear grabbed Star's skipping rope and looped one end, tying it in a knot so he had a mini lasso, the kind you might use to catch a horse – and Hero was almost big enough to qualify for that.

Hero didn't move away as they both slowly approached him, Meadow waving a large piece of chicken at him, Bear holding out the rope. He was actually wagging his tail. Bear inched closer and Hero spotted the chicken, licking his lips. Meadow broke it into two pieces and held one piece out. Hero took the first piece gently and, as he swallowed it and Meadow offered the second piece, Bear carefully slipped the lasso over his neck and pulled the knot gently so the rope was secure. Hero didn't even flinch, he only had eyes for the second piece of chicken. Meadow fed him.

'Let's get him some more food and water, poor thing must be so hungry,' Meadow said.

Bear gently tugged the dog towards the kitchen but surprisingly he was more than happy to come. Meadow quickly filled a bowl with more chicken and a bowl of water which Hero ate and drank from greedily.

'Let's have a look at that cut too,' Meadow said, grabbing a bowl of warm water, some cotton wool and the first aid kit.

Bear smiled as he watched her. God he loved this woman.

CHAPTER SIXTY-ONE

Meadow surveyed the cut, it wasn't deep and now she had cleaned it up she could see it was OK. 'Shall we put a bandage on it?'

'Let's get him in the shower first,' Bear suggested. 'He's so dusty.'

Meadow nodded and she grabbed a bit more chicken to persuade Hero to come upstairs into the bathroom. She was surprised how compliant he was being but maybe he was just done running. He knew he was safe here, plus there seemed to be an unending supply of food, which she guessed was helping. Star was going to be over the moon they had finally caught him.

They got him in the bathroom and shut the door behind them in case he tried to do a runner once he knew what was in store for him. But when they switched on the shower, Hero wagged his tail as if he'd done this before. She watched Bear strip off down to his shorts. God he was divine. She grabbed a couple of large towels from the shelf, laying one down on the floor, then she stripped off herself so she was just in her sleep shorts. Bear stared at her, his eyes darkening with need.

She swallowed. 'We should...' she gestured to the shower.

He nodded.

With a bit of cajoling they got Hero into the shower and they washed his thick fur which, judging by the colour of the water in the shower tray, seemed to hold a lot more dirt than she'd thought. After a while they switched off the shower, got the dog out and dried him, which he obviously loved, wiggling his bum around, a big smile on his face.

'Let's see if he'll settle down in the bedroom,' Meadow said, grabbing a few more towels.

Bear gently tugged Hero towards Meadow's bedroom and once they were inside they shut the door. Meadow lay a towel down on the floor and Bear removed the lasso. Hero sniffed around the room and then, as if he knew he was home, he lay down on the towel and went to sleep.

Bear stripped out of his wet shorts and she did the same. She passed him a towel and he wrapped it around Meadow. She smiled as he rubbed her dry. When she was, she took the towel and did the same for him.

'I love you,' she said.

He smiled and pulled her into his arms, holding her close against him. 'I love you too.'

She held him tight. 'God, the last twenty-four hours have been an emotional rollercoaster.'

They stood like that for the longest time and she understood what Leah had said about loving Charlie with carousel and rollercoaster love. Bear was solid, dependable and she loved him as a friend because of that, but the excitement she felt because he was her future, the desire she felt standing here naked in his arms, that was definitely rollercoaster love.

'Come on, get into bed, we have a few hours of sleep before we need to get up,' Bear said.

She looked up at him and smiled. 'I really wasn't thinking of going to sleep right now.'

He grinned. 'As much as I would love to take you to bed and make love to you for the rest of the night, I haven't got a condom with me. It's not the kind of thing you take with you when you're searching the woods for your niece at four o'clock in the morning.'

'Fortunately, I do. I bought some the day of the kiss speed dating.' She pulled away and grabbed one from the packet in her drawers.

'Because you were hoping one of those kisses would turn into something more?' he asked.

'Because I knew once I started kissing you, I wouldn't want to stop.'

He grinned and then climbed into bed, holding up the covers so she could get in too. They lay on their sides facing each other.

She kissed him, pressing herself close against him, and his hands caressed her everywhere making her desperate with need for him. His touch was gentle but confident and her orgasm was just there, bubbling beneath the surface. As the kiss continued, he moved his hand between her legs. She clung to his shoulders as that feeling exploded through her. He held her close, kissing her hard.

'I've figured out why you love those sparkly vampire films and stories so much,' Bear said.

'Why is that?' Meadow said, her breath heavy.

'It's about eternal love. But we have that, we have that kind of love that will last a lifetime. I have no doubt about that.'

'Me neither, I know what we have is forever.'

'Then marry me.'

She let out a little laugh. 'What?'

'Marry me. I've waited eight years for you and I don't want to wait a moment longer. We can buy that wedding dress we saw at Dwelling, we can get married in the little chapel in the woods just like you dreamt of. I want to make your dreams come true. Marry me and I will spend the rest of my life trying to make you as happy as you make me.'

Her heart soared with happiness. 'The dream wasn't really to get married in the woods, as lovely as that would be, it was to marry you. As far back as I can remember, when I thought about marriage, I always knew it would be to you.'

He smiled. 'So is that a yes?'

She stared at him. It should be ridiculous and silly but nothing in the world felt as right as when she nodded. He was her love story, her beginning, the middle and her gloriously happy ending, she knew that. 'Yes, I will marry you.'

He grabbed the condom, ripped it open and after a moment he was hooking her leg over his hip and sliding carefully inside her. They moved together slowly, with no rush, no desperation because they both knew that what they had was forever. His touches were gentle, treasuring her body with his own. He kissed her shoulder, her throat and when he kissed her on the mouth he slid his hand down to her bum, holding her tighter against him. That feeling started to build and she pulled back to look at him.

'I love you so much, I always have, always will,' she said.

His face lit up in the biggest smile and he kissed her again, rolling her underneath him as he started moving against her. That feeling suddenly exploded through her like a thousand fireworks sparkling through her body and she knew she had never felt so completely happy as she did right then.

EPILOGUE

Meadow pulled on her sparkly cream dress and looked at herself in the mirror. It had taken weeks to make but she couldn't have been happier with how it had turned out. The dress itself was quite a simple style, gathered around the bust and then loose to the knee, but the embroidery and sequins had been the things that had taken so long. Tiny little flowers and jewel-coloured leaves danced around the fabric like they were caught in an autumn breeze.

Fortunately, she'd had plenty of time to get it right while Heath and River finished the wedding chapel treehouse and they'd waited for the wedding venue licence to be approved. They'd had their first wedding in there the week before, when River and Indigo got married. Today was the second one. Although autumn was well under way, the colour of the leaves in beautiful tones of scarlet and gold, they were experiencing a hot spell, the sun streaming through the windows and sparkling off the emerald sea.

The day couldn't have been more perfect to marry the love of her life.

Bear stepped out of the bathroom, fixing his tie. Seeing him in a suit made her catch her breath. He was so handsome.

He spotted her in her wedding dress and stopped, his face filling with complete love for her.

He'd seen the dress before. When Star was in bed or at Heath's, on the nights they weren't tearing each other's clothes off, they would sit in the spare room together where she made her dresses, including the one she was wearing, and he sat and wrote his stories. He hadn't seen her wear it before though.

'You look incredible,' Bear said, softly.

'Thank you. You're looking sexy as hell in that suit.'

He laughed. 'Thank you.'

'Will you zip me up?'

Bear moved behind her, his fingers deliberately grazing her skin as he slowly zipped up her dress. He kissed her shoulder and then her throat.

'Bear Brookfield, you've already had your wicked way with me twice this morning, we haven't got time for a round three.'

'Well, maybe we can sneak back here before the reception,' Bear said.

She turned round, looping her arms round his neck. 'That can be arranged.'

'So we need to talk about the bet,' he said, wrapping his arms around her.

She frowned in confusion for a moment and then she remembered the silly bet they'd made when she had embarked on dating for the first time. 'It hasn't quite been three months, I'm not sure if we can class this as a serious meaningful relationship yet.'

'Hmm,' Bear said thoughtfully. 'I moved in with you pretty much straightaway, we're getting married today and you're carrying my child,' he moved his hands to stroke her almost flat stomach with his thumbs. She hadn't started to show just yet but she knew she would soon. 'That sounds pretty serious to me.'

'Yeah you're right. But the man I'm marrying today is the man I've been in love with all my life, not some guy I met online, so you owe me twenty pounds.'

'Hang on a minute. We matched online, ninety-six percent match. I know you never met AstralSurfer but, if you had, I feel pretty confident you would have hit it off.'

She smiled. 'What would you have done if you'd gone on a date with Twilight, not knowing who I was, and then I walked in?'

'I'd have walked right across the restaurant and kissed you hard so you'd never be in any doubt about how I felt for you and then I'd have brought you back here and made you forget your own name.'

'I like the sound of that. So I guess, in some weird way, we both won.'

He kissed her. 'I know I have.'

She smiled against his lips. 'We should go.'

'One more thing, after we're married, you promised to show me that video of you singing, 'There's a Hole in my Bucket'. I'm going to need to see that video,' Bear said.

She grinned. 'And because I trust you're never going to run away, despite how bad my singing voice is, I may even show it to you. After we've consummated the wedding. It can be my wedding gift to you.'

'You and our baby are the only gift I'll ever need.'

He kissed her on the forehead and her heart melted with love for him.

'Come on, let's go, everyone will be waiting for us.'

She took his hand and they walked the short distance through the woods to the wedding chapel treehouse. The sunlight streamed through the coppery bronze leaves above them, a warm autumn breeze swept around them and then danced out to sea, taking a few red leaves with it.

The last few months had been the happiest of her life. She and Bear just fitted together like two halves of a whole. He had moved in with her after just a few days, which Star was over the moon about. They hadn't told her about the baby yet, but as she'd been dropping hints about having a baby brother or sister since they'd got together, Meadow knew she'd be absolutely fine about it.

After the success of her first wedding dress, she'd had requests for a few more. It was something she loved doing. She'd even been brave enough to send those couples who had booked to have their wedding in the little wedding chapel links to her Etsy page to see if any of them were interested in the kind of wedding or bridesmaids' dresses she could make. She knew she could very easily go down the wedding dress route if she wanted to, making extravagant beautiful dresses. She felt like she was finally making her dreams come true and she wasn't the only one.

Bear had received an offer for a three-book deal from a small digital first publisher, which meant if his books sold well in ebook first, then they would go into shops in paperback later. It was very exciting and Meadow couldn't have been happier that people were going to be reading his work and enjoying it too.

They approached the chapel which had a perfectly wonky bell tower on the top, in keeping with all the other treehouses. Little fairy lights glittered from the eaves and white flowers were wound around the stairs as they climbed up. It was charming and beautiful.

At the top of the stairs, Indigo, looking gorgeously huge in the last few weeks of her pregnancy, Tierra and Star were dressed in purple bridesmaid dresses. Heath looked dashing in his suit and he had the biggest grin on his face as they approached.

Star ran forward and gave them both a hug. Bear kissed her on the head and Meadow knelt down and hugged her little girl.

'You look amazing, Mummy,' Star said.

'You look beautiful,' Meadow said and then smiled at Tierra who looked so adorable. 'You both do.'

She stood up and Bear kissed her on the cheek.

'I'll see you in there.'

She couldn't help the grin that spread on her face. 'You can count on it.'

Bear disappeared inside and Heath offered out his arm. She slipped her hand into the crook. 'Thank you for giving me away.'

'I could not be happier right now, you two were meant to be together.'

Music started playing inside and Meadow heard 'A Thousand Years' by Christina Perri, the song from the last *Twilight* film, and she smiled hugely that Bear had chosen that for her to walk down the aisle.

She stepped inside and Heath walked her up the aisle towards her future, standing at the top under the glass ceiling with River by his side.

There were only a few guests: Amelia, of course, with Marco, her latest boyfriend, Leah and Charlie were there, Leah wearing a very large hat. Greta was also there with her husband, Felix with his boyfriend, Alex and Lucien. They didn't need a big affair.

They got to the front and Heath handed her to Bear.

'Take care of her,' Heath said.

'Always,' Bear said.

Meadow smiled as she took Bear's hands, turning to face him as the bridesmaids came in and took their seats in the front row.

The registrar stepped forward. 'Friends and family of the bride and groom. Thank you for being part of this glorious occasion. We are here today to celebrate the wedding of Bear and Meadow. Before we go any further, do you have the rings?'

Meadow looked over at River and Heath and frowned slightly when both of them starting patting their pockets but neither of them producing the rings.

She glanced back at Bear and he smiled, giving her a wink before turning to the door and letting out a loud whistle.

Hero came bounding through the door, bow tie around his neck, tongue lolling, smile on his face. He skittered to a halt in front of Bear, and Meadow couldn't help smiling when Bear removed the rings from Hero's bowtie.

'Couldn't have our wedding without our dog,' Bear said.

Meadow stroked Hero's head and the dog snuggled up to her. 'Absolutely not, he's part of our family now too.'

Star called Hero over and he went and sat next to her, the bond between the two of them undeniable. Most nights Hero would sleep in Star's bedroom, it was clear he adored her and the feeling was very mutual.

The registrar smiled. 'Well, now we are all in attendance, let's start.'

Meadow turned back to face Bear again and as the ceremony started she knew that all of her dreams had finally come true.

*

If you enjoyed *The Wisteria Tree Cottage*, you'll love my next gorgeously romantic story, *The Christmas Tree Cottage*, out in October

ALSO BY HOLLY MARTIN

The Wishing Wood Series
The Blossom Tree Cottage

~

Jewel Island Series
Sunrise over Sapphire Bay
Autumn Skies over Ruby Falls
Ice Creams at Emerald Cove
Sunlight over Crystal Sands
Mistletoe at Moonstone Lake

~

The Happiness Series
The Little Village of Happiness
The Gift of Happiness

~

The Summer of Chasing Dreams

~

*

Sandcastle Bay Series

The Holiday Cottage by the Sea

The Cottage on Sunshine Beach

Coming Home to Maple Cottage

~

Hope Island Series

Spring at Blueberry Bay

Summer at Buttercup Beach

Christmas at Mistletoe Cove

~

Juniper Island Series

Christmas Under a Cranberry Sky

A Town Called Christmas

~

White Cliff Bay Series

Christmas at Lilac Cottage

Snowflakes on Silver Cove

Summer at Rose Island

~

Standalone Stories

The Secrets of Clover Castle

(Previously published as Fairytale Beginnings)
The Guestbook at Willow Cottage
One Hundred Proposals
One Hundred Christmas Proposals
Tied Up With Love
A Home on Bramble Hill

∽

For Young Adults
The Sentinel Series

The Sentinel (Book 1 of the Sentinel Series)
The Prophecies (Book 2 of the Sentinel Series)
The Revenge (Book 3 of the Sentinel Series)
The Reckoning (Book 4 of the Sentinel Series)

STAY IN TOUCH...

To keep up to date with the latest news on my releases, just go to the link below to sign up for a newsletter. You'll also get two FREE short stories, get sneak peeks, booky news and be able to take part in exclusive giveaways. Your email will never be shared with anyone else and you can unsubscribe at any time
https://www.subscribepage.com/hollymartinsignup

Website: https://hollymartin-author.com/
Email: holly@hollymartin-author.com
Twitter: @HollyMAuthor

A LETTER FROM HOLLY

Thank you so much for reading *The Wisteria Tree Cottage*, I had so much fun creating this story and including all the magic of living in a fairytale wood. I hope you enjoyed reading it as much as I enjoyed writing it.

One of the best parts of writing comes from seeing the reaction from readers. Did it make you smile or laugh, did it make you cry, hopefully happy tears? Did you fall in love with Bear and Meadow as much as I did? Did you like the little treehouses in Wishing Wood? If you enjoyed the story, I would absolutely love it if you could leave a short review on Amazon. Getting feedback from readers is amazing and it also helps to persuade other readers to pick up one of my books for the first time.

If you enjoyed this story, my next book, out in October, is called The Christmas Tree Cottage and follows Heath's story.

Thank you for reading.
Love Holly x

ACKNOWLEDGEMENTS

To my family, my mom, my biggest fan, who reads every word I've written a hundred times over and loves it every single time, my dad, my brother Lee and my sister-in-law Julie, for your support, love, encouragement and endless excitement for my stories.

For my twinnie, the gorgeous Aven Ellis for just being my wonderful friend, for your endless support, for cheering me on, for reading my stories and telling me what works and what doesn't and for keeping me entertained with wonderful stories. I love you dearly.

To my lovely friends Julie, Natalie, Jac, Verity and Jodie, thanks for all the support.

To the Devon contingent, Paw and Order, Belinda, Lisa, Phil, Bodie, Kodi and Skipper. Thanks for keeping me entertained and always being there.

To everyone at Bookcamp, you gorgeous, fabulous bunch, thank you for your wonderful support on this venture.

Thanks to my fabulous editors, Celine Kelly and Rhian McKay.

To all the wonderful bloggers for your tweets, retweets, facebook posts, tireless promotions, support, encouragement and endless enthusiasm. You guys are amazing and I couldn't do this journey without you.

To anyone who has read my book and taken the time to tell me you've enjoyed it or wrote a review, thank you so much.

Thank you, I love you all.

Published by Holly Martin in 2022
Copyright © Holly Martin, 2022

Holly Martin has asserted her right to be identified as the author of this work.
All rights reserved. No part of this publication may be reproduced, stored in any retrieval system, or transmitted, in any form or by any means, electronic, mechanical, photocopying, recording or otherwise, without the prior written permission of the author.
This book is a work of fiction. Names, characters, businesses, organisations, places and events other than those clearly in the public domain, are either the product of the author's imagination or are used fictitiously. Any resemblance to actual persons, living or dead, events all locales is entirely coincidental.

978-1-913616-40-3 paperback
978-1-913616-38-0 Large Print paperback
978-1-913616-39-7

∼

Cover design by Emma Rogers

Printed in Great Britain
by Amazon